I0603432

Jono Pech is an award-winning writer and former journalist with a background in daily newspapers. He now works as a marketing and communications adviser in Geelong, Victoria, on Australia's south-east coast. Jono's work has been published in *The Age, Sydney Morning Herald* and on IGN.com. He also hosts several podcasts for ATEBIT.net, including *Comedy Rewind* and *Puttin' In Work*.

The Maven Effect is Jono's second novel and is the sequel to *The Spy and the Maven,* released in 2017.

Follow the author
twitter.com/jonohimself

~∞~

facebook.com/themavenseries
twitter.com/themavenseries

THE MAVEN EFFECT

A NOVEL

JONO PECH

For baby Pech
In memory of Zion

~∞~

Acknowledgements

Thank you to everyone who read *The Spy and the Maven* - your kind words, enthusiasm, support and feedback made this book happen.

Thank you Dad, Mum, Hannah, and Colin, for all of your help and support. Thank you Trey Zink and Jesse Cusworth for your contributions behind the scenes.

Foreword

We live in an age much like any other in human history, where what you do defines you. But if you ask my friend Jono what he does, he might have a hard time parsing it all down. A comms and marketing guy by day, his true passion actually comes out when he's away from his nine-to-five, when he flexes his creative muscles behind a podcasting mic or in front of a blinking cursor. It's this very fact that's always impressed me about him, even from half a world away. Perhaps it's because I know precisely what it takes to want to do it all, and the amount of focus and energy it requires. And maybe -- just maybe -- I say that with just an inkling of jealousy, because while I find my creativity regularly sapped, Mr Pech seems to have boundless reserves. This book is the proof.

When our beloved author was gearing up to release his first novel in 2017 (to which this tome is a sequel), I offered him encouragement and a platform to get the word out, not knowing what the book was really about, the quality therein, or a whole lot about its author, other than that he was a fan of mine. I readily understood just how hard it was to burn so much fuel making a paycheck, only to dig deep and find the fumes necessary to complete what perhaps mattered most: A true passion project that, in Jono's case, came in the form of The Spy and the Maven. Writing a novel is no small feat. How many of us have half-a-dozen incomplete documents sitting somewhere on our hard drives or in the cloud that we one day hope will become The Next Great Book? Our boy delivered, and from that point on, I became a fan of his.

I don't mean to undercut the toil we all put into the extraneous things that make us all tick. Parents sacrifice everything for their children; a radically changing economy forces many into taking multiple jobs to survive; some even act as caretakers for siblings, or older moms and dads. Our world isn't an easy one to navigate, and everyone has a story to tell. What impresses me, though, is when someone undertakes an optional side quest in their busy and often overwhelming life, lacking any guarantees, with barely a photon beaming through the other end of the tunnel, pursuing something that doesn't have to be done, but simply needed to be through sheer will alone. It takes a unique sort of person to not just tell their story, but a story, something concocted out of whole cloth in a reality that doesn't necessarily demand it. It's this sort of reverse supply-and-demand that exists at the genesis of many a work of art. It's why we're so impacted by painters like Vincent Van Gogh or Johannes Vermeer, who created even when the world around them didn't yet understand them, or wordsmiths like Herman Melville and Edgar Allen Poe, who didn't live long enough to see just how famous and beloved they would become. Will Pech become the next Melville? I don't know. What I do know is that he's now harpooned his white whale twice. That's twice more than most.

Within the pages that follow, reinsert yourself into the world of journalist Andrew Maven, who finds himself on another unexpected and exciting adventure. But as you read, don't only absorb the words on the page, but see what's so clearly between the lines, too: The work, sweat, and selflessness that goes into the craft when you don't have a publisher, when you didn't get an advance, when you already work 50 or 60 hours a week, and when you simply love to write to write. It's this kind of creative purity that sits at the center of all of us, but that only some of us have the ability to tap, goaded not by the promise of capital, fame, or prestige, but because some people -- like Jono Pech -- simply cannot contain what they do best.

Colin Moriarty

Richmond, Virginia

November 23, 2019

The Maven Effect

~∞~

Investigative Espionage Adventure

Chapter 1

Coffee and Burritos

It's hard for me to admit this: I'm afraid I may have messed up my life.

I'm in two minds about it. There's a sense of relief as I lie here in an unfamiliar queen-sized bed, feeling the most comfortable I've been in more than a year... but I think I might throw up if I allow my thoughts to travel further than these four walls.

Outside my hotel room stand two Panamanian police officers taking guard shifts. I call them all Hector and Pablo, since they haven't introduced themselves. I haven't said it to their faces though – not because it might come across as racist (although that's a strong possibility), but mostly because my Spanish is less than mediocre. They've also barely said two words to me since they burst into my home screaming *"Maven, Maven, alto, Maven"*, which I've learnt has nothing to do with saxophones.

That was the end of my year-long authority evasion. A year of looking over my shoulder, a year of wondering if things would ever change. As much as I'm terrified to face the US government, an American prison cell is probably better than the conditions I've endured on the run. I guess after everything I've been through, I'm still a "glass half-full" kind of guy.

Don't get me wrong. It's been hell. I've walked down into the valley of depression and out again. For the longest time, no matter how I processed our situation, I couldn't seem to shake the dread. Sleep really shoots its way up Maslow's Hierarchy of Needs when you're not getting any of it, when anxiety is stealing your rest. No matter what, I felt like I was either trying to sleep or struggling to stay awake during the day. Mars was the same. He's not the most expressive guy, but if we found our way to a case of Coronas, he'd talk about it. I remember a few months ago, he explained how he would close his eyes and hope for sleep to end the day, only to wake up and face the drama all over again. I don't know how I've avoided a breakdown, honestly. This stress steals your energy and keeps you up all night. But we got through it. We started to fall into a more consistent routine and slowly I learnt to live with the terrible cards we've been dealt.

I arch my back and roll over in bed, turning away from the clock radio reminding me I have nothing better to do with the best part of the day. A slight movement catches my attention, but without looking I know it's just the silhouette of yet another police officer, beyond the closed curtain hiding a pleasant view over the fifth storey balcony. This is how I know they're serious. Depending on your perspective, they're either guarding or protecting me at every possible entry, no matter how ridiculous it seems. I don't know if they expect Spider-Man to drop by, or maybe they're just not taking any chances with their American bargaining chip. After all, I have a couple of friends who would assimilate fairly well into the Marvel Cinematic Universe. Part of me hopes the reason Mars abandoned me was to bring his father, Agent Rust, back into our runaway crew, doubling our number of capable former secret agents. This is an optimistic theory at this point, considering it's been more than forty-eight hours here without a peep from the Metric agency rogues. I'm starting to think no one is coming for me.

Here's my new theory.

Despite changing my appearance, someone must have recognised me and alerted Panama City police. They saw it as an opportunity to trade with the US government, so they captured me as a bargaining chip, hoping to negotiate some kind of goodwill offering in return for the journalist and conspirator Andrew Maven. I'm the news reporter who dared to shine a light on the corruption of the evil New World Order, along with Metric, previously the USA's most secretive espionage organisation. That's got to be worth something.

Maybe I'm a little biased, given Metric's history of trying to kill me. Maybe you can't trust my views on the White House, after its complete cover-up of the news story that should've changed everything. But here I am and that's the best theory I have.

I finally plant my feet on the carpeted floor to start my busy day of doing nothing. This initiates my daily routine of regretful thinking, just like clockwork. Things were going so well before this all went down. I was busy, but successful. I had an awesome podcast and plenty of freelance writing work, which landed me a sweet apartment on Long Island. The Andrew Maven brand was strong. I had thousands of fans, the first 4K TV of all my friends, and a Siamese cat that respected me enough to leave me alone most of the time. I also held relatively no fear for my personal health and safety – as much as anyone can feel safe in modern America.

But that all changed.

Four chaotic days in 2017 flip-turned everything upside-down, and I'm still trying to figure out exactly where I went wrong. I don't even know if I'd do anything differently. It all seemed like the right thing at the time. I still stand by my actions. But I wonder if there was a way to find a better outcome, another combination of actions or words in the English language that would've resulted in anything different from this.

Don't get me wrong – I've had incredible moments of doubt. When you reveal a worldwide conspiracy, accusing the US government of heinous crimes, colluding with multi-national corporations and powerful organisations as puppets for a New World Order, you're going to question yourself. Sometimes I think about it and I realise it sounds crazy. The White House, the Vatican, Wall Street, the Five Eyes alliance, all under the thumb of an elusive shadow government. Should I have perhaps sat on the information for more than twenty-four hours before broadcasting it to the entire world? Possibly. But there was no clear alternative – it was either die with that information or risk our lives to get the truth out. Desperate people take desperate action.

If it was a bad idea, I would've expected Rust and Mars to say so. Metric agents surely aren't recruited into a life of espionage without knowing a good idea from a terrible one. Instead, the father and son spy team led me through the biggest story of my journalism career. People died in our effort to escape the clutches of Metric and reveal this information. Bad people, I'm told. Metric's monstrous leader, Scarpino, was the one I would've said I wouldn't lose sleep over, but ironically her death in front of my very eyes is the one that haunts me at night.

I pull the curtains open and wave to the officer on the balcony.

"Coffee?" I mimic a drinking action and he pouts in response. "I know, it's bad. But coffee is coffee, right?"

There's a good chance he can't hear me through the glass, or his English just isn't great, or maybe he's more of a tea drinker. It doesn't really matter. Human interaction is what I'm lacking and if that means this cop has to take an earful, I'm OK with that.

I promised myself I'd appreciate coffee of any quality after going so long without a hot beverage. My first six months on the run were nomadic, as Mars and I bounced between South American hotels, safe houses, yachts and camping grounds. In that time, I would've done terrible things for a chai latte.

Rust had disappeared. We knew he went to search Metric HQ for information before the government wiped it clean, and then we presume he took that information to find his missing wife, long feared dead. Scarpino's dying words cast doubt over this theory, but being the crusty old romantic he is, I imagine Rust won't stop until he knows for sure. We hoped the government would co-operate and shed some light on her whereabouts. I just kept waiting for clearance to return to the US. I thought surely it would become obvious that our accusations were founded, but communication is difficult when you're a fugitive. Mars made sure there was no way for us to be found until we were ready. Stealth is his speciality, but he's never had to hide a civilian for months as well.

It's still crazy to me. I honestly thought Wall Street would shut down, almost overnight. I don't wish harm or loss on anyone, but I had hoped our revelations would send shock waves across the world. I expected the truth would summon another global financial crisis and I'm a little disappointed to say the world just blinked and carried on with its daily grind. Sure, I guess I knew the government would deny the incriminating testimonies, but I truly believed the public outrage would be enough to take them down. This obviously didn't happen. On the outside, the White House ignored us completely. We knew they would disband Metric – partly due to most of its agents being killed or traitorous, but also to cover their tracks. To the informed American, however, Andrew Maven was just another nutter spouting off about the Illuminati, viewing the world through cellophane eyes. To the misinformed, I was the patron saint of conspiracy truthers, while the people I needed to believe me just didn't want to. I don't know if they saw me as a desperate liar or mentally ill, but even my friends in the mainstream media were sceptical of the stories I told. Only a handful of reporters did their best to champion the cause. Without support from their editors or the public at large, the news cycle replaced our tell-all video with a sneezing panda or whatever was the next viral meme to pull people away from the depressing reality of Trump's divided America.

"Gun smoke, Bob. That's what we need. Did you see our video, Bob?"

This is the name I've given the outdoor police officer, as I pull out a chair at the balcony's small table.

"We put up an eight-minute YouTube clip. Mars and Rust revealing the truth about Metric and the New World Order. It was crazy. We got about twenty million views in a month."

Bob keeps staring out across Panama City, diligently continuing his surveillance job.

"I think that's pretty impressive. *Saturday Night Live* did a sketch on it. Joe Rogan did, like, a ten-minute rant on his podcast.

Every frame of that video was broken down and analysed by YouTubers and bloggers looking for hidden information... or a hot take on the conspiracy community. But you know what? They all came down to the same conclusion – there wasn't enough evidence. No smoking gun. And it's true. We needed that gun smoke. That's where we went wrong, Bob."

You can't argue with a person's experiences, and that was the main crux of our message. Mars and Rust had seen enough to know the truth. They'd done the research to uncover the corruption, and any sceptical reporter who sat down with them for ten minutes would be swayed, the same way I was. But that's not how this works. No one knew who Rust and Mars were, and there were no receipts to prove their service to the country, their assassinations of warlords, or their amazing feats of espionage over the years.

"We had one chance to break the news, Bob. One golden opportunity. That's what I thought. But it was more of a... I dunno, what's the opposite of golden? Iron. Paper? It was like a plasticine opportunity. And with the time and information we had at that point, we did the best we could. It just wasn't enough."

Bob's silence is appropriate. The US government has basically treated us as treacherous, un-American conspirators, without even publicly acknowledging our existence. We're like Edward Snowden without the recognition and street cred. Snowden had the receipts he needed to make a change. That's why we talk about "the Snowden effect" – he woke up America to legitimate concerns over privacy and government surveillance. He woke them up with a splash of cold water to the face. Despite our best efforts, everyone is still sleeping on the New World Order.

"So, yeah, Bob. You could say it's a precarious and unfortunate situation I'm in. I wouldn't argue with that, Bob. I did the right thing and I'm paying for it now. Keep staring and ignoring me if you agree."

In our year on the run, I've become fully dependent on Mars. Honestly, I have no idea what I'm doing, for starters, and no one else could understand how it's been. I would've gone crazy and handed myself in without his survival expertise, or even without his constant company. By now I've heard every war story, every Jason Bourne-esque adventure he's survived. Each of my struggles have been just another day on the job for him, except his former employer has become the enemy.

For the past eight months, we've settled in Panama City's outskirts, where there are almost no American tourists. It turns out there's a lot more to Panama than just a canal and large hats. We've been living in a humble shack, eating tons of Mexican food, playing chess, watching soccer with Spanish commentary, and trying to make our own pasta. I don't even like soccer.

"It hurts, Bob. Even though it's trying to kill me, I miss America. I miss golf and basketball, and French fries with ketchup, and Netflix with super-fast internet. Can you believe I haven't even seen *The Last Jedi* yet? The wi-fi is terrible here, and it's so hot. We should've fled for Alaska. I don't know if the internet would be any better in Alaska, but at least I wouldn't feel tired and sweaty all day. It's like, how am I supposed to prove a worldwide conspiracy when it's ninety degrees and humid?" I wipe my brow and dry my hand by running it through my shaved hair.

"I'd kill for an iced coffee, you know what I mean? But I promised myself I wouldn't complain about coffee, so this is great. This instant coffee... it's great. I'm not even lying. I can make you one, Bob. Just say the word."

Bob turns finally, making brief eye contact, then continues moving his gaze across my body to the other side of the landscape behind me. He's either very anti-social or he brings a Queen's Guard level of professionalism to his job. He'd rather squint into the beaming sun than look my way.

"The Mexican food here almost makes up for the heat. It might be better than Mexico itself. And yeah, my life is basically over. Thirty-four years down the drain. But I will say this: burritos bring me moments of contentment. Despite everything, I know I have a clear conscience and beef burritos to comfort me. Usually. Just not this week."

Every Monday morning, Mars ducks out for groceries, and

every Monday afternoon he returns. This week, he never came back. This week, I was alone for the longest period since Metric agents first came knocking on my door on Long Island more than a year ago. This week, I have no comfort.

It freaked me out. Mars wouldn't do this to me. I knew something was wrong, but I had no way to investigate. Every noise at night made me wonder "Is Mars coming back or is a SWAT team here to kill me?" The four days alone plunged me further into fear and anxiety than the entire experience leading up to his disappearance. I could feel my weakening grip on my own sanity slipping away. I was praying to God for his safe return and wishing I'd paid a lot more attention in high school Spanish class. I was so fearful that I slept with a handgun beside my bed, and if you know me well, you understand how much I hate guns. My palms sweated as I awkwardly loaded the Glock 17, just at the thought of having to use a gun again. I've learnt the Glock is like an iPhone camera. Anyone can use it. You just point and click. It really made no difference though. The night they came for me, I didn't hear a thing until there were three screaming voices and three guns on me.

"You know, Bob, I do like the green uniform. Cops back home, we call them the boys in blue, but a lot them are black or brown. You've really got that Che Guevara resistance look going on here with the khaki and the cap. You know about Che Guevara here?"

Bob finally looks at me, pressing his bottom lip firm against his thin moustache and possibly holding back words he shouldn't say. If I knew him better, I might think he's mad at me, but I really don't know him at all. I imagine he would rather be busting drug smugglers than babysitting a runaway journalist. I think he might still be mad about the US invading Panama in 1990.

"*Basta!*" he shouts, breaking his silence, before calming himself. "Mister Maven..."

"Please, 'Senor Maven' is fine. I'm a visitor in your home."

"Yesterday was a good day. No talking." Bob squints and spreads two fingers through his moustache in opposite directions. "Let's go back to yesterday, yes?"

"Yesterday… Well, I'm sorry, Bob, but it seems as though your troubles are here to stay." I drink the last of my coffee, pretending I'm not intimidated and wondering how long I need to stay seated to save face.

"You will stop talking, or I will stop you from talking, Andrew Maven."

Bob places his hand at his hip, right beside his handgun, making my pulse accelerate and my chest feel fifteen pounds heavier. I swallow by reflex, tasting the instant coffee still coating my throat.

"Sir," I start, not knowing exactly what I'm going to say. "I can sit inside if you would prefer. And your English is great, by the way."

"I will not tell you again."

Now I want to stand up and leave, but I'm afraid if this police officer is trigger-happy he'll take my movement as an act of aggression.

None of this matters because before I can even make a decision, Bob drops to the ground, convulsing from head to toe, his eyes rolled back in a state of rapture.

A figure I can only describe as "translucent" drops out of the sky, landing beside the shaking body. It's a familiar shape, but one I haven't seen for several months.

"Took you long enough, Mars. Where the heck have you been?"

The figure begins to take a more visible form, deactivating his suit's stealth camouflage effect to reveal the Metric agent in hiding, back turned away from me.

"It ain't Mars, Maven," says a deep voice I don't recognise. "It's your guardian angel."

Chapter 2

____

Freebird

"Who are you?"

I feel like a wartime codebreaker as my mind races to unscramble the available information before me. This guy is wearing a Spectral Suit, the trademark espionage and physical enhancement outfit of Metric agents. We know the agency was essentially disbanded after our video released and Rust killed Scarpino.

So, who is this guy?

"And where's Mars?"

"I don't know," he says as a matter of fact.

"Who are you?" I ask again.

"I would've answered the first time, but you cut me off." He bends down to check Bob's pulse. "Just be cool, OK? I'm former Metric. I'm here to help."

"You serious?"

"What's wrong, never seen a black dude in a Spectral Suit?"

"I haven't, but to be fair, I've only seen it on Mars. And I know I keep mentioning him, it's just–"

"You can call me X. And we can talk later. We gotta move."

The agent is a decent five inches taller than me, bald with a consistent black scruff across his dark jaw. His brown eyes dart with intensity as he analyses our surroundings, both outside and inside my hotel room. My instinct is to trust him, and what choice do I really have?

"Is that like the letter X or as in 'ex-girlfriend'?"

"Does that matter? You ain't writing a book about me. How many in the hallway?"

"Cops? Two, maybe one. It depends on the time, but I haven't been taking notes. Hey, what did you do to Bob? Is he dead? He's not moving."

"He's stunned. I knew you'd take issue if I came in guns blazing, you know?"

"True. Stun gun." I nod, piecing together Bob's physical reaction. "Thanks, I appreciate that. See, why couldn't Rust use a stun gun? He always told me–"

"Maven." X grabs my arm and drags me inside through the sliding door. "You're not listening. We have to go."

"Right. Lead the way, X. If that is your real name."

"It's clearly not."

He proceeds with caution through my spacious hotel room, activating his Spectral Suit again to investigate the area. Mars has explained the technology to me several times and I can never quite get my head around it. There's something about metamaterials and "active" camouflage. I know it has built-in stimulators that make the wearer stronger and more durable, stabilising balance and reducing injury risks. That's all good, but the near-invisibility was always the coolest thing to me. Mars' suit ran out of juice a couple of months into our time in Central America, but before then, I was amazed every time he used it. My eyes couldn't believe what they weren't seeing. He compared to clear water flowing over a rock in a stream, but I found he was almost impossible to detect unless I was actively searching for him. It certainly wouldn't be discernible at night, in shadows or in grainy security footage.

"No cameras in here," I say, my voice lowered. Mr X ignores me and I see his camouflaged figure move across the room, turning over several innocent household objects. Eventually the toaster flies past my head and off the balcony to the street below.

"I guess you've eaten today."

"With all due respect, Maven, you wouldn't know a hidden camera if it was attached to your glasses."

"I think I probably would, but I take your point."

X deactivates his stealth effect and takes a deep breath, now facing the front door. I thought the Spectral Suit looked cool on Mars, but seeing this huge, mysterious black dude geared up in the sleek material takes it to another level. X's confidence assures me he's been in this situation before. He must be close to forty years old, if the grey in his beard is any indication, but I've been told I'm not great at picking ages with other ethnicities.

"So definitely just the one cop outside?" he asks me again.

"Two. Or one. I mean, they don't let me linger. But there's Pablo and Hector taking shifts. From what I can gather."

"Pablo?"

"That's what I call them."

"You really shouldn't have named them," he says, like a farmer scolding his son for bonding with the livestock. X reaches for his shoulder holster and pulls out a gun that looks just like the Custom M1911 that Rust fondly holds dear.

"You know what, I'm actually not that fond of Pablo," I admit. "Hector is fine. If you can avoid blood, that's great. But you know what, do what you gotta do. You guys have corrupted me."

"Believe it or not..." X fastens a suppressor to the barrel of his pistol, confident the close range combat won't require the precision of unhindered sights. "I don't kill police officers unless I absolutely have to. Even in Panama."

"That's... very noble of you."

Before X can talk me through our plan, the door flings open from the outside. I hit the deck, instinctively hiding behind the giant bed as Spanish shouting takes me back to that night in my cabin. The thud of a skull connecting with drywall cuts out one voice, and similar noises continue, becoming quieter as they grow more distant, until the sound of approaching footsteps brings me back into the action.

"Get up, Maven. We're outta here." X stands above me, eyes on the door and gun extended into a firing position. "Move. We gotta hustle."

I have a lot of questions, but now isn't the time. I rise to my feet, spotting Pablo propped up against the wall with his face nestled into the plaster. Beside him are several more cranium-shaped imprints, as if X was creating his own twisted Goldilocks tale until he found a spot that was *just* right for Pablo's face. At the door, we step over another unconscious officer and I can see the rest of X's handiwork along the hallway.

"Just a bit of redecorating."

"Move."

There are a lot more cops than I expected, as we stride through the corridor. Taking out Bob must've triggered some kind of alarm. X freezes up and stops me with an outstretched arm across my chest.

"What now?"

"Shh. Listen."

Before I can figure out what I'm meant to be hearing, X pushes me against the wall and takes a knee.

"One set of footsteps..." he says to himself, changing back to his stun gun. "Small frame."

"*Alto! Empezaremos a disparar!*" A young police officer emerges from the stairwell pointing a gun with intent. Before I can heed her warning, she collapses in a heap, the victim of a taser to the neck. The ionised bolt looked rather painless, but I can see a small burn mark on her neck showing she's going to wake up with a story to tell.

"X gonna give it to ya."

"Hustle, Maven."

X leads the way to the elevator with fearless confidence, gesturing for me to enter first.

"Ground floor? Or basement."

"Roof," he says without explanation.

"The roof?"

X hits the button himself, finally lowering his gun as the doors close behind him.

"Trust me. I know what I'm doing."

"Yeah. I'm sure you do," I laugh, waiting for the penny to drop. "But I'm not exactly Metric material, if you're planning to paraglide home or something crazy like that."

"Something like that."

I wait for a descriptive outline of our escape plan, but X keeps me hanging. The elevator opens at the top floor and we navigate to the stairwell. I guess I'll find out when we get there.

"This hotel... is really understaffed."

"Keep going," X commands, following me upstairs.

I push on the door leading outside, setting off a fire alarm as I'm hit with humidity once again.

"What now?" I shout over the blaring noise.

"Just stay close." X charges in front of me with purpose, reaching a set of huge air-conditioning or ventilation units casting a shadow over the rooftop. I follow, looking back to the door and expecting police officers to charge through at any second.

"I thought there would be a pool up here."

"This hotel ain't that nice," X says, producing two metal rods I can only compare to miniature tent poles, if you replaced the elastic with some kind of super spy polymer microfibre material thing. I'm clearly not a scientist.

"What's this?"

"We're zip-lining."

"With that?"

X sets the first rod up into a coathanger-like trapezoid contraption with hand grips across the longest bar. He locks each part in place, around the metal cable extending from head height to the streets below.

"See this? It's one hundred per cent safe and secure."

"Isn't there electricity running through that thing?"

"You're going to hold on tight to the grip. It'll be five, ten seconds tops, and you'll hit the next building. I'll meet you there and set you up again."

"We're doing this again?"

"Stress less, Maven. "

X spins a nut around each of the zip line device's connections for extra security, then passes it to me.

"Careful. Take a few steps and jump. Hold it tight. Twenty seconds and it's all over."

"Didn't you say ten seconds?"

"You ready?"

"Yeah. Just, let me psyche myself up." I take a deep breath and feel X's supporting hand on my back, preventing me from losing balance as he pushes past with urgency.

"No time to wait, man. Go!"

My mouth opens in protest until I notice X's pistol is drawn, pointed towards the ajar door we just used. The sight of two armed police officers sprinting towards us is enough motivation to get me out of here. I push my glasses up on my nose, take hold of the zip line and shout the only words that come to mind as I leap off the seven storey-building.

"Play *Freebird* at my funeral!"

Chapter 3

One Beer

My insides are all messed up. The echo of gunshots behind me accelerates my already thumping heartbeat. My stomach rises with the quickening motion of descent, as I horizontally traverse Panama City's rooftops.

Don't look down. Keep looking up. Just focus on the cable ten feet ahead. This is actually pretty cool. I bet I look awesome. Don't think about sweaty palms. Don't think about loosening grip. Almost there!

I brace for my landing and realise there's no safe way to slow down. Panicking, I consider letting go before I notice a button between my two straining thumbs. With nothing to lose, I follow my compulsion to push the ambiguous red switch.

"Whoa. Whoa."

The zip line stops and starts with jerky movement for the final twenty feet of my decline, allowing a safe dismount onto the rooftop below. Left to gravity's control, my handheld contraption continues sailing for another few feet, falling to the ground like a horseshoe thrown over a stake. I inspect my red, sore palms before looking back to the hotel roof. It's too far away to make anything out, and for all I know X has gone invisible again. I decide standing around is less productive than removing the zip line device for my next jump. X screwed those nuts in pretty well, but

I'm able to undo them and force the rods apart. Now I just have to decide my next move. There are two cables descending from two corners of the roof. Neither goes straight to the ground, but I'm sure one of them was X's intended escape route.

"Left! Go!"

I peer over my shoulder to see X flying towards me, barking at me like a movie director between takes. I don't waste time waiting for details as I try clipping into the next zip line.

"Thanks for telling me about the brake button, X," I shout across the roof.

"I was a little distracted," he says through gritted teeth, as he detaches his own device. "Looks like you figured it out. Just quit whining and get gliding."

"Where does this one go?"

"That there's a two-storey parking lot," he says, gesturing as he approaches the cable. "Head for the stairs on the left. And hustle. You're slowing us down."

"Yeah, well... I'm Batman."

I jump again, this time enjoying the shorter ride and the security of knowing I have a dismount strategy. The scent of hot concrete welcomes me, as my Nikes hit the earth. If I hold my breath, I can still hear the fire alarm sounding on the roof of the hotel towering behind. It feels good, as if the drama and impending danger are both literally and figuratively behind me.

"Move!" I jump out of X's way and he doesn't even pause as his glide seamlessly transitions into a jog towards the stairs. "Quit staring and get moving."

"You want this zip thing?"

"Hustle, Maven."

"What are we doing?"

"We're hustling." X reaches the ground level ahead of me and stands facing the alley towards our destination. "Don't suppose you have any friends nearby?"

I follow his gaze and see a police barricade at the street joining the alley, presumably blocking our most direct route to safety.

"This isn't really my part of town. Is an Uber out of the question?"

X looks left and right. He peers up to the skyline, then at me, trying to formulate a plot. I use the time to catch my breath, standing to the side and making use of the shade. Despite his tight, long-sleeved Spectral Suit, X doesn't seem to have broken a sweat.

"I remember somewhere," he says, straight-faced and reluctant. "There's an American dive bar around the corner. C'mon."

"This a friend of yours? Friend of Metric?"

"It's complicated. I used to go there a lot, before they blacklisted me."

"Blacklisted? Is it... safe?"

"Yeah, yeah, yeah. Don't worry. Things got rowdy one night. Too many Coronas. I haven't been there in fifteen years, so they probably don't even remember me. They definitely won't remember me."

~∞~

"Jacoby, you hellkite, you think I don't remember you? Step out of my bar."

"No love for an old friend, Sammy?"

If the seated bartender of this empty bar is surprised, she's doing a good job of hiding it.

"Friends, we are not."

"C'mon, how long has it been? It's good to see you."

"I wish I could say the same thing," Sam says, looking X up and down. "No, I don't, on second thought. Take your kung fu military suit right on outta here."

We're standing in the entry of Whammy Sammy's Paddy Bar & Grill, which can't be more than twelve feet wide. The floors are sticky and the whole place reeks of beer-stained furniture. I step in line with one of the bar's three cooling fans, each running on high and placed strategically throughout the long venue.

"I really just need to be here for, like, ten minutes, Sam," X says, with humbled body language.

"Great. I don't want you here. Obviously!" Sammy leans back in her chair, an elbow resting on the bar with a look that says she wouldn't pour a beer on X if he was on fire.

"By my count, it's been fifteen years. Long years."

"Jacoby…"

"Let's move on. From one American to another."

"We're closed, padres."

I chime in with a simple: "You don't look closed."

"Oh, we are definitely closed… especially for him. The black-list is final," Sam says, her grey, braided ponytail swinging with every exaggerated gesture. "Once you're on my list, you're blacked out forever."

"Is this because he's black?" I interject, hoping a dabble of humour will cut the tension.

"Shut it, Maven," X responds without turning his head.

"The blacklist. Is final."

"I bet Dee's been back since that night."

Sammy keeps her mouth shut, but her eyes tell a story that doesn't need to be spoken. Nothing will change her mind. "I don't want to say it again, J."

"Maybe we should go," I say. "There's other places. Next door looked quiet enough."

Sam squints at me, her lips parting slowly as her mind processes several unspoken details. "Wait, did you say Maven? Is that Andrew Maven?"

I look to X for permission to identify myself and he nods towards Sam.

"At your service, madam. We'd really love to just hang out here for ten minutes."

"Twenty minutes," X interjects. "Half an hour tops."

"As in, the Andrew Maven?" Sam stands out of her chair and leans across the bar towards us, squinting away her near-sightedness. "You've shaved your head and grown a beard, but I'd say it's you."

"I'd… say that too. Thank you, Ms Sammy."

"Call me Sam. I'm a big fan of what you did, man. I left America twenty-two years ago and I can see it's still a hornet's nest. And that's coming from someone who picked a dump like Panama to call home. Do you want a beer? One beer on the house."

"That's generous, but I could use a glass of water, actually. And I'm glad to hear there are some believers out there. You're one of... not many."

"I can give you half an hour, Jacoby. But you can't drink. And you gotta replace anything you break. Got it?"

"Sure, one hundred per cent. We'll just take the back room for... forty-five minutes tops. Maybe an hour."

We walk towards the back, through the kitchen to the rear section, which is as cramped as the bar. It's filled by a round table with two chairs, a closed laptop, and a TV set resting on a filing cabinet. X looks a little stressed, clearly frazzled by his unplanned encounter with Sam and whatever else has backfired as part of his rescue plot.

"So, thanks, I guess. For saving me."

"You're welcome."

"Now what?"

"Now you listen to me."

"I don't get to ask any questions?"

X pauses, considering his options. He has to understand a happy Maven will be a co-operative Maven. "One question. You get one to start with."

"OK. Let's see." I take one of the seats as X opts to lean against the wall, as if chairs are merely a crutch for the weak. "I'm going to ask something you're probably not going to tell me if I don't go ahead and make you. Who are you? X, Jacoby, Metric. What's the story?"

He explains his codename X was mentioned out of habit and it technically expired along with the collapse of Metric, which happened exactly how we thought it would. After Rust and Mars defected, we took out Scarpino and several of her Metric henchmen, so there really wasn't much left of the small specialised secret service. Jacoby assures me he knew nothing about Scarpino's dirty deeds or Metric's role as the muscle of the New World Order. He seems genuine enough.

"So, all these gadgets, the Spectral Suit..."

"I call them retirement gifts."

"Most people swipe a stapler or maybe an office chair on their way out."

He lets out a chuckle. "You ain't seen nothin' yet. Are we done with this round of speed dating?"

"Hm. Neither enemy, nor friend."

"Come again?"

I gesture to his outfit and the array of weapons and devices fitted to it.

"I'm thinking out loud. You've come from Metric and my only two allies this whole time have been former Metric agents... but then you guys are also the ones who have repeatedly tried to kill me. That's the baggage I'm carrying right now, just so you know."

"Hey, it is what it is. For what it's worth, I'm not here to be your friend. I'll agree with that part. But I'm definitely not your enemy."

"Prove it."

This flippant response hits a nerve with Jacoby and I can see he didn't anticipate having to justify his intentions so soon.

"Man, I just saved your unshowered fugitive ass. You got any-one else in your corner right now?"

"First of all, I showered yesterday. I didn't have time to grab an overnight bag when the cops dragged me out of bed. And secondly, saving me... That doesn't mean anything. I've been used by Metric before. How do I know you're not just, you know, run-ning the same manipulative scheme I got caught up in with Rust last time?"

Jacoby pouts, knowing there's little he can say to convince me. "I mean, you just have to trust me, Maven. That's up to you. Sometimes you gotta look a man in the eye and make a decision about him." He crosses his arms and stares at his feet, probably wondering what it's going to take for me to play along. "Tell you what, I'll give you one more personal question. I know how much you're into that kind of thing."

"Sure. OK. You got a last name?"

"It's Hirano."

"Is that Mexican?"

Jacoby cringes and I fail to hide my curious expression until he goes on to explain his mixed heritage. "Dad's half-Japanese. Mom's black. Obviously."

"Half-Japanese? What's the other half? It doesn't matter, I'm just a curious cat."

"I think we're done playing the family tree game for now."

"Well, yeah. I hope you can still explain–"

"I'll explain everything you need to know, eventually. Just listen for now. I didn't come to rescue you. I came to finish what you started."

Now he has my full attention.

"You've got proof? Of the NWO?"

"I don't really know how to tell you this, but the New World Order is here to stay."

"No, come on. Don't say that."

"It's the truth." I can see Jacoby genuinely believes this. "Nothing we can do will ever take them down. Ever. They're too big. Too powerful. Too ingrained. They were never gonna just go away because of a YouTube video."

"That's not the plan, man. The plan is to expose them and save the world from their manipulation... from their evil. However that manifests. Rust and Mars and me... I mean, we have to be patient and stick to the plan."

Frustrated with my stance, Jacoby takes the seat opposite me, leans forward and looks me straight in the eye.

"The plan. Is not. Working. Just look at yourself," Jacoby scoffs, pointing to my face. "I've seen how you used to be. The shaved head, the beard. You've lost fifteen, twenty pounds. You know how I found you? I could smell you from the roof. Has that haggard-ass T-shirt ever been washed? You look like every other damn conspiracy nut turned hermit in hiding."

"Well, yeah. Those old photos of me have to be on every federal bulletin board from San Antonio to Fargo."

"And now you're gonna be on every Panamanian police bulletin board too. The whole world is just waiting for you to screw up. It's time to change your perspective and try something new."

Jacoby pauses briefly, continuing just as I start to respond. "It's you against them right now, and I know, man. I know. I get it. They're all wrong. You're right. It's not fair. But what are you gonna do? Something's gotta change."

"Then the *world* has to change," I say with conviction. "Not me."

"You'll go insane waiting for the world to change, and I can guarantee, if you stay on your own you won't last another week out here."

"I'm not on my own."

Jacoby stops himself from responding, pausing to look around our empty room for dramatic effect.

"I don't see any of your friends in here, Maven. I don't see anyone else knocking down doors, jumping through windows, taking out police to get to you."

"You jumped through a window?"

"I'm gonna be honest with you. The way I see it, you don't have a lot of options. If you think Rust or Mars or Captain America are walkin' through that door anytime soon, you might as well hand yourself in."

I open my mouth to argue, but the words escape me. When I'm out of words, I know I'm definitely in trouble.

"Look. I'm here to help. There's no hero to save the day. Just my black ass... and you can kiss it if you think I'm gonna wait for you to check my references before we split. What's it gonna be?"

"So, what's the point then? Of all this." I gesture around our surroundings, referring to the situation and the purpose behind our meeting.

"We can't take out the New World Order. But we can hurt them. Weaken them. Expose them. I know it won't solve anything. It's like cutting out a cancer that's already spread through the whole body. But you don't give up and let it kill you. You fight it."

"So, you want to chemotherapy the crap out of them?"

"One hundred per cent."

"So the New World Order will keep doing its thing..." I can't help ruminating aloud, convincing myself this plan makes sense.

"But we'll expose elements of their work that point back to your story being true. We can prove Metric existed in a way that can't be ignored. And that might just be the seed we need to plant to start the whole revolution."

"That might be a little naïve," Jacoby grins, heartened by my sunny disposition. "But sure. The sooner we put out every Metric candle, the sooner we can finally go to sleep. And I really need to sleep."

"Don't we all. So, what's the plan?"

"We clear your name. Find this evidence – just like you said. And from there, who knows. Maybe there's more to be done, maybe it becomes someone else's problem."

"That sounds like a good place to start." Now that I've accepted Jacoby's plan, I've let go of the ideas and pressure that have weighed me down for months. Optimism beams out of my face for just a split second as I imagine returning to the simpleness of my Long Island apartment, before reality sets in. "But how are we going to do it?"

Jacoby screeches his chair back and stands to his feet. "We're going on a trip."

"Can it please be somewhere colder?"

"You're out of luck. We're going to the land of smiles." Jacoby's stiff face makes me wonder if he's ever smiled.

"Disneyland?"

"Thailand. You better pack some SPF." He looks down at my sun-weathered Coca-Cola T-shirt, the one he could apparently smell a mile away. "First stop in Bangkok is gonna be the markets. I want to see you haggle for some new clothes."

Chapter 4

In-flight Entertainment

The handful of possessions I've acquired on the run through Central America are sitting back in the hut I called home. There's nothing worth going back for and I haven't even had a working phone for the past year. Mars wouldn't let me keep one for obvious privacy reasons, but I'm sure it would've been destroyed, lost or stolen by now anyway.

Now that I'm free from the dopamine of social media notifications, there's been nothing to distract me from my grim reality. I'm seeing clearly, for the most part, clouded only by the anxiety loops in my own mind. For the first few months, I'd occasionally check my Twitter mentions when I could find secure internet access. I'd catch glimpses of people's theories back home about why I disappeared. There were always references and allusions to theories on Reddit and random message boards. As you would assume, the misinformation and speculation is rampant when everyday internet commenters decide to discuss a journalist's disappearance following an attempted government conspiracy unveiling. The old Andrew Maven wouldn't be able to resist the urge to jump in there, pore through the comments and set the record straight. But now, it just hurts too much. It makes me feel like a lunatic, knowing I'm one of the only civilians to hold the truth, as anonymous trolls snicker and flame my reputation.

It's sad how much I relate to every movie fugitive accused of a crime they didn't commit. I'm John Kimble, minus Harrison Ford's dashing good looks. The stress and Central American humidity have taken a toll on my appearance, but if I'm going to be considered a nutjob enemy of the state, I might as well look the part.

"Is it far?" I shout over the roar of passing traffic.

"Not long."

After lying low in Sammy's bar for a good ninety minutes, Jacoby resumed his original getaway plan and took me to a motorcycle he had stashed on the other side of the hotel. We're a few miles out of Panama City, en route to a small airfield in a town I can't pronounce.

All I know is we're going to meet someone in Bangkok. There will be plenty of time to find out the rest when we're stuck in a plane together over the the Pacific Ocean. I don't recall Rust or Mars ever mentioning Thailand and I still hate that I don't know their whereabouts, especially after Mars' sudden disappearance. With no way to communicate, I'm stuck with a tense feeling of uncertainty, lingering like hungry house guests overstaying their welcome. As much as I try to ignore it, waiting for it to leave, it's still there and it won't leave. Metric's Nano GEAR was our original form of contact, but that's been defunct since we've had targets on our back. Even the in-ear technology's closed channels weren't secure enough to use in hiding. The Nano became a gamble every time. It was like Frodo wearing the One Ring – it could get us out of a jam every now and then, but every time it would pinpoint our location to anyone who knew what they were looking for.

We turn into the airfield entrance and stop at a manned boom gate. When Jacoby kills the Triumph Bonneville's engine, I realise how quiet it is out here, compared to the Panama streets I've recently called home. The birds and bugs are going about their drama-free lives, enviably avoiding the pressures of government conspiracies. I can hear an excited Spanish soccer announcer on a radio, then the distant sound of a plane engine brings me back to reality.

"Senor." A security guard approaches us with the urgency of a middle-aged man browsing a car dealership lot. "*ID. Por favor.*"

Jacoby hands over a licence and some papers, as I sit behind him, feeling the heat emanate from each side of the motorcycle. I lose track of their Spanish conversation after the first couple of lines. I stare into Jacoby's back, wondering how well the Spectral Suit can pass for motorbike apparel. Every few seconds, the guard glances at me. It started off fairly natural, but I'm becoming more and more the subject of his attention.

"Is it cool, Jacoby?"

Their dialogue ends as I've become his main focus. I look away, totally failing to look discreet, but I'm relieved when my darting eyes notice he's begun a tense stare-down with Jacoby. A couple of heavy heartbeats pass before the guard breaks into nervous laughter, relaxing his firm stance. He skips back to his booth, presumably having told us something along the lines of "I'm just doing my job".

"Is it cool?" I ask a second time, still waiting for an update.

"Nah. We've got some work to do."

"Work?"

I look over to the security guard, hoping he'll open the boom gate for us. Instead he has a phone to his ear, his eyes still fixed on my face. This wouldn't have happened if Jacoby brought me a helmet. My spider sense is tingling.

"When I start the bike, run around the gate," he tells me. "Keep running to the left and don't stop until I'm in front of you."

"The gate's closed."

Jacoby hits the Triumph's "start" button and I do just as he said, sprinting past the gate and ignoring the shouting security guard.

I can hear the roar of the bike engine trail off as Jacoby presumably goes looking for another entry point. Still running, I glance over my shoulder, distracted by the sound of accelerating commotion. Arms raised, the security guard gives up on blocking the boom gate and dives just in time to avoid the hooning bike. Jacoby pulls up on one wheel, splintering the gate into a dozen broken pieces. I turn again, facing forward and sprinting as fast as possible until the bike pulls up beside me. The second I'm seated, we take off with an acceleration that almost sends me to the tarmac.

I clutch uncomfortably tight to Jacoby's body as we speed up, surely more than a hundred miles an hour to close the gap between the entrance and the airfield's most distant hangar.

Jacoby yells something I can't hear, but I assume is along the lines of "hold on". He brakes fast, skidding for fifteen feet until we stop dead at the side of a small red, white and blue airplane.

"Whoahh-kay. Can we take a breath?" I ask, as Jacoby wastes no time stepping towards the cockpit door.

"No time to waste. Could be cops here within minutes. You don't want to hustle, you want to stand around, you may as well walk yourself back into custody."

"A simple 'no' would have been fine."

I approach the modest twenty-five-foot plane to see two cushioned seats waiting for us. "This thing literally has a propeller. Are you sure it's cut out for trans-Pacific travel?"

"Don't you worry about that."

"Is this another one of your parting gifts from Metric? I think I took a coffee cup after my internship at CNN."

I climb into the cockpit as Jacoby explains the Beechcraft Bonanza G36 is more than capable of our overseas flights – given its Metric modifications.

"It's faster, it's got purpose-built tanks, has better efficiency on gas, and..." He raps his knuckles against the solid fuselage. "Bulletproof. More or less. All of this, with the unassuming exterior of a legendary charter plane. Same reason the FBI uses them for surveillance."

"What's the plan for fuel though?"

Jacoby closes the door behind him and flips a few switches before checking the supplies behind us. "I pulled out two seats back here to make room for extra gas. Stress less."

"Yeah. I mean, I know nothing about aviation, so I'm asking more out of curiosity."

"You know what they say about curiosity."

"It killed the cat."

"It's killed more than that."

I buckle my seatbelt as Jacoby returns to the cockpit and messes around with switches until the propeller starts spinning.

"And away we go. I hope you packed some snacks."

"We're not in the clear yet," he says.

As the Bonanza moves out of the hangar, I can see what Jacoby is referring to in the distance. Police sirens. I can't hear them, but there are two flashing cars heading towards us.

"What are the chances?"

"Of cops showing up? It seems to come with the territory."

"But we've only been here, like, five minutes?"

"Panama, man. I'm gonna miss it."

We're picking up speed as the police cars draw near. One of them has turned away to match our direction, as the other swerves across our path.

"They're blocking us."

"I can see that, Maven."

Jacoby banks to the left, slowing us down to avoid the cop car.

"Is he pulling a gun? He's pulling a gun!" I can see two approaching officers outside their car, shouting at us with their weapons drawn. Jacoby grits his teeth, bracing for the consequences of his actions. The plane banks right again, right for the cop car, fast enough to scare the officers into fleeing until we straighten up again.

"We're running out of runway."

"Maven. Just shut up for a minute."

The second cop car has been waiting patiently, now driving alongside the plane. It swerves closer and closer, gently nudging the Bonanza landing gear and shaking the whole aircraft as metal grinds metal.

"These guys are nuts!" I say, looking down at the officer, making awkward eye contact.

"Take this. Fire off a couple rounds." Jacoby hands me a pistol, knowing exactly how much I detest guns and violence. "Everyone's hands get dirty eventually."

"How does this window even work?"

"Good point," he says, biting his lip and internally improvising a solution. It's possible the window can open, but not with the ease we need at this second. "Just, show them the gun. Hold it up."

I hesitantly bring the pistol to the window at eye level, grimacing towards the police officer in hopes of scaring him away. He turns his head like an inquisitive puppy, occasionally glancing back at the shortening tarmac in front. The confusion buys us just enough time to gather the speed required for take-off, leaving the ground with only a few hundred feet of runway left.

"That was embarrassing," I say, handing the gun back to Jacoby, who gladly returns the weapon to its holster.

"It's done now."

"It is. So, do I get the safety demo? Where are the emergency exits?"

"Every exit is an emergency exit."

"That was a joke. Or are you gonna show me how to inflate the life vest?"

Without reacting, he flicks a switch and banks the plane on course for our next destination.

"Do you do anything besides crack wise?"

"Not really. I might get us out of a jam, now and then."

"I look forward to that."

He takes the initiative to explain our flight path will take us to Cabo San Lucas on the Gulf of California, then somewhere in Hawaii before our longest leg to the Philippines – our final stop before Bangkok.

"And how long's all that going to take?"

"If we fly without stopping... two and a half days."

"Wow. I'm suddenly feeling very claustrophobic."

"Just look out the window."

I instinctively follow his instruction, watching the scenery below grow smaller and smaller until it looks like a Google Map. I don't know that it's helping, but it is cool to see the Panamanian landscape in a new light. It makes me a little sad to leave this part of the world behind. As much as my life has been a mess here, it was my sanctuary. It feels strange to say, but it was my home. I never had a chance to explore the green and orange mountains scattered in front of me. I'd like to come back one day as a tourist, if I ever have that luxury again.

I marvel at the fluff balls of cloud scattered below us, as far as I can see. Each one forms its own dark shadow, like a thousand lakes across the terrain. I watch them change shape and disappear out of view, the way I used to gaze into my uncle's lava lamp as a kid. I keep staring until the clouds merge into a blanket of solid haze.

"You good now?"

"Yeah, I think so. Except you just interrupted a really comfortable stare. One of those satisfying stares, you know what I mean?"

"I'm surprised to say I actually know what you mean."

"Nothing makes you feel more insignificant than seeing the world from this height."

"Ain't that the truth."

I look over to Jacoby as he slides on a pair of black Maui Jim sunglasses, straight out of the 1990s, shading his eyes from the setting sun before us. He looks like an action hero, still dressed in the dark Spectral Suit and matching combat boots. A shaven head makes it harder to judge his age. He has the smooth cheeks of a catalogue model, but I can see some telling grey hairs speckling his beard and eyebrows like stars in the Milky Way.

"Those sunglasses infra-red or something?"

"Nope."

"Super optical zoom?"

"Just polarised."

"Oh. That's disappointing. You seen that *Mission Impossible* where Tom Cruise has the ones that explode?"

"I missed that."

"It's a good one."

"I don't see a lot of movies."

"I haven't seen one for a while. My life kind of became like a movie, funny enough. You ever thought about who would play you in a Metric movie?"

"Denzel," he replies, without pausing. "One hundred per cent, Denzel."

I can't help laughing.

"You've thought about that before. I could see Laurence Fishburne doing a good job."

"I don't know him."

"*The Matrix?*"

"Hm. Must've missed that one too."

"You're doing better than Rust. James Bond was the only movie reference he understood."

"Sounds about right."

I make a mental note to delve into Jacoby's history with Rust. In the days we spent together last year, the older Metric agent revealed a few details of his life, but he's such a closed book that I'll take any information I can find. It was a huge revelation to discover Mars was his son and his wife had gone missing. There's still so much to dig into about Mars and Rust, or David and Bryan Fox as they're otherwise known. My life's been turned upside-down since I met them, I'll admit. But even if they're the reason I'm in trouble, they've saved my life enough times to leave me eager to unlock as much as I can from their treasure trove of knowledge, overflowing with years of espionage adventures. Now I'm starting to feel that uncertainty come back, that itch that just won't go away. Where are they? Hopefully Jacoby has a theory.

"So you knew I'd be in the hotel, but what about Mars?"

"What about him?" Jacoby leans back from the plane controls, finally relaxing into his chair.

"Am I supposed to think him disappearing this week has nothing to do with you being here?"

"I caught the chatter between Panama police and the US. They all know you're down here, but lucky for you, I was in the neighbourhood. I had the jump on 'em. You know they were getting ready to trade you in, right?"

"So you have no idea where he is? Don't you Metric guys have a sense for this kind of thing?"

"It would depend on a lot of factors, Maven. I didn't know the guy. We work isolated, remember? Sometimes it was years at a time, one location. I've heard of him, sure. Heard he was good."

"And Rust?"

"Him. Yeah. I know that old, grumpy bastard. Everyone did."

"You know they're related?"

"The *Fox* boys," Jacoby retorts, shaking his hands in the air with an exaggerated, sarcastic pizzazz. "Sure, I knew. Fox junior, Fox senior. Making spying and killing into a family business." There's an awkward pause as I choose not to disagree, while refraining from speaking ill of my friend and his father. "Look, I know you care about those guys. But I don't have any good theories. Maybe something spooked Mars. Maybe he could see the police were coming for you."

"That was a couple days later though. He wouldn't just leave me like that. You think they might've found him too? He could be in a different hotel."

"A dude like that?" Jacoby scrunches up his face, unconvinced. "I mean, maybe. They would've needed shackles to keep him down though. Even then, he'd still find a way out of there... I know I would."

Wherever Mars is, I think he'd be proud to see me taking action to clear my name. The thought of seeing my family again, of working and having a functioning bank account... being a journalist again, playing video games, watching American sports, walking a golf course on a sunny day. All these things are motivating me, but above all, I want the world to know the truth. This backfired last time, but the truth is something I'll never give up on, at any cost. Jacoby was right – taking down the New World Order might be impossible, even if people believe they exist. But the first step to hurting them is for people to know about them. I exposed them before, but our stories will have so much more gravity with tangible proof. I'm not naïve enough to think Jacoby's plans in Thailand will be a quick-fix solution, but it's better than watching soccer and waiting for the world to catch up.

Chapter 5

___

Luau

Hawaii is beautiful. Kauai is the smallest of the main islands, and no less spectacular from the air. I can't fight the urge to hum the *Jurassic Park* theme song as we fly over the pristine beaches and green mountains. The opportunity might never come along again.

"Cut that noise out," Jacoby barks.

"It's been a long flight without music. Plus, look around. Have you been here before? It's amazing."

"It sure is. Doesn't matter how many times I fly over. It's still damn impressive."

Jacoby says we're refueling at the Port Allen Airport, a small commuter airfield with no public facilities and no security guards to chase us down. This will be my first time back on American soil in a year, so I'm glad we're doing it under the radar.

"You've spent a lot of time here, then?" I ask.

"You could say that. Mostly on Oahu. You heard of the Marine Corps Air Station Kaneohe Bay?"

"No."

"Never mind then."

Jacoby brings the Bonanza down on the asphalt runway surrounded by forest – a single strip of black contrasting against the green island. As the engine slows down, the relative silence washes over me for the first time in more hours than I can count, with the simple sounds of distant birds and crashing waves enticing me from the cockpit.

"This won't take too long," Jacoby says, as I stand to follow behind him. "But you should stretch your legs."

"It'll be nice to escape the constant smell of gasoline for a few minutes."

"Don't wander too far."

"Well, this is my first time in Hawaii, so I'm gonna breathe in some of that good old American *freedom*."

Jacoby chuckles at my sense of irony and pushes the door open onto the tarmac. The nearby beach immediately hits my senses as I taste the salt in the air and hear the tide rolling in. It's the purest oxygen I think I've ever inhaled, so far from civilisation and surrounded by nature. I circle around the plane, feeling the combination of humidity in the atmosphere, sun reflecting off the asphalt, and heat generated from our overworked aircraft.

"Why does it always have to be so hot? Everywhere we go."

Jacoby ignores me, returning to the Bonanza to retrieve a couple of fuel canisters. I look through the nearby trees for a few moments, taking in the natural beauty around us.

I ask Jacoby about the object fidgeting in his hand as he stands idle, fueling up the plane. He looks down, as if he hadn't consciously realised what he was doing.

"Bullet."

"Bullet?"

"Lucky bullet."

"Can I see it?"

"That's not a bad idea while I fuel up," he says, tossing it to me. "It's an incendiary round."

"Oh. Like, tracer ammo?" I hold up the gold bullet, inspecting its blue tip and trying to make out any lettering.

"Exactly."

"I thought this stuff was just from video games."

"You thought wrong."

"What's the point of it? Starting camp fires?"

"Usually armour-piercing. That one's got some extra kick, but I've never had to use it, obviously. That's why it's my lucky bullet."

"You believe in luck?"

"I don't know. Sometimes."

"I took you for more of a nihilist than anything else. But the concept of good luck? That definitely goes against random chance."

"I don't align with any 'isms. Fortune favours those who go with the flow."

"You can't explain luck without appealing to metaphysical phenomena, or in my case, the whole concept that everything happens for a reason. It's kind of the anti-luck."

"I'm kind of bored of this conversation," Jacoby says, turning away to focus on pouring the gas. "Go stretch your legs."

I decide not to argue like I usually would because nature's bathroom is calling me. After briefly experiencing the liberty of the outdoors, I return to find Jacoby moving onto the second tank of gas. It seems a good time to do some digging.

"So that marine-bay station thing you mentioned... That's your back story?"

"Hm?"

"Hit me with the whole process leading up to Metric. How'd you start out?"

"Do we have to?"

"You can tell me now or you can tell me tomorrow. We've still got a long way to go."

Jacoby sighs, reluctant to share but resigned to the fact that boredom is even worse than talking. "Where do I start?"

"Where'd you grow up?"

"Englewood."

"In LA?" I raise an eyebrow, trying to pick up any hint of a west coast accent.

"Nah, man."

"Chicago?"

"That's the one."

"Right. Yeah. I've heard stories about that neighbourhood."

"Fair to say everyone has." I wait for Jacoby to offer up more details, but he remains silent.

"Don't take this the wrong way, but that must have been rough sometimes."

"Yeah, it was... most of the time," he responds, more forthright than expected, but I suppose it's no surprise. Englewood is a notoriously dangerous district where drive-by shootings and gang violence are common occurrences. "Big family. Real big. Dad ran the corner store. Mom handled the kids. I wasn't plucked out for Metric like your boy, Mars. It was a pretty gradual progression. Chicago PD. Air Force. Marines. Special Activities Division. That whole thing. You know how it is."

"I don't, but sure. You must've had a lot of exposure to the police there."

"One hundred per cent. The blue lights were part of the furniture on my street. When I was growing up it was maybe ninety-nine per cent black. All the white folk bailed in the '70s, and you know what that means. No funding, no investment. They left us to fend for ourselves. Drive-bys, drug raids, all that *gangsta* nonsense. It's the way of life."

What Jacoby is telling me is clearly being framed as a terrible thing, but I can sense an element of boasting. If I'm right, it's coming from a place of pure pride in surviving that environment and the strength it must have granted him from an early age.

As we're talking, a German Shepherd wanders over to us, straight out of the bushes to say hello. To my surprise, Jacoby's face lights up and he drops to one knee to heap attention and belly rubs on our new wagging friend.

"He likes you."

"I used to have one of these."

"You think his owner is here?" I look around again, but can't see any sign of human activity. The dog looks well fed and too domesticated to be wild. Jacoby scratches its neck, pulling his hand away every time it sniffs at the petrol fumes coming off his skin. "Hey. Hey."

"Can we take him with us?"

The dog bounds away, leaving as quickly as it arrived, as if responding to a whistle we couldn't hear. Jacoby's smile fades and I realise it was the only genuine one I've seen on his face since we met.

"A lot of the crew I ran with hated the cops. The worst thing you could be was a cop. But I always secretly looked up to them. Think I valued stability as a kid, and Chicago PD was the only thing trying to bring that to Englewood, as far as my family was concerned. I could tell they didn't want to be there. But they tried anyway, day in and day out. The only people I could see trying to make a difference."

"And look at you now."

"Look at me now," Jacoby mumbles, standing up and tossing the empty gas cans into the back of the Bonanza. There's something significant being left unsaid, but I know when to push and when to let it rest. I say a mental goodbye to the beach and forest before returning to my leather seat. I slam the door behind me and watch Jacoby run through the rigamarole of takeoff yet again.

"I grew up in Grand Rapids, so I spent my share of time in Chicago."

Jacoby nods, focused on the menial task at hand.

"Do you ever go back? See your family?"

"In Englewood? Not for years. Not. For. Years." As his voice trails off, I wonder what it would be like to rise above your surroundings, only to leave behind everyone you know. I can relate a little. I've left everyone behind too. I didn't have a choice.

~∞~

I wake up from a deep sleep and open one eye to inspect the avionic display screen in front of me. Throughout the trip, I've spent hours reluctantly staring at it, through lack of alternative, and I'm no closer to understanding the different numbers and frequencies. I can see the graphical 3D representation of our terrain and the overhead GPS, which has mostly been pure blue since leaving Central America. Despite hoping to see some pixelated land displayed, it's still just ocean around us. I open my other eye and turn slightly to peer out the window, but the clouds beneath us give no further insight into our position. All I can see is white, like an ocean of cotton wool. It's another world up here, peaceful and unpopulated.

"Where are we at?"

I look over to Jacoby and my heart drops when he's not there. Do I grab the controls in front of me? Do they even do anything? Do I grab his controls? The plane is doing fine without him. Perhaps we're fine. I turn and see Jacoby at the rear of the plane, hunched around the low ceiling with his back to me, standing motionless.

"What are you doing?" I ask with an accusing tone.

"We've been in the air for seven hours and you haven't been to the bathroom."

"What?"

"I don't know about you, but a man's not a camel, Maven. When I gotta go, I gotta go."

I don't think that's the meaning of the expression, but it's not the time to set him straight. I explain that I'm a bit more concerned about the self-flying plane.

"Stress less." Jacoby returns to his position as the pilot, allowing the plane to continue flying itself. "I don't know how you lasted this long filled with so much anxiety."

"That's what I liked about Mars. He understood how normal people think."

Jacoby nods, conceding his lack of empathy. "You guys really went through hell together, hey."

"You probably don't know the half of it."

"Fill me in, then. Last I heard, he went rogue from Metric. Next minute, he's on the news with Rust telling all our secrets. New World Order. Bang. I'm out of a job."

"Scarpino roped me in, teamed me up with Rust to find Mars. They told me there was some terrorist threat and I had to act as a whistle-blower to gain his trust... basically bait to rope him in. That's when he told me all about the NWO, all their control across the world, from the White House to the Vatican, Wall Street and everywhere in between."

"Yeah, I caught up on that. The secret society. Illuminati kind of stuff," Jacoby says, more interested in the details than I expected. "Truth be told, I always assumed that was going on. Never thought we'd ever know for sure though."

"Right. You probably know the rest of the story. Rust confronts Mars, they fight, Mars appeals to his conscience. It's like a Luke and Vader situation. I try to mediate, Rust throws us both in a military base prison cell."

"That's cold."

"But then he busts us out, we blow up a helicopter, yada yada yada... release the video, upload it, kill Scarpino. We've been on the run ever since."

"Huh. So that's how it went down."

"More or less. I totally thought it would change the world, you know what I mean? But everyone turned a blind eye. Not enough evidence, I guess. But that's why we're here now."

"I'm surprised Mars and Rust went with it, to be honest."

"There wasn't much choice. It was get chased down and locked up, or shake things up. It's like you throw the facts against a wall and see what sticks – usually it strikes a nerve when it's something that big, but I dunno. Trump's 'fake news' era kind of kicked us in the butt. No one wanted to publish it without digging around, and no one wanted to dig around. If they did, Metric did a good job of covering its tracks and they couldn't find a damn thing."

"People believed you," Jacoby says, with an informative tone. "You aren't the first reporter to get a whiff of Metric – you're just the first with the stones to dig into what we were doing and tell the world about it."

"Is that so?" I'm surprised, but it makes sense. Rust warned me that anyone who heard of Metric was smart enough not to talk about it.

"If you think everyone is sitting there back home just ignoring you, it's because they know better than to pull on the thread. No one wants to look behind the scenery to see what's really happening, because it's easier to go along with the lies our parents passed down from their parents, generation after generation, than it is to actually change. How often do you think about ways to make it all better?"

I resist the urge to respond, knowing it's a rhetorical question. Jacoby has a clear passion for this topic.

"My point is it's easier to be outraged at the puppets and the muppets on the TV every day than to figure out exactly why or how they're holding office. You took those extra steps and look what happened. You can't win."

"That's what I realised. It's systematic. The system isn't set up to take in new information that rattles the cage."

"I agree. And yet, the *system* doesn't owe you a damn thing, Maven," Jacoby says, becoming more animated. "The *system* didn't set you up for success as a journalist. You worked through it and found something no one else was doing. I don't blame the *system*. Society defines the system – not the other way around. And society is broken."

Five to ten seconds pass before I decide to share my perspective. It doesn't take much for me to give unsolicited opinions, but I've always got something to say on these matters.

"That's the thing, if you want to talk about society. Mankind is dark. People blame media, drugs, mental health, the economy, religious differences, bad parenting... but I think messed up stuff happens when you don't have a centred belief system, or a hope in something greater, something attainable. For me, it's–"

"God, right?"

I pause, trying to think of something insightful to say.

"Well. Yeah. Changed my life. Gives me peace in my darkest moments... and my faith has taken a hit since this all went down. You know, I was so sure it was my purpose to bring the truth to the people, expose the evil. So when that truth went unheard, or ignored... that kind of threw it all out of whack. I dunno. It's been hard."

"No doubt."

"I keep thinking it's all part of the plan, you know. The struggle. Like that slow metamorphosis inside the cocoon. Maybe it's still a work in progress."

"Hey. Whatever it takes to get you through the night."

I know it's meant as a statement of open-mindedness, but Jacoby's response is a little deflating.

"It's a bit more than that. Two or three glasses of wine will get you through the night. It's my whole... worldview. Things make a lot more sense to me when there's a reason for everything."

"Like I said. Whatever gets you through the night."

"So cynical."

"I just... can't buy into it. I'm sorry. You joked about me being a nihilist before, but that's kind of true."

"You think life has no meaning?"

"Not that I've observed."

"What's the point then?"

"Just... gotta play the game. We're making up the rules as we go along. When it's all over, we'll find out the score. Who won, who lost, who was on the same side when they thought they were opposed. Who was actually opposed, but always thought they were on the same side. But let's not pretend like there's a defined meaning when no one can agree on a single damn thing. We're just here trying to make the world a better place to die."

"Like I said. Cynical."

"It's my worldview." Jacoby says, throwing my words back at me.

"Whatever gets you through the night." I say, throwing his back too.

Moments pass as we silently agree to disagree. Jacoby breaks the tension, hitting a switch that changes the screen display to show our full journey's trajectory.

"We're almost there. Should hit Bangkok in an hour."

"Can we talk about that?"

"We can talk about anything you want. We're sitting right next to each other."

"So now you want to talk?"

"You asked if we *can* talk."

"OK, whatever. So why Bangkok?"

"I said we were meeting someone."

"Yeah, but... why Bangkok?"

Jacoby takes a deep breath and exhales, presumably because there's so much to tell. "Thailand and the United States have been close allies and diplomatic partners for decades. You know, everybody's talking 'bout China, but the Thais are our best help in the Asia-Pacific. Side by side in every major conflict since World War II."

"And that means what to us?"

"America's been withholding military aid to Thailand since their military coup in 2014, so Metric took it upon itself to plant a research facility there. Circumnavigate the government, unofficially keep our ties going. Not only was it free from US regulations and restrictions, but it's far away from prying eyes and snooping noses. Like yours."

"So it was, what, doubled up as Metric's olive branch to Thailand?"

"Something like that. I'm not sure it worked. RTP Special Branch still isn't the biggest fan of Metric." Jacoby reads my blank expression and clarifies: RTP – Royal Thai Police. "So even without a free trade agreement, our two-way trade is over $35 billion year-on-year. America's got investments here worth more than $11 billion on the books. This factory, this facility is only one of those investments."

"So whoever we're meeting, they're a contact into that facility?"

"You catch on fast." I can't tell if this is a genuine or sarcastic remark. I'm leaning towards the latter.

"I thought Metric was shut down."

"It was. Every site. But Metric control in Thailand was more or less by proxy. Metric staff, Metric research, helped along by local suppliers and security. A ton of security. So when Metric pulled the pin, of course the Metric suits and management followed. The lab techs, researchers, the engineers and scientists got left behind to carry on the work."

"And why don't they bail?"

"I thought they did. Makes sense. But I got a call out of the blue. This lab tech tells me the local security company put the squeeze on 'em once Metric cleared out, basically taking over the operation and keeping things running as they were. Metric staff, same Metric research, only they're selling on the black market instead of direct to US intelligence."

"Right. Right. That sounds really dangerous."

"It's not good."

"What's my role in this, though? You could've come here without me, gone through with this on your own and cleared my name from a distance. It would've been a fun phone call to receive from my padded cell back home. *Mr Maven, it turns out you're not insane and you were right all along.*'"

"I thought of that. Believe it or not, they won't talk to anyone but you. So you're like a key. A password to get what we need."

I shrug, having grown accustomed to Metric agents using my reputation to get what they need.

"Last time I was bait, so I guess that's an upgrade."

Chapter 6

Twenty Questions

Why couldn't it be New Zealand? I always wanted to go there. I could've visited my parents when this was all done. I haven't seen them since everything happened a year ago. Once the writing was on the wall, I scared them enough that they moved to a New Zealand dairy farm in the middle of nowhere. Initially it was just the neighbourhood gossip that bothered them, or the occasional news reporter calling after 6pm when Mom was in the kitchen trying to get a stew going. Then the surveillance began. Men and women in black suits asking questions. Hiding in the south Pacific Ocean, they can keep a low profile on a remote property with family friends who moved there a while ago. They can relax, drink coffee, and try not to stress about their son's espionage adventures. Plus, Dad has been looking for an excuse to move to New Zealand since the first *Lord of the Rings* movie.

The second I step outside our hotel, I instinctively recoil in Bangkok's humidity, like I've walked face-first into a spider's web. I squint down the street as the tropical sun starts to boil the moisture around my eyeballs. My overnight stay in an air-conditioned room made me forget about the sticky heat and bizarre smells of the street. I have no idea what time my body thinks it is, but after two days in a cramped plane, a good night's sleep in a comfortable bed was just what I needed.

Bangkok is a city of extremes – dirt poor and wealthy, side by side. Walking from my four-star hotel to the meeting point around the corner takes me past not one or two, but three beggars, plus countless desperate taxi drivers harassing me even more shamelessly. The amazing aromas of exotic curries, fried noodles, spices and oils waft through the air, clashing with the stench of loose rubbish and filthy stagnant water. Don't get me wrong – I'll gladly take that funky odour combination over the gasoline smell inhabiting my nostrils after two days stuck inside the Bonanza. In the distance, I can see the beauty of modern architecture and beautiful temples contrasted with hovels and tin sheds turned into homes for less fortunate Thai families. A city of extremes.

I can see why they call it "the land of smiles." The people are kind. They seem willing to help strangers any way they can. The level of poverty is impossible to ignore, but there's an admirable shamelessness about their desperation and willingness to do anything to provide for their families. I know that sounds terrible. It's just a fact. The resourcefulness needed to make it in this culture void of social welfare has made Thailand's underclass a tough and adaptable group. It would be easy to make fun of this old woman on the street trying to sell knock-off Nike sunglasses with a reversed logo. Her eyebrows are drawn with a biro, but she's near fluent in a second language and that's more than I can boast.

"You know where you're going, Maven?"

I turn back to Jacoby and confirm I have no idea.

"I haven't been here for, like, fourteen years. I came over with two of my cousins. We stayed at a hotel called the Bel Aire Princess. Funny, right?"

A motorbike short of a muffler passes us, making conversation impossible for the next five seconds.

"Why is that funny?" Jacoby asks.

"Bel Aire Princess. Like, the *Fresh Prince*. What are the chances? It's so close."

"I don't know what you mean."

Jacoby's Spectral Suit is finally gone, replaced with a Hard Rock Cafe T-shirt, khaki shorts and Birkenstock sandals. That's right – Jacoby's civilian disguise includes Birkenstocks. I want to make fun of him, but I know he'd still outrun me in soft leather sandals. I'm dressed exactly the same as before, only with fresh underwear, socks and a knock-off navy blue Ralph Lauren polo to replace my stale outfit. In my time gallivanting across South America, I've shrunk down from a large to a medium – the benefits of running for your life and being too stressed out to eat.

"Are you telling me you don't know *Fresh Prince*?"

"Just because I'm black, doesn't mean I'm a Will Smith fan."

I crack into a smile and laugh, as Jacoby realises the hole in his argument. "I knew it. Don't try going all blaxploitation on me."

"You got me. It's fun making you squirm."

"The joke's on you. I don't know how anyone your age could grow up without *Fresh Prince*."

"We're crossing over here. Hustle." We pick up the pace to make it across the street before the lights change, letting through a loud tidal wave of road rule-flaunting motorists. The air pollution is strong, but the waft of fried chicken fills my nostrils as we hit the pavement. I wish we could slow down and take in the sights and sounds of Bangkok, even with our strict schedule. I'm smart enough to be sceptical of foreign street food's hygiene standards, but when the locals are lining up you know it has to be good.

I realise Jacoby's lucky tracer round is still in my pocket and I try to return it. He tells me I'll need it more than him for now, suggesting I should be more nervous for my meeting. I can't tell if he's messing with me or just teaching me to stay on my toes.

"It's just a scientist, right? They wanted to see me, so I'm not expecting anything volatile."

"You never know," Jacoby says. "Can't be too careful."

It feels so good to walk around freely in public, knowing I'm completely off the US government's radar here. I know no one recognises me and I definitely know there's no one hunting me. There are some US tourists here, but I look quite different from my last confirmed public appearance.

"Do you need to be here? You said they didn't want you

there."

"I gotta do everything I can to make sure you don't fail. I'll be nearby, just if you need me. Bring her outside when you're done."

"Her?"

"We're here."

"Here?"

I look up at the store in front of us – a run-of-the-mill massage parlour. They're as common here as banks are in New York City. It's impossible not to notice them, thanks to the women parked out front constantly coercing or harassing passers-by into stopping for a massage.

"Maybe we've got some time for reflexology."

"Just don't come out until you know where that research base is, or she agrees to take us there."

"And who is she?"

"*Jintara Kasetsin.*" A small Thai woman steps forward, her hand outstretched to greet me the way we do it back home. "The Americans call me Jin. You must be the guy."

"I'm the guy," I say, shaking her small hand, realising how sweaty I am already. She lowers her head and shoulders into a small respectful bow.

"You're the... lab technician?"

"Come inside and we'll talk, Mr Maven." She turns to Jacoby, standing quietly to the side, arms folded and ignoring the nearby Thai women requesting his business. "Thank you for your correspondence, Agent X. I know it's been a long journey, but it will be very worthwhile."

"Thank you. We'll talk when you're done, I'm sure." Jacoby gives me a final nod before walking away, just in case I felt any anxiety about this situation. The old Maven probably would've been hesitant. I feel like I've evolved, either through experiencing a lot of weird stuff, or maybe I'm desensitised after a prolonged period of fear and unpredictable circumstances. Trailing behind Jin, I step inside the massage parlour and breathe in the pleasant aroma of oils and scented candles.

"Thank you for picking a place with air-conditioning."

Jin smiles politely and tries to catch the eye of the manager. The room looking out to the street is lined with leather chairs, most occupied by tourists enjoying a foot, hand or head massage. A loud woman in the corner is speaking French on her phone while two Thai women manicure her free hand and feet. I feel like she's missing the point of this experience. Everything about this place is tailored toward relaxation, from the ambient music playing on the stereo to the dim lighting and peaceful water features bubbling away.

Jin says something in Thai to the manager, who nods and points to the back room. Another employee leads us to an isolated and sparse square room, with only two floor mats, matching pillows and chairs.

"Oh, we're actually getting massages?" I ask, somewhat surprised.

"Couple's massage," Jin says with a straight face, as a second masseuse enters the room holding a square pile of clothes. She leaves them on the floor, bows with her hands folded in front of her face, and says something to Jin before leaving with her colleague.

"What's happening?"

"We need to change." Jin picks up and unravels one of the two folded gowns, making it clear I'm meant to replace my entire outfit with the cotton robe.

"Turn around, please, Andrew."

"Sorry, I wasn't... I haven't done this before."

I can hear Jin giggle as I face away and change into the robe as fast as I can. I'm going to wait an extra five or ten seconds before facing her again, just to be safe.

"It's OK now." She laughs again and I turn to see her dressed in the same robe, only looking a hundred times better. It fits her, for starters. "I'm sorry, that was abrupt. I didn't mean it like that."

"No, it's fine. I didn't... It's fine." I laugh as well, shaking my head.

"That's made me less nervous." She untucks her dark hair from inside the back of her robe and explains we have about an hour to go over the details of her plan.

"Is it safe to talk here?"

"I asked for girls who don't speak much English. But I don't think they would care anyway."

As if summoned, the two women return and instruct us to take a seat. They waste no time beginning to massage our extremities, beginning with some painful but relieving pressure to the pad of my right palm.

"Do we really need the whole gown for this?"

"Where's the fun in that?"

"Right. Fun. I suppose after two days on a plane I could do with a little less tension."

"See, I'm looking after you already."

"Right. Thanks. So, you're a Metric scientist?" I ask, knowing the answer but needing to get our meeting on topic. I want to ask the right questions in a friendly way that will naturally reveal why Jin has called me and Jacoby to Thailand. I don't need her feeling interrogated or uncomfortable, even though I'm the one who has been summoned.

"I'm a senior lab technician and project manager. I oversee some of the major research undertaken at the SWAN – our research facility."

"SWAN? Like the bird?"

"Special Weapons and Nanotechnology."

"Oh. Cool. What have you worked on?"

"Everything Metric. A lot of weapon modification and vehicle designs. You might have seen our physical enhancement stealth suit and communications tech."

"Did you guys design the Nano GEAR? I love that thing."

Jin nods, keeping her eyes closed as the masseuse rotates her wrist in a circular motion. It looks remedial and somehow relaxing too. Why isn't mine doing that move? She's only just moved from my palm to my fingers.

"Before Metric folded, my team was working on an in-ear communication device to surpass the Nano GEAR."

"Like, the Nano GEAR II?"

"Something along that line. The project was abandoned, like many at the time."

"So, without Metric..." I pause, wincing and holding in a gasp as the masseuse pulls my toes in a direction I never expected they could go. It distracts me enough to momentarily lose my train of thought. "Without Metric, what happens to the tech?"

"No one is truly sure, but I'm told it's moved directly to black market arms dealers. Whoever can afford it."

"That sounds... catastrophic. Does the US government know?"

"I think they would have to. I assumed we were forgotten about, or they just expected we would disassemble when Metric folded. But it's been going on for too long for them to stay in the dark."

"Yeah. Your English is really good, by the way."

"Thank you," Jin says without smiling. I suppose by a certain point this stops being a compliment and becomes patronising. She's cute, I've decided, and her non-threatening demeanour makes her easy to talk to.

"So why would the US allow special intelligence tech to go into the hands of the highest bidder?"

"Any number of reasons. It could justify extreme military measures." I look over to Jin hoping she'll elaborate, staring until I make it clear that it's still her turn to talk. "It would be easier to accuse a nation of holding weapons of mass destruction if you have developed and sold them those weapons of mass destruction. Just for example. But I'm only a lab tech."

"Right. I get it. And how big is this SWAN facility?"

Jin explains there are almost one hundred staff, including the armed security that make up about a third.

"That's... a lot of security."

"I know."

"So if Metric is gone now, where do they come from? Private contractors?"

"More like a private military. Have you heard of the militia group in the south called Runda Kumpulan Kecil?"

"Hm. Sounds familar." I catch the eye of my masseuse and feel a slight concern that she can sense I'm lying, even though she doesn't speak my language.

"They're militant Islamic insurgents. But four years ago there was a splinter group that began operating in the north – much less concerned with religious terrorism."

"So what's their deal?" I ask.

"No one really knows how it works behind closed doors, but from the outside, they seem focused on capitalist prosperity. I've seen no indication of any political agenda. Just greed and chaos. But in simple terms, they are just as bad as the RKK. Maybe worse."

I think Jin's English might be even better than mine, but I hold back from repeating my compliment. Although it's quite common outside of America, bilingual communication is so foreign to me. Hearing someone speak a second language this well is as impressive as watching a musician master a concert harp. As much as it's typical for Thai women to speak English, her fluency and general attitude seem so... American.

"What do we call these guys?"

"The KIL Unit," Jin says.

"Ooh, scary. Very bold. And not subtle at all."

"It's K-I-L. Letters of a Thai phrase."

"Ah."

"They're what keeps us all working there. You know, some of us are OK with what's happening. Some need the money, and some people like me just don't want to see anyone come to harm. I'm one of the only ones allowed to leave the district. But if I ever ran away, I know it would cause pain for people left behind up there."

"That's my next question. Where is it? When can we get there?"

"The SWAN is hidden in the Chiang Dao district, about halfway between Chiang Mai and the Myanmar border."

"My Thai geography isn't great."

"It's in the jungle. Deep in the forest. Many hours from Bangkok."

I grunt to myself, anticipating another long plane ride. At

least this time I might have a Thai scientist to keep me company. She'd have to be more inclined than Jacoby to indulge my requests to play Twenty Questions.

"This will be interesting."

"Yes."

"I'm glad you contacted us. How did you get in touch with... Agent X?"

"We made the comms technology, so we can manipulate it," Jin says, watching the tenacious movements of her masseuse working over her ankle. She explains one of her colleagues has ties to Metric and said I was the only person who could be trusted to bring an agent to the SWAN. Jin made contact to the former Metric communications channel and "Agent X" responded.

"It's hard to find someone you can trust," I say. "But you made the right call."

"I hope so. Alison has spoken very highly of her experience with these agents. The relationship seems confidential, but she's willing to bet her life and the lives of others on this."

" Alison. Alison?"

Jin smiles, nodding once in affirmation.

Alison... *Alison.*

The cogs start spinning in my head, breaking free from the rust and cobwebs that have built up over the past months.

"Is it Alison *Fox*?"

"Fox? No Fox. Smith."

"Really? Dark hair, American, late... forties to early fifties?"

"Yes."

"And has she been here since... about three years ago?"

Jin swivels in sync with her widening eyes and for a split second I wonder if she could be choking.

"How do you know her?" she whispers, as if our silent masseuses have learnt English in the past fifteen minutes.

"You've got to be kidding me."

I pause for a moment to take a deep breath and double-check the facts flying around my brain. "It sounds like you're talking about Rust's *wife.*"

"Alison..."

"I think that's *Mars'* mom, Jin. We thought she was dead."

Chapter 7

Dogmeat

"Rust and Mars – they were the agents in your video?"

"Yep."

"And Alison is that boy's mother? The old one's husband?"

"It's shocking to me too, Jin. But damn, if that isn't an awesome story."

"I don't know. It could be a coincidence."

"What are the chances though? And Smith, I mean. I don't know. Maybe she never changed her maiden name, maybe it's a fake name. The rest of it works."

"I can't believe it," Jin says, staring deeply at nothing in particular. "Now I see. Two Metric agents."

"Former Metric agents."

Jin has bought into my theory without much convincing.

"It makes sense. She never wanted to reveal her personal life. I knew there were family, but she never talks about them."

"You think..."

"It would make her a target with the militia. I have no doubt about it."

"If Alison is at the base..." I pause to calm and lower my voice, realising my excitement has the best of me. "If she's there, it's not impossible that's where Mars and Rust have gone."

"I sent a cryptic message and it was your bald friend outside who responded."

"Yeah, but... Rust has been busy somewhere for the past year."

As we make eye contact, I realise Jin has no idea what I'm referring to and I'm just thinking out loud at this point. I've covered off the who, when, where, and why of this whole situation, so there's only two questions left to reveal the plan.

"Sorry," I say, trying to get back on track. "What's, what's... you know... What do you want us to do? And how are we doing it?"

"We want you to close the SWAN. If it's exposed, it can no longer operate and we can all leave. The illegal operations will cease and you'll have your story."

I assure her that Jacoby is capable of shutting down the facility, and much more, but I'm going to need my proof of Metric. That's what I came here for, after all. Definitive evidence. Jin explains there's no shortage of official documentation available, which is more than I would need to prove the paper trail of Metric and the NWO.

I pause, allowing myself the luxury of time to think before I respond. Just as I'm about to speak, my masseuse slaps her fingers across my back to finish the session, bowing and thanking me before the two of them leave us alone.

"Surely, the records are gone now. And surely Metric has done this all under the table." An odd look from Jin reminds me this idiom might require some explanation, despite her English proficiency. "Their business, I assume, is mostly off the books, undocumented and undercover."

She shakes her head with a wide-eyed contrary expression. Maybe I should know better than to disagree with a scientist. "No. It's all documented. Everything. Funding, blueprints, directives, everything. Encoded and encrypted, but I know where to access it."

"But how? How did they not wipe it when they wiped everything else?"

"I don't know. But I know we have documents. All digital. Things work differently here. It goes back several years. We wouldn't call you here for nothing, Andrew."

"You seem pretty sure. On a scale from one to ten, how–"

"I'm as sure as the sky is blue. Or as sure as your face was red when I met you outside. But how we do it, that's up to you and your Metric friend."

"Firstly, I don't do well in the heat. I'm from Michigan, so don't judge me. Secondly, Jacoby's not really my friend. We just met two days ago. He's former Metric."

"Oh, I'm sorry. You look like you need a friend." Jin bursts into an over-the-top giggle, probably realising how harsh this sounds. "I'm sorry. I know I'm a bit rude. Sometimes I just say what I'm thinking."

"You don't want to know what I'm thinking, right now."

"Oh. You're funny, Andrew. A little funny."

"Truthfully, the closest thing I have to a friend right now is Mars. So if I can help out his Mom and somehow get them back together, bring her back to Rust... And clear my name, prove I was right about Metric. I mean, wow. I'm kind of blown away how well this has come together."

"It does sound too good to be true, when you put it that way."

"I know we just met, Jin, but I don't need that negativity in my life."

~∞~

I miss dogs. I still see them around, but aside from that brief moment in Hawaii yesterday, I haven't been in the state of mind to mess around or play with them in a long time. Plus, I was always afraid of rabies and other diseases in Panama, given I wasn't a citizen and my understanding of the health care system was nil. It's probably not much better in Thailand. There are so many abandoned dogs here. I've heard smugglers often round them up to sell to China or Vietnam for meat. There are something like three hundred thousand in Bangkok alone, if the newspaper article I skimmed this morning is to be trusted. For a ninety-four per cent Buddhist nation, turning your stray dogs into yum cha dumplings doesn't seem very Zen. But that's just one of the many disgraceful animal rights problems more or less ignored by Thai authorities, I'm sure, favouring general stability over social issues. I'm getting a bit off-track here, but I do miss dogs and Jacoby has reminded me of my old roommate's hyperactive pug. His lower jaw protrudes into the same kind of underbite when he's utterly confused and struggling to process the information before him.

"You mean they didn't wipe it when they wiped everything else?"

"That's what I said. Apparently not."

We've moved to a nearby hotel bar on mutual turf, out of the tropical downpour. Now that Jin trusts us enough to be seen in public. It's perfect because no one here would likely recognise us, and more importantly, they're selling cocktails for what I think is close to $6. I have no local currency to spend, so I feel better asking Jacoby to buy cheap drinks. It's early to be drinking, but our body clocks are all messed up and I've been awake since 4am. I don't know Jin's excuse. Calming her nerves? Maybe she's just a high-functioning alcoholic.

"I'm not sure this SWAN place could be in a more inconvenient location," Jacoby says, leaning back on the two-seater couch he has all to himself. Jin and I are seated opposite each other on low stools, with a small table between the three of us to hold our icy drinks. This is the part where I sit quietly while the grown ups talk.

"That's the whole point. It's hidden from the skies. You would never find it because it's underground, built into a mountain and below the trees."

"I'll need you to describe the entire layout if we're meant to infiltrate."

"You need to do more than that," Jin says. "You need to shut it down."

"What are our options? You want to get creative? Explosive?"

"I don't want anyone hurt."

"And I don't want to *get* hurt," I say.

Jacoby scoffs at our naivete, as if avoiding cracking skulls and setting fires would be impossible, like walking naked through the rain outside without getting wet.

"Ma'am, I'm a professional. I can minimise fatalities, but when you make an omelette, you have to break a few egg shells."

"With all due respect, Agent, we're not making an omelette. We're talking about liberating some of the most brilliant minds in research and development. And please, don't call me 'ma'am'. It sounds weird."

"She's got you there," I say, earning a subtle scowl from Jacoby. "On both points. I mean, I'm sure we can put our heads together to think of something that clears the SWAN before it's shut down. You know what I mean?"

Jacoby finishes his scotch and slams it down a little harder than I expect from someone relatively sober.

"That's it."

"That's it?" It's rare that one of my tactical suggestions is so well-received.

"You said it's underground, right, lady?"

"It's OK to call me *Jin*."

"So we can trigger a mass evacuation. That clears the facility."

"And then blow it up!" I say, using both hands to gesture an expanding mushroom cloud.

"Now you're speaking my language," Jacoby says, pointing at me with the enthusiasm of a football coach designing a game-winning play. I can't tell if he's gesticulating for dramatic effect or if he's actively trying to convince us to go along for the wild ride he's proposing. "The only problem is gonna be procuring the bombs. We need some serious stuff."

"Wait, is that really the option we're going with?" Jin asks, looking to me as a voice of reason. "You're cool with this too?"

"Um... Sure. I'm down for that." She looks a little surprised. "Who doesn't like a nice explosion every now and then?"

"That's so American of you. I can't believe that's the best idea we have."

"Well, hold on," I say, resisting the American stereotype. "I can put it a bit more poetically, if it helps... Think about it this way. I would rather see this SWAN place burn to the ground than let it stand to flaunt the reality that I know. The reality no one else will believe, as long as the SWAN is running. It's a symbolic thing as much as it's, you know, practical. You know what I mean?"

"Well said, Maven," Jacoby jumps in before Jin can answer. "Now, I could make some low grade, basement-style explosives. Any farmer's gonna have some ammonium nitrate lying around, but for something like this? It's going to take a lot of firepower. I'll need a few days to find enough materials, unless you've got C-4 lying around the lab."

"We don't. And we don't have a few days either," Jin says. "We have two days. Exactly."

"What are you talking about?" Jacoby motions to our bartender for another scotch, as if he's one drink away from unlocking a solution.

"In two days... I forgot to mention, but the system is due for an encryption upgrade."

"So when we said we couldn't believe the data hadn't been wiped yet–" Jacoby starts.

"I should have said, it isn't wiped, but we only have two days before it's inaccessible."

"Listen, lady–"

"Enough. Call me Jin, or don't speak to me at all."

Jin's boldness has caught Jacoby off guard. He smirks as if he's not sure whether to be offended or impressed.

"Are you sure you're Thai? You know, most women in this country have a little more respect for..."

"Old men?" she says, with a burn that's so painful it hurts to witness. "Sorry, but I'm not like most Thai women... Agent."

"I can see that. Jin, it is."

"We could hack it," I say, bringing the conversation back to the SWAN. "Jacoby, could you hack it?"

"You can't hack this," Jin says.

"But we could–"

"No. She's right." Jacoby picks up his glass and downs a mouthful of scotch. "We're talking about Metric software designed by Metric programmers. It's like a magician trying to trick another magician."

"So we have two days," Jin repeats.

Jacoby and I sigh in perfect unison, like the world's most depressed synchronised swimmers.

"Well. The time is right then. Two days later and we'd be out of luck. You still think the world is random coincidences, Jacoby?"

"Sure."

"Right. So... what do we do?" I ask, sensing someone is holding back the obvious solution that would tick all of our espionage boxes. By my understanding, we need to somehow retrieve an entire network of top-secret data, while safely evacuating and destroying a Metric base at the other side of the country, all while avoiding the trigger-happy Thai militia. This is happening in the space of two days, with no resources other than a two-seater airplane and a bag full of stolen Metric gadgets. Is it even possible? I wish Mars and Rust were here to help, but I don't even know if they would have the mettle to pull this off.

In my moment of uncertainty, Jin clears her throat and points to her phone resting on the table, reminding us that phones are always the magic machines holding the resolutions to life's greatest conundrums.

"Give me ten minutes to make some phone calls. And please don't blow up anything while I'm gone."

Chapter 8

KIL Unit Special

Tourists love bargaining with the Thais, trying to save $2 on a pair of $12 sunglasses that would cost seven times more back home. Truth be told, I think the Thais love it too. They know the Rolex watches will break in six months and the Apple EarPods will barely make the flight home. It doesn't matter how many times the government pretends to crack down on counterfeits. They always make a way back to the street markets. I guess it's a way of life for people who have no better option.

"Hurry up. You're so slow."

Jin is bustling through these crowded Bangkok streets like my mom navigates the supermarket before a national holiday. It's hard not to get distracted every few yards. If there's not a man bopping away to music as he carves tiny, coloured soaps into stunningly realistic flower shapes, there's a city worker welding without a face mask, standing on a run of cables and wires, elevated two storeys above the traffic. I see a woman selling plastic bags filled with soda and ice. I see a single motorcycle with four fearless passengers on their way to work and school. There's so much to observe and no time to take it all in. Jin reminds me of our short deadline, and I realise I could be sub-consciously delaying the inevitable hardship before us.

"If I'm your bodyguard, am I meant to be speaking Thai?"

"You'll be speaking as little as possible."

Jin's evening plans have been revealed as the solution to our problem. We need explosives and she knows exactly where we can get them. The whole purpose for her leave of absence from the KIL Unit facility was to meet with the group's leader, Bhandit Kaypradee. He seems to prefer his progress reports in person – just one of his many quirks. He's wealthy, powerful, a little bit crazy – all of the clichés, apparently. As much as I've tried to gather background information, the only way Jin can describe him is as the classic arms dealer, motivated by money and whatever else that brings. Since Metric vanquished, she's visited Bhandit on a bi-monthly basis, providing timelines, test samples, prototypes, and anything else that can help him sell to his sources. He's eccentric enough to do this in person, but clever enough to keep the operation functioning and very profitable, so he's not one to underestimate. Jin says their meetings usually take place at his home in the mountains, but this month he's holding a small get-together with unknown guests. As fortune would have it, the location is exactly where we need to be.

"Remind me why you need a bodyguard?"

"I'm not meant to leave without a chaperone. But I'm not even meant to be in Bangkok right now, so I had to make the trip without one."

"Right."

"But I can't turn up to this meeting alone. I planned to use Agent X."

"But he's going to be busy grabbing the bombs."

"The explosives, yes."

The meeting is an hour out of Bangkok at a small vineyard. Apparently the humble horticultural setting is a front for the KIL Unit's black market storage, with underground cellars full of ammunition, weapons, explosives and Metric tech developed at the SWAN. The research and development weapons and technology are transported from the northern facility down to the vineyard, where they're held until a buyer comes forward. With the choice between posing as a bodyguard or thieving enough explosives to clear an entire research base, I chose the option that didn't involve accidentally blowing myself up.

Don't get me wrong. I'm still terrified. But it's relative. I'll be less scared than I would be handling bombs, and compared to my espionage experience a year ago, this will be easy enough. This time I have months of evasion and impersonation experience, plus some absorbed spy knowledge to keep me company through my paralysing insecurity.

"This is the place," Jin says, gesturing to a tailor's store front. This one looks like the rest of them, but she seems to know something that's made it our destination. There are two white mannequins in the front window wearing full suits with a shirt and tie, showing passers-by what they might look like after a shopping spree, minus any facial features or skin tone. Tailors are almost as common as massage parlours in the tourist-friendly parts of Bangkok. It's a city of eight million people, but a large amount of the small businesses cater exclusively to foreigners looking for a bargain and an experience they couldn't afford back home. It's like a fantasy land.

"They all wear these black suits. Red tie, white shirt."

"In this heat?"

"Don't be like a baby. Everywhere we go is air-conditioned."

She's not wrong. I step inside to an instant greeting from the Indian tailor, introducing himself as Rahil. He's dressed head to toe in a deep purple three-piece suit, so dark that it's almost black. I'll be honest – he looks good. Rahil follows his over-the-top welcome with a spiel about his costs and special combinations on offer, showing Polaroid images of past satisfied customers. It's all very unnecessary, but he seems to be enjoying the process too much to interrupt.

"Is this your girlfriend? Wife?"

"Her? No," I respond, pointing at Jin. "We just met."

Jin folds her arms and shoots me an unimpressed look. Why, I don't know and don't really want to assume. Was it the way I said it?

"Oh. Of course." Rahil gives a polite nod and smile, confused but hesitant to dig any deeper. I realise too late how commonly foreign white guys would wander in here with pretty Thai women they just met under far less noble motivations than mine.

"We work together," I add.

"Right. Of course. I only like to ask the wife what they prefer, because they're the one who has to stand beside the suit, of course. They're the ones who have to look at it." He gestures to the wall of fabrics behind us, each rolled up and ready to be cut, pinned, hemmed, and turned into any sort of stylish apparel. "Sometimes the man and his wife come to pick up the suit and she says 'This is what you decided?' It's very awkward."

"I think I'm just going with a black suit, white shirt. Red tie."

Rahil's upper lip and moustache curl into a reserved smile. "But of course. And you can't come to Thailand and not pick up a tie."

I can't tell if that's an innocent pun or he's referring to Jin. Either way, it's a bad joke so I pretend to laugh. I'm sure they see all sorts of bizarre arrangements between foreigners and local women, but this isn't one of them.

"Please give us the KIL Unit special," Jin says.

Rahil's coyness is replaced with an austere professionalism as he realises we're connected to Bhandit's troupe of merry men. As their preferred supplier, I'd imagine he's met his fair share of humourless henchmen. While he disappears into the back of the store, Jin says something I don't understand.

"This Thai is special. Very special. Metric secrets, you know?"

"He looks Indian to me, but OK." I consider that there could be tie/Thai confusion here, but neither is interesting enough for me to clarify. "Jin, I just realised he's gonna make me look like Agent 47."

"Is that Metric?"

"No. He's fictional. From a video game."

"You don't have to tell me everything that comes into your head."

"I don't have to, yes."

Rahil returns with some fresh material and Jin asks how long it will take to tailor the outfit. He says if we can finish taking the measurements now, it will be ready in two or three days.

"We'll pay extra to have it today," she says, before I can respond. In cartoonish fashion, she produces a thick wad of Thai baht from her bag, flashing a bright grin and a raised eyebrow. "We would like it right now. Please."

"Yes, yes, of course." This makes Rahil very happy. I can see the dollar signs flashing in his brown eyes as he proceeds to engage with even more attention, catering to every minor detail of the outfit. Looking buff is my top priority, I tell him. I need to be believable as a minder. Losing a bit of weight and sharing meals with Mars for a year isn't enough to give me the complete look of a meathead bodyguard, but a good disguise and solemn disposition will do the rest.

"For what you want, the KIL Unit special as you call it..." Rahil winks with an embarrassing confidence. "If you're not concerned about a particular lining or extra buttons, I could have it done one hour after measurements. Approximately."

"That fast?" I ask.

"One hour," he gestures with a single finger. "I'm very fast. The tie is premade, of course, one size fits all. I am very meticulous in my preparation, so it will not take long."

"It seems impossible. I'm impressed."

"Trust me, I'm so OCD that I'm CDO, because I like it alphabetical. That's a joke, sir, of course. I'm sorry. The suit will not be the same quality as the usual. That would be several hours. But for what you've described, I can do one hour."

"I hope so," Jin says, glancing at her wristwatch, probably calculating the travel time to the vineyard and the duration of Jacoby's burglary. The Spectral Suit will make it a piece of cake, as long as we can keep the ship afloat with Bhandit. How hard could it really be to pull off the "silent henchman" look?

As Rahil measures my waist and legs, I look into the wall mirror reflection, giving my most brooding "tough guy" squint. I stand straight and push out my chest, relaxing my shoulders just to see what I'm working with. Jin catches me in the act and exhales a tense breath of air.

"Oh boy. This suit needs to be really good."

~∞~

The highway outside Bangkok is busy with traffic and it's hard not be amazed as it flies by at breakneck speed. I thought Jacoby was driving fast, but every now and then a car will overtake us and disappear ahead, flaunting the relaxed road rules and ignoring the wet conditions. It's not unusual to see six men crammed in the tray of a pickup truck, or a motorcyclist in bare feet and children in front. I've heard it doesn't rain a lot, but it does rain hard at this time of the year. At every overpass, there's a crowd of huddled scooters and bikes in shelter, waiting for the rain to pass.

"It's close. Take the next exit."

As I've watched traffic and mentally prepared for my role, Jin has been directing Jacoby to the vineyard. He was adamant about commandeering her Toyota Corolla Altis and she seemed happy enough to take the navigator role.

"Remember, these are bad people, Maven," he tells me. "Just say as little as possible and avoid confrontation. They think you're on their side, so there's no reason to get caught up in anything."

"I know."

"And remember, I'm not gonna be there to save you."

"I know," I say louder, as if my first response wasn't heard.

"If anything happens, just find a good excuse to leave and hustle on out of there."

"I've met with Bhandit many times," Jin says, patting down her black jeans, the most I've seen her do to prepare her appearance for the meeting. "There's never been a problem."

"Something tells me this'll be different. And we can't afford for any delays to our schedule, according to your timeline."

"I thought of something, guys," I say, raising my voice to be heard from the back seat. "How are we meant to stay in touch while you're loading the back of this car with explosives? My phone's not working, remember. We didn't get time to pick up a new one."

"We don't need phones, Andrew." I lean forward to see what Jin is referring to. She remains silent, digging around in her bag like she's searching for eyeliner, until she produces a familiar object. "We're in the business of espionage, remember. Let's do this in style."

"Nano GEAR?"

"It's the latest prototype. We've been working on this version for about a year."

"Hell yeah," Jacoby says, doing his best to keep an eye on the road. "That's the new model?"

"Well, you'll remember the previous in-ear device was on Metric private channels." Jin passes me the small cashew-shaped item, giving me flashbacks to a year ago when Rust first introduced me to the concealed Nano GEAR. "There's no market for a stealth comms device the US government can monitor, so we had to reprogram the tech to be secure and untethered to Metric HQ servers."

"Even though they're technically shut down. So these are are programmed individually?"

"Each set comes with a unique server and a passcode that can be provided to a wider network."

"Like wi-fi," I say.

"More or less. But as I said, this is a prototype. It's not ready for distribution. Technically, it's not yet undetectable from similar models."

"So the old models won't be able to hear us?"

"No one's using the old Nano anymore, anyway," Jacoby says, displeased like an audiophile mourning the decline of vinyl records in the 1990s. "They're so easily tracked that you'd have to want Uncle Sam to know your every move if you were still rollin' with it."

"Correct. It is a prototype, but that's my understanding." Jin places a Nano GEAR inside her ear and leaves another in the car's central console for Jacoby. "You need to let Andrew drive this last section. We'll drop you around the corner. As long as that Spectral

Suit still works, you won't have any trouble navigating through the property. If you have any questions, just remember we'll find it hard to respond while I'm in the meeting."

"I've had enough of talking. It's time for some action." Jacoby drops his foot on the accelerator as if he wasn't already speeding for the past two hours. The storage facility is his candy shop and he's a fat kid just busting to explore it.

Chapter 9

P-A-R-T-Why?

Thai pop music blares from a PA system to welcome guests as we walk between two fish ponds, leading to the open entrance of the vineyard's main building. It's unbearable. I don't mean unbearable like bad pop music back home – this is a whole new level of awful. It's like the Thais have invented an instrument designed to keep foreigners from sticking around too long.

"Is this good music here?"

"This song?" Jin asks. "It's a huge hit. You don't like it?"

"I'm more of a rock fan."

"Me too." Jin leads the way and I follow very close behind.

"What's Thai rock like?"

"Not great. I prefer US and UK artists."

"You get that over here?"

She nods, squinting as we face into the setting sun. "And plus, I spent many years in America. Boarding school, university and my first job."

"Really? That's pretty cool. We'll come back to this." I have to cut the conversation short as we trot up some stairs to the vineyard's function room. With every step, the distant ruckus gets louder as the roars of laughter and good times begin to drown out the fountains and pop music at the bottom of the stairs.

"This tie. It's weirdly heavy." I can feel it pulling at my neck as it swings with every step as we ascend.

"I told you it was special."

"What?"

"The tie. From Rahil."

"Oh." I laugh, feeling really stupid. "Yeah, I thought you were saying 'Thai'. As in Thailand."

"Yeah, I remember you looked confused."

"Because Rahil is Indian. So tell me about this tie."

"It's made from graphene microfibres. Covered in silk, but underneath is the strongest light material known to man."

"So, great, I'll be strangled twice as fast when we get into a throw-down"

"That is a drawback, yes. But I'm told it has many practical applications in the field. It could save your life."

"Let's hope it doesn't come to that."

"Yes. But for now, are you ready, Andrew?" Jin stops before we enter the room, turning to face me straight.

"I think so. How do I look?" I plant my feet and close my right hand over my left wrist, security guard-style, but feel more like an awkward NBA rookie posing on media day.

"I think the suit is working. It's a shame about your face, isn't it? You're a little too cute to be the tough guy." She claps her hand against my cheek, but her smile fades before I can respond. "You need to remove your spectacles."

"I... Do I?"

"Everyone knows Andrew Maven's famous photo. The one they used in the newspapers last year. Especially in Metric circles."

"You're just thinking of this now?"

"You look very different compared to then. But the glasses are the last thing remaining. Too recognisable."

"Do I need to be able to see, though? I feel like I should be able to see."

"Just..." She reaches to my face and removes my glasses with care. "Stay close to me and it won't matter too much."

I take a deep breath and hope she can't feel my beating chest as she places the glasses in my jacket's inside pocket.

"Hm. Or maybe you should keep them on. You look strange now."

"I know, I know." I've heard this before.

"It's like a turtle without its shell." She laughs and makes two circles with her hands, holding them up to my face around my eye to marvel at the difference.

"Are you done?"

"Sorry. Let's go. You look good."

"Yeah, OK. Now it feels like you're my Mom sending me off to prom."

"Good luck, you two," Jacoby chimes in, reminding us he can hear everything.

"Oh, so you do believe in luck then?"

"Just a figure of speech, man."

"Let's leave luck to heaven," Jin says, pushing open the door way to the party. I step up the final stair and instinctively take a deep breath as I walk in. There aren't as many people as the noise had suggested, but I'm more taken aback by the party's extravagance and the wall of cigarette smoke hitting me like a Sahara sandstorm. It's possible the task at hand distracted me on the way in, but this place is visually breathtaking. The wood panel walls are scattered with a mix of landscape photographs, Thai artworks, and western-influenced stained glass windows that don't really fit in. Two rows of Chinese lanterns are hanging from the high ceiling, mirroring long tables along the length of the room. Tables are placed in semi-circles around the open spaces, most of them covered in a plethora of finger-food platters and filled wine glasses. Bhandit's party planner has secured every form of edible fountain you can envisage – fondue fountain, chocolate fountain, and what appear to be several alcoholic fountains. Cider, maybe wine, punch. It's hard to tell without my glasses. It could just be cranberry juice.

I'm probably focusing too much on the drinks. I should be figuring out if the two full-grown tigers watching over the room are real or fake. They're lying flat on a small stage overlooking the rest of the party and people don't seem to be paying them any attention at all. As we get closer, I can see they look heavily sedated, possibly asleep, and most likely chained up... but they're still tigers. Behind them, stretched across the width of the room, is a reclining Buddha statue, shimmering in the flickering light of the lanterns.

"That's the second biggest Buddha statue I've ever seen."

"That's nothing," Jin says.

"It's like... Sagat's stage in *Street Fighter II*."

"It's what?"

"Nothing."

The room's occupants are mostly Thais in traditional formal wear. There's only a few women, and each is dressed in colourful shiny dresses. The men who aren't dressed like me are wearing an outfit that Rahil called "chut thai". The pants are dark, contrasting what looks like a bright, high-collared, thin suit jacket, buttoned all the way to the top. I've seen politicians wear them, so these guys are either important or super rich. Perhaps they're playing dress-ups. It doesn't matter. As the sound of Thai dialect fills my ears, I'm hit with what feels like a large oversight on my part.

"Wait. Jin. Am I meant to be American? What's my name?"

"Um. Whatever you want? It doesn't matter." She's vastly underdressed for the occasion, but if it bothers her, she's not showing it. I don't imagine scientists are a great deal concerned with fashion, especially when there are diseases to cure and technologies to render obsolete.

"OK... If you have to call me something, call me Drake."

"Like the rapper?"

I try to shrug with my mouth, keeping my body language as neutral as possible in case anyone in the room has noticed the two of us conversing. "He's OK, I guess. I'm more of a Logic guy. It's just a cool name."

"If you say so."

"I do say so."

There are large foreigners dressed like me are mostly minding their own business in the corners of the room. I wonder if I should copy them or stick with Jin. I just don't know how a henchman should behave at these things. Do we mingle amongst ourselves and swap henchman stories, trading henchman tips? I catch the eye of one of them – a Pacific Islander with a better fitting black suit than mine. He nods at me with a sense of mutual respect for the trade, with a shared kinship for our commitment to the cause. Mercenaries in arms, we are. I bet he'd follow me into battle at the drop of a hat. What a champion. I nod back at him and revel in the satisfaction of my made-up backstory, full of bodyguard heroics. I've seen a thing or two. I might even have taken a bullet once or twice. He doesn't know any better. I'm a good fifty pounds lighter than him, so he's probably assuming I know kung fu or something awesome to compensate.

"Hey. You need to look where you're going." Jin grabs my elbow and squeezes, stopping me just short of a woman rushing across our path with a wobbly drinks tray. Despite the surrounding noise, her voice is crystal clear through the Nano GEAR. It's as convenient as it is unsettling, but it's bringing back memories of my introduction to espionage with Rust last year.

"Sorry..." I raise both eyebrows and blink, hoping to telekinetically convey that this wouldn't be an issue if she hadn't taken away my glasses.

"It's fine."

"Quick question, are these guys all about weapons? Or is there drugs and stuff too?"

"Officially? No one really knows."

"Mm. I don't like that," I say, as if it matters what I like.

We make our way across the room, approaching the largest group of people huddled together by the main bar. Jin waits patiently on the outskirts of the crowd, diligently passing up an opportunity to snack on the smoked salmon rillettes and spinach puffs circling the room. They'd be hard to resist if I wasn't so deep in character.

The conversation revolves around the smallest of the laughing Thai men, which indicates he could be Bhandit. They're all hanging on his every word and cackling the way one might when a powerful militia leader tells a bad joke. He looks about thirty years old, with a wispy goatee and shoulder-length hair. He couldn't be more than five foot six, even with a serious heel on his boot. As I look around the room, I can see several sets of eyes locked onto him, which further cements my theory. His only other defining characteristic is the white silk scarf draped around his neck like a Roman Catholic priest, setting him apart from his friends in similarly vibrant chut thai outfits. Honestly, a scarf. In this weather. Even if it's merely decorative, that seems to fit the bill for "eccentric".

The small man lights a cigarette and spots Jin through the rows of heads and shoulders, then excuses himself to pass through. I can't understand what he says to her in his native language, so I'm left to analyse the way he says it. The conversation begins with a welcoming smile, a greeting of familiarity. I wouldn't say it's warm, but it certainly isn't impersonal. I get a very short look of acknowledgement before Bhandit goes into a long exchange that involves a lot of hand gestures leading Jin to nod about twelve times in a row. For all I know, he could be explaining his new internet data plan or the plot of the latest *Avengers* movie. Unlike his friends earlier, Jin doesn't smile or feign laughter. She just nods and nods until he stops talking, then gestures away from the crowd. Now it's his turn to nod. The two of them begin walking over to the quietest corner of the room, occupied only by another suited westerner. Just as I begin to follow, Jin turns and gives me a "wait" sign, followed by a brief smile of assurance. I'm getting a bit antsy, so I'm happy for them to get this over and done without me. They're moving too far away now to read any body language, and if I keep squinting people will think I'm nuts.

I glance at the tigers. They're still sleeping. I subtly cover my mouth, scratching my beard, and check in with Jacoby.

"Just working on a lock right now," he says. *"It sounds like you had to let your lady go."*

"She's talking to the guy. I can't really see that far…"

"The farther away you are, the better. You're not actually there to protect her, remember? You're just a walking costume."

"I know."

"This goes without saying, but you've got to keep your mouth shut. And if you get jammed up, don't mention my name."

I hear a clang of metal before Jacoby mutes his end of the Nano GEAR again. I take a deep breath, adjust my tie, and fold my hands in front of me, assuming a classic bodyguard stance. Now to wait and stay out of trouble. It should be simple, but I know better than to assume simplicity at an event like this.

A quick movement across the wall in the corner of my eye distracts me. I squint at the blurry shape until it moves again and I realise it's a tiny lizard, a pinkish grey gecko. I scan the room and spot several more, each relaxing and eavesdropping on the party below, capitalising on the bugs attracted to the light. In a way, the geckos are like the people in this room. Thailand is a beautiful nation, but so many criminals are able to operate freely – child prostitution, human trafficking, animal abuse, drug trade, police corruption, sexual abuse, black markets, and rampant piracy to name a few. I know these things exist in America too, but I think our citizens have enough clarity and privilege to be outraged and motivated to fix it. Maybe it's through the inevitable failings of Thailand's class structure or through neglect from leadership that these things continue to happen. I don't know, and that's not for me as a visitor to decide. You can spend a lot of money on a nice venue, make it pretty, fill it with catered food, alcohol and dopey tigers, but you can't keep the hungry lizards from infiltrating and doing their thing.

"American?"

While I've been staring at the walls, an elegant, older woman has sidled up to the bar nearby. She appears interested in talking to me, which is not what I'm here to do. Even in America, I wouldn't be interested in socialising with someone of her ilk. Her burgundy sleeveless dress is definitely worth more than everything I own. The language and cultural barrier are one thing, but we've got a class and income gap to overcome if we're going to find some conversational common ground. I pause to think of how I'm supposed to react, long enough for her to ask if I speak English.

"Yes."

"I lived in America for seven years." I nod several times, slow enough to show I'm listening. This woman isn't Thai. I'm not confident to guess where she's from, but I feel like she could be Kurdish or Egyptian. Something like that. Her accent is American-influenced, but I can sense English is her second or third language. "My first husband died there."

"I'm... very sorry to hear that."

She takes a glass of champagne from the bar and holds it below her chin, considering her next words. "He was hit by bus in Modesto. Right before my eyes."

"I've never been to Modesto. I've heard it's... worth avoiding."

I instantly regret my informal choice of words, realising I've ignored the key part of her story. There aren't many women in the room, so I know she's important to our host. To my surprise, she reacts as if my flippant response was something she's been waiting to hear. Her laughter is loud enough for a few people to turn their heads, much to my regret. I shoot a quick eye towards Jin and Bhandit, but the view is obstructed. It really would be useful if I could see properly. Jin can bet this is coming up in my mission debrief.

"You're funny," the woman says, demanding my attention. She seems too important for me to scare away with rudeness. "Seher." I don't know what this means, but she extends her hand and several silver bangles rattle against each other on her tiny wrist. Even with my eyes fixated on her jewellery, I realise she's just introduced herself and I instinctively shake her hand.

"Drake... is my name."

"Drake," Seher repeats back to me. "Like Sir Francis."

"Sure." I glance at Jin again, hoping I'm not in trouble. I can see their blurry shapes and imagine the glaring daggers that may or may not be burning a hole through me. I'm afraid I'm left with no choice but to engage like a normal human being.

"What brings you to the vineyard?"

"I'm... That's confidential, madam."

"Please don't call me 'madam'. It's Seher. And you can talk to me – I'm with Bhandit. We're lovers."

She points her champagne glass towards the two blurry shapes at the side of the room, confirming my presumption that the small man is indeed the notorious Bhandit. This is not a conversation I want to have.

Chapter 10

Russian Roulette

What are my choices here? Ignore Seher and draw the scorn of Bhandit's lover, or engage in chit chat, potentially drawing the jealous wrath of Bhandit himself, a known eccentric and unstable bad guy. The old Maven would be paralysed with fear, but bodyguard Maven is all about action.

Who am I kidding? As much as I'm meant to be in character, it's just not in my nature to be rude. I have to hope Bhandit sees our innocent banter for what it is.

"He seems like a fun guy."

"A fun guy? Yeah, real fun guy." Despite the sarcasm, I don't sense any hostility toward her special friend. "He's fun when he's not killing people. Or selling the guns that kill even more people. Oh, he also kills people with his own hands. Fun guy."

I tilt my head in affirmation, like this news isn't a huge deal, because to Drake the bodyguard, this is old information. We're talking a lot about Bhandit, but I'm learning more about Seher – the fact that she's able to live with a murderer, that she knows about his business, and is brazen enough to discuss it with a strange foreigner at a party. She's a little nuts.

"Well... This is a lovely place you have together. And... a nice spread." I nod my head towards the drinkable fountains going largely ignored by the party guests. "Everyone is dressed so nice."

"Yes, indeed," she says. "Like captive beasts walking around in their cages, just measuring the lengths of their chains. We're all captive to something, wouldn't you say?"

"I would say... the tigers are a nice touch." I chose to ignore her philosophical analysis in form of a more close-ended topic, much to her amusement.

"Oh, they're too much, I know. Bhandit takes them just about everywhere. It's incredibly inconvenient. More than you would think. Try finding tiger food at midnight on Koyao Island."

"I can only imagine."

She laughs again, louder than before, and I start an internal panic. I'm not even trying to amuse her, but she won't stop cackling at everything I say. Something is wrong. I know I'm not this funny.

"I never expect the security to have such a dry sense of humour," she says. "I love it."

I chuckle out of a nervous politeness, and turn my body slightly away from Seher, hoping she finds some form of shiny object to distract her.

"Who did you come with? Don't tell me it's the Pattaya group."

"It's not."

"They're such a bore. Don't get me wrong, they're crazy. But it's so predictable, so trite, the antics they get up to at these events."

I silently nod and roll my eyes, like I know what she's saying. Totally, those Pattaya guys... If only they'd start with their antics right about now to pull her attention away from me.

"You should have a drink or two, Drake. Loosen up a bit."

"I probably shouldn't."

"I'm giving you permission."

"Well, I... have to drive soon, actually. Long drive up north, through all of the... terrain. You know what I mean?" It's obvious what I mean, but I'm a bit nervous she's going to insist on taking our relationship from "jovial awkward banter" to "bonding over an alcoholic beverage", and that's a level of closeness I'm completely unprepared for.

"Oh, you're not staying? You have to stay. You have to."

"I do?"

She raises one of her too-perfect eyebrows in classic mischievous fashion, leaving me to wonder what her dead husband would think of all this madness.

"Drake. There are a lot of violent people in this room. I'm sure a man like you will find plenty of amusement from what happens next."

"I can't tell if you're kidding," I start. "But I've had plenty enough fun already."

"Oh, Drake. It's not fun until someone gets hurt. You never told me what you're doing here, by the way."

Yes, there's a reason for that. She's smiling like Grinch in the middle of stealing Christmas, confirming this woman is more than nuts. She's bananas. Whichever is the worst of the two. But it's too late to back out now. I need to keep the conversation as mundane as possible.

"So, Modesto?"

"Tell me, what's so funny?" I feel a firm hand on my shoulder, pulling down to turn me around. It's Bhandit, trailed by his huge bodyguard, dressed just like me. Behind them is an outwardly nervous Jin. "I'm trying to conduct business over here and all I can hear is my woman laughing, laughing, laughing."

"We were just... I was–"

"He's just picking on you, Drake," Seher assures me, taking her lover by the arm. She stands several inches taller than Bhandit, but without heels they'd both stand a flat 5'7". His scowl slips into an earnest grin for a split second before resuming his interrogation act. I realise Jin's concern isn't about Bhandit throttling me, but rather that we're even conversing at all.

"Bhandit, this is my minder today..." she says.

"Drake." I lower my head in the style of the traditional Thai bow, but realise I've forgotten to fold my hands together. Whatever. It probably doesn't matter.

"You're quite small for a minder. Not like Coppard. I've got the best." Bhandit gestures over his shoulder to the giant protecting him. At the mention of his name, Coppard's mouth moves ever-so-slightly in his strange version of an acknowledgement. I nod, hoping to secure some sense of kinship with my fellow henchman, but he gives me nothing in return. A true professional, I suppose. He's burly, like a strapping overgrown bulldog, shaved down and shoved into a black suit. I'd have to hear him speak to guess his nationality, but his porcelain skin, light buzzed hair and handlebar moustache give him a European vibe. He looks like the kind of guy who brings his own ball to the bowling alley. If push came to shove, I'd think twice about punching him, for fear of bruising my own fist and seeing him laugh in my face.

"We come in all shapes and sizes," I say. "All with our own specialities, I'm sure."

And you can underestimate me at your own risk, buddy.

That's what I wanted to say, but this particular lie would be best unspoken. As weird as it is to have a smaller man question my physique, Bhandit clearly has a tall ego to support his own lack of self-awareness.

"I'm sure that's true, Mr Drake," he exclaims, lighting another cigarette with a smile. Bhandit's flawless General American accent suggests he's a westernised Thai who wants to conduct his shady business the American way. For no discernible reason, I assumed he was some thug who worked his way up through the slums to become a crime boss, but his temperament could convince me he's a college-educated entrepreneur. "Regardless of your stature, allow me to welcome you to my party. I am Bhandit Kaypradee. This is my winery. You've met my partner, Seher." She beams a smile, as if she hadn't just been telling me her boyfriend was a murderous maniac. "And what is it the two of you are finding so incredibly humorous?"

"It's just American humour, my love," she tells him, running a finger through his long hair. "You know how I adore a dry wit."

I smile politely, not sure how I ended up here or how to continue. Jin's mouth is wide open, as if she knows it's time to interject but her tongue is lagging behind her impulses.

"I don't typically do this with the muscle, but would you like to sit down for a drink?" Bhandit asks, although I sense it's not really a question I'm expected to answer. When a man like this makes you an offer, you accept it to keep on his good side. As much as I'm flattered to be described as "muscle" without referring to my lack of them, every instinct I have is telling me to get out.

"Get out, Maven. Hustle outta there."

Even Jacoby is telling me to get out. I look to Jin for her input, as a bodyguard should, and she's finally ready to breathe words into the discussion.

"I really would prefer for us to get going. It's a long way back to the SWAN, you know?"

"Nonsense. You can leave tomorrow morning."

"Bhandit, there's work to do, as we've just discussed, and I'd like to get back to my team to–

"It's my pockets funding the research, so I know I can afford it. And if you have a problem with that, I can replace that problem with another problem."

Jin is a terrible actor and has made no attempt to hide the disappointment from her face. She looks like she's been asked to work an extra Saturday shift and her excuse has fallen flat. She should've said she's not feeling well. That usually works. No one wants to catch the flu.

"I'm actually very tired and would prefer–"

"We insist," Seher says, clinging to Bhandit's arm like a magnet on steel.

"Yes, we do." There's no avoiding what looks like a delightful time with Thailand's "it" couple of the underworld.

"You're not actually doing this, are you?"

Unable to respond, Jacoby's voice rings like an inner monologue or conscience I have to just ignore.

"Don't be an idiot. I can't be bustin' in there to save you when this goes south."

I sigh, wishing Jacoby could understand our predicament, or

that I could at least explain it. I hold a chair out for Jin, which draws a head shake from Bhandit.

"We have somewhere more quiet to sit down. There's business left for me and Jin to discuss, and I'm bored with most of my guests here. This way."

I nod, attempting to look neutral instead of completely terrified. Most would aspire to confidence or fake excitement, but I'm realistic enough to just aim for neutrality. Bhandit tells Coppard to stay behind to make sure no one messes with his drowsy tigers, then he leads us through a small crowd. We pass a card table holding a bowl of potato chips, poker chips, a handgun, and what looks like a pile of the drugs that killed River Phoenix.

"Last time, we played Russian roulette and it was a great time," Bhandit says. "Great party. So I just left this here hoping we could do it again. But I still want it to come up organically. You can't force good times."

I nod, yet again, because how else can you respond to this madness? We reach a door I hadn't noticed in my literal short-sightedness. Bhandit takes a deep drag from his cigarette and swipes his phone over an electronic lock. We follow him into a short hallway with doorways on either side, leading towards a separate area at the end. Again, he swipes his phone and unlocks the entry to a room that hopefully doesn't become my final resting place. I'm not sure anyone would hear us scream from here, but then again, I'm not sure there would be much concern anyway, given the moral fibre of Bhandit's party guests.

The music and chatter fades, replaced with the patter of our shoes on the hardwood floors. With the food and fountains now separated by two closed doors, the strong scent of wood hits me in this study scattered with antiques, artefacts and artworks on display across the mahogany panel walls. I take a minute to examine some of the eclectic feature pieces on display – a stone tablet with Hebrew text, an ancient samurai helmet and sword, a signed copy of the Communist Manifesto, just to name a few. Of course, there's also the obligatory national flag, framed photograph of the king, and Buddha statues that you seem to find on display in every Thai building.

The far end of this peculiar room has a flat, stone feature wall with a stained-glass window overlooking a single mahogany desk, and a semi-circle of leather chairs waiting for our warm bodies. Two flat-screen TVs to the side are broadcasting CCTV footage from the party and parking lot. It would be a great set-up for some late-night *Call of Duty,* but I imagine it will never reach its entertainment potential.

"Have you seen *Scarface?*" I ask Jin quietly, drawing an obvious comparison to Tony Montana's mansion office.

"I don't know," she says, clearly distracted and confused by the question's relevance. "Maybe."

"Doesn't matter."

"This is my personal workroom," Bhandit says, gesturing needlessly. "It's where I conduct my legitimate business."

"I'm not sure there is much business left for us to discuss, sir," Jin says, reluctant to sit down or mention that their business falls well short of the "legitimate" nature.

"Well, Jintara. If you have nothing left to report, you've got time for a drink. You're not expecting, are you?"

"Don't be silly," Seher says. I'm not sure if she's being condescending or trying to save Jin the obvious embarrassment of awkwardly responding to such an unnecessary intrusion of privacy.

"Exactly," he says. "So, let me pour you a drink."

"You can pour a drink," Jin says, finally sitting alongside me and Seher. "But I'm not thirsty."

She's not backing down, despite Bhandit's obvious power play.

"I'm working and driving," I add.

"And I'm paying your wage, Mr Drake. Scotch?"

"Sure."

"You need. To leave. Maven." I can hear the concern in Jacoby's voice, but there's nothing I can do. I'll finish my drink, make nice conversation, and we'll be gone in ten minutes. That's my plan.

"Where are you from, Mr Drake?"

"Michigan." I see no reason to lie about this, and it's definitely the type of question you need to answer without hesitation.

"Ah, Detroit. *8 Mile.* Much like my lady, I have a fascination with American culture, you see. I perfected my English from watching *Everybody Loves Raymond.* I have every season on DVD."

"It's a great show," I say, telling a bold-faced lie, knowing it's merely a good show.

"It's the best!" Bhandit swishes the ice around in his drink, making me increasingly uncomfortable with his lingering stare. Even though I feel like the least interesting person in the room, to him I'm a novelty of some kind.

"Have you been to America?"

"Many times. But not for many years. I'm not allowed back, you see. Tell me, how long have you been working with our KIL Unit, Mr Drake?"

"I'm new." This feels like a safe answer. I can't be expected to have a deep knowledge of anything in particular.

"New?" He hands me a glass overflowing with ice and what appears to be barely an ounce of alcohol.

"Thanks. Fairly new."

"And the two of you." He points to Jin.

"This is our first day working together," she says. "He's a good driver."

I nod along, as if this is my well-established reputation.

"I bet. What are you carrying?"

"Carrying?"

I look at Seher and notice she's quietened down, deferring to Bhandit and almost uncomfortable with the line of questioning.

"Your weapon."

"Oh. The usual." Bhandit raises his head in a slow nod, a reaction so vague that I can't tell whether he believes me. This is bad. I swallow and feel my mouth going dry. If I licked a stamp, I think my tongue would rip it in half. I didn't even bring a gun. We never expected I'd do anything more than stand at the side of the room. As I hold eye contact with Bhandit, I can see Jin's nervous hand in my peripheral vision, tapping on the arm of her chair. Her agitation is growing, like a nervous parent in a hospital waiting room.

"Darling," Seher places a hand on Bhandit's arm. "I was telling Drake about my time in Modesto."

"I'm sick of hearing about Modesto," Bhandit says, shutting her down with abrupt aggression. He leans forward on his desk, arms stretched out, pushing an overflowing ash tray out of the way. "And I don't care about your dead husband. I'm sorry, not sorry, as the kids say."

This is super awkward. I take a casual sip from my glass and realise why Bhandit poured such a small drink. It burns, from my lips to my oesophagus. Are these ice cubes made from pure ethanol? Seher's dejected expression forces me to break the silence.

"Your English is great, sir. Both of you... actually."

"Thank you, Mr Drake."

"And I'm no expert on antiquities, but your collection here is very impressive."

"Thank you, again. Would you believe I never paid for any of them?"

I smile, feeling this is meant to be impressive, and he grins back in delight, eyes almost closed. He pushes back his long hair and pours himself another drink, this one twice the size of our first, then lights a cigarette in the same hand as his glass. I'm keeping count and that's three in ten or fifteen minutes.

"At my home in Bangkok, I have a blue parrot. Beautiful creature."

"That's nice," I say, unsure where he's going. They did say he was eccentric. "They're super smart, those birds. I've heard."

"Not this one," he says. "Sometimes I open the cage. I want her to fly around, feel free. Explore the house. Half the time she doesn't realise the door's open, you see. Doesn't even leave the cage. Every week I open it. She sits there on her perch. Week after week. She's so used to her environment that she has no desire to leave it."

"Or maybe she knows even if she leaves the cage..." Seher

starts. "She's still not free."

"You're giving her too much credit. It's not a philosophical decision."

"You don't know her full intelligence."

"I give her an opportunity and she ignores it. That's not intelligence. She will never reach her potential, stuck in that cage. It makes me sad." Bhandit's free hand slides over his chest, as if this proves he has a functioning heart capable of positive emotions. "The bird has created a cage for itself. And it stays inside. Just like you." He points in my direction, prompting me to look at Jin for an explanation.

"This has been nice," she says. "But we should be going." Bhandit responds in Thai, gesturing at me, Seher, and unseen objects.

"Is there a problem?" I ask.

"There is a problem," he spits back, standing up straight with his glass still in hand. "I don't like to be wrong. I hate it. Can't stand it. It doesn't happen very much, you see." He knocks down his scotch, and tosses the drink into the wall, shattering into tiny, indistinguishable fragments of broken ice and glass. The three of us recoil at the sudden noise, then watch Bhandit for an explanation of his violent action.

"You're like the parrot, you see," he says, looking me dead in the eye. Beneath a calmed voice, there's no mistaking his simmering rage, ready to overflow again. My hand is gripped tight around the leather arm of my chair, my elbow shaking with adrenaline. "You made this prison for yourself. You could have flown away, but you've caged yourself, unable to fly free, as you probably should."

He's lost it. He's making no sense. Even Seher is showing subtle signs of concern, like an attentive dog owner ready to pull back as they recognise the early signs of an unfriendly exchange. As she stands, Bhandit gestures for her to remain seated and she obeys. When it was just the two of us, she was so free-spirited and talkative. It's stating the obvious to say there's something clearly wrong with this man. Seher isn't innocent in this, and clearly condones the majority of his actions, but I sense Bhandit's overbearing presence has turned her into a passive observer. Classic oppressive patriarchy, some might say. If she's enjoying his antics, she's certainly keeping it to herself.

"Like I said. I don't like to be wrong." Bhandit circles around his desk and leans forward, with both arms resting on its rich brown surface. "And I assumed you were dead. But if you were somehow lucky enough to survive this long... what are you doing here, Mr Maven?"

He stands up straight and calmly reaches to his desk drawer as I do my best to look baffled. My rapid beating heart is so strong that I look down to make sure it's not visible through my shirt and jacket.

"Are you here for me?" Bhandit asks, lighting yet another cigarette, as if it's only the first few puffs that count for anything. "Because you should know I'm not going without a fight. And if you wish to fight me, I wish you to at least admit your intentions."

Bhandit produces a small, black submachine gun from his desk and places it down next to the drinks tray, just daring me to react. As he notices me eyeing it off, his chest begins to shake up and down in bizarre silent laughter.

"This... This is a Steyr TMP machine pistol, 9x19mm. It's Austrian, not Israeli, of course. But I still call it my Uzi. I know it's technically not an Uzi, but it's just so fun to say. Uzi. Oooh-zeee. That's what I've called all SMGs since I was a young boy."

With his head lowered and eyes fixed forward on me, I can tell he's anticipating some kind of movement.

"I'm sure, Mr Drake, you are very familiar with this weapon in your line of work. Would you clean it for me?"

"Excuse me?"

"Clean it."

He tilts his head toward the gun, probably expecting me to reach for it. I look to Jin and she gives me a slow wide-eyed nod. I know exactly what to do. I take a deep breath and visualise my plan of attack.

With perfect accuracy, I throw my cold empty glass at

Bhandit's face, staggering him.

I reach for the SMG, click back the safety and point it at Bhandit's bloody forehead as he flails.

"Be careful what you wish for, fool."

At least, that's what I should've done. That would've been really cool... but that's not who I am.

Chapter 11

Proposition

"I'm sorry, sir. I don't know what you mean."

This is my measured non-violent response to Bhandit's threat. He's seen through my bad disguise, but I'm still hopeful I can walk him back, and at least buy some time for Jacoby to somehow save the day.

"Please," Jin starts without finishing, as Bhandit uses a sharp head turn to stop her short. I don't sense any fear for her own safety, but she's certainly not dumb enough to think we're not at risk.

"Don't act the fool. I know it's you."

"Bhandit, what's going on?" Seher is as clueless as I'm acting.

"It's painstakingly obvious, Mr Maven," he says, rudely ignoring his lover. "You're not like my other security officers. There's something off, you see. And then *Michigan...* That's right. I've done my research."

A drawn out breath escapes me as I loosen my tie with one hand, and reach inside my jacket with the other. I take out my glasses and slide them onto my face. Vision, at last.

"What can I say? I wanted to see how the other side lives."

"That's what I'm wondering, Mr Maven. What brings you all the way to Thailand? You know if you wanted to meet me, you only had to say so." He smiles a mile wide, easing my tension a little. At least he doesn't seem likely to shoot me dead right here in his office. "I harbour no ill will to you. Shutting down Metric has been a boon for business."

"Well... First of all, you're welcome," I say, realising Bhandit had to take a great deal of interest in the story I broke with Rust and Mars last year. It set off the course of events that increased his power and gave him total control of Metric's SWAN facility. Still, I need to minimise the risk here and keep the tension from creeping up again.

"You kind of just blew my cover with this one, though." I point to Jin, who's sitting quietly and expressing as little emotion as possible. Her overt nervousness is gone, replaced with a stoic neutrality. Poor Jin. This is her boss grilling us, and it's my fault, but I know enough about her to expect she'll be feeling responsible for the tense situation. She can't plead ignorance and excuse herself, leaving me behind, and there's no benefit admitting she's in on the charade. I've put her in a no-win situation.

"What's your play then? Following around my scientist? Infiltrating the SWAN?" Once these words leave Bhandit's lips, his eyes expand from crescents to full moons. "You've come here for proof. New World Order proof. How bold. Fortune favours the bold. I could help you with that."

"Y...you could?"

"But I can't have you bringing attention to my work. I work hard to stay off the radar of the Five Eyes. Look at me – I know how to play their game. But it's in our best interest to remain free from influence and political obligation. The devil resides in the houses of parliament."

"I'm really not sure what that means, but honestly, I'm just here for a news story. And I can see that's not happening without your input. I'm guessing nothing happens around here without you knowing about it." Bhandit nods carefully in response. I can't tell if it's a nod of agreement or if he's not quite buying my attempt at flattery. "I can craft this narrative however you like, or I can leave now and beat the traffic. Perhaps I've come a little unprepared, but it sounds like I need you in my corner if I don't want to be going home empty-handed."

"Yes, partly true." He doesn't elaborate about how I might be wrong, instead choosing to apologise to Seher about breaking the glass. Apparently it was a gift. She doesn't hesitate to say she forgives him, but she still looks incredibly uncomfortable. This doesn't quite add up with the way she was acting at the party, when she was thriving off her lover's violent reputation. I can sense she's sobering up and realising she might see some bullets fly tonight.

"Which part is untrue?" I ask Bhandit, attempting to clarify whether I'm getting closer to a pardon or just digging my own grave.

"The part you said about going home empty-handed. You see, I wouldn't say you're going home."

"I'm not?"

I throw Jin a confused look and notice she's wisely remaining silent and letting this play out. It feels rude to ignore her, but in this instance I think keeping the attention on me is the safest option. I don't know how she's keeping so calm. Most people in her position would be freaking out, yet she's sitting quietly and concealing her reaction like a high court judge, obligated to hear both arguments.

"Mr Maven, what do you think of me? No, perhaps don't answer that. You don't have to. I know how people like you see people like me."

"I might surprise you. I can be very open-minded."

"We are the scum of the earth. Preying on violence and war, profiting from murder and misery. Am I close?"

When he puts it like that, it's hard to disagree. I must've hesitated a fraction too long, as he continues.

"You look around my country and see the poverty and wonder who is helping these people. I am. It's me. You see, bad guy buys gun and kills other bad guys who buy guns. We're down one or two bad guys, yes? In Vietnam, in India, in Tibet – whoever is buying, they're all the same. Every weapon I sell makes less evil. Only the most foolish will expire."

"But that doesn't make any *sense*," I say, finally allowing an emotional response. Bhandit's drivel got to me and I've poked him back instead of thinking about a way out of here. "They're just bad guys killing more bad guys? What about all the innocent people, they're always spared, are they? That would be a strict moral code for a 'bad guy', sir."

"Don't talk to me about morals, Mr Maven. I know all about your American traditions. I paid attention to your stories, so I know you're well aware. The New World Order is breeding violence and America is complicit. This is how it needs to be. Weapons and technological warfare are our greatest symbol of evolution. He who holds the biggest gun is the most advanced civilisation. Throughout all history, the greatest armies have controlled the world."

I part my lips, trying and failing to interject before he continues. He's on a rant that can't be stopped.

"You have the biggest army and the rest of the planet falls in line. What happens when they don't? Look at Iraq. Afghanistan. North Korea. It's a death wish to go up against the dominant world power – unless you have the weapons. Count the guns. Think about the expenditure, all while your citizens go without food, without homes, without shoes. Your government doesn't look at the needs of the people. They just happily feed the war-cannibalised animal and rub its belly. You see, everyone knows it's more profitable to let people kill each other than to feed them."

"Not everyone thinks like that, and I still believe a lot of people back home are gonna help me change this. I just need to get my story heard. If you really want to help the poor like you say, help *me*."

Bhandit exhales a long drag of smoke and chews the side of his mouth, pondering my proposition or wondering how much mess it'll make to feed me to his tigers. "I mean, yes. I can talk about philanthropy all day. I put my money back into the community. But if I'm honest, Mr Maven... Can I call you Andrew?" I would've said "yes" if he left me any time to react. "The truth is that I like this. All of it."

Bhandit grasps his pistol and thrusts it in the air to emphasise every statement. "My home. My vineyard. My army. My collections. My status. My women. My guns. Helping my people. It feeds me. And I'm not letting you take away my dinner."

"I'm not here to take anything from you," I protest, leaning forward in my chair, attempting to be nonplussed by his lackadaisical gun brandishing.

"We'll see."

"Will we? Surely nothing can prove it, at this point. You either believe me or you don't. Sir."

Bhandit rises from his chair to stand over me and prove his dominance – a very necessary move given his lack of physical stature. If it weren't for the gun, I think I could take him. "I've given this a lot of thought, as we're sitting here. I believe I won't take your life today."

That's a relief. My eyes dart to Jin to check that her poker face is still reactionless.

"But I can't let you go either. You will stay and work."

"Err, what? Here?"

"You're a man of many skills. My ventures extend far beyond weaponry and wine, Andrew."

"I... OK? Sure?" I don't know what to say. The path of least resistance would be to roll with it until Jacoby can bail me out.

"But you, *Jintara Katetsin*." He turns his full attention to Jin, including the barrel of his gun. "This betrayal I cannot allow."

"Bhandit, I can assure you I knew nothing of this," she says with confidence, breaking her silence and raising her hands in a peaceful gesture.

"Hey, hey, no, no no." I'm not so calm with the gun pointing. "She's absolutely in the dark on this. Trust me, I needed her to get to you, and that's the only reason she's here. So please, let her do what she does best, and... you know, keep doing the scientist things. Please."

"Bhandit," Seher says gently, raising her voice to speak her mind. "Whatever you're doing, just please hurry. I feel like this has been a giant waste of my time and not at all the conversation I was expecting."

I'm a big fan of the theory that behind every great man, there's a greater woman, but Seher is failing to be the voice of reason we need right now. It must be my turn again.

"I haven't seen your annual report, but I feel like she's got to be one of your greatest assets, if she's running that research division. Don't do anything rash." Even as I get emotional and desperate, Jin continues to stare down the gun without batting an eyelid. She either has a lot of trust in Bhandit's reasoning process or she's insane.

"You have been a great asset," he says, still stretching out his arm, clutching the weapon in front of his chest. "But you have either betrayed me or been completely blind to a spy operating right under your nose. Both of these crimes are unforgivable."

"Hey, man," I interject. "You can forget about me working for you if this is how you dismiss your staff."

"Then I'm going to need two bullets instead of one."

Seher places hands over both of her ears and turns away. "Just do it already!"

Man, Seher is the worst.

Actually, Bhandit is the worst, but she's a close second.

"I have to say, I'm close to losing count of the people I've killed. It's never an easy thing to do. But I've never regretted it."

"There's a first time for everything," I say with a confidence in stark contrast to my total lack of an escape plan. Maybe now is the time I throw my glass at him. Could I get over the desk in time? His gun is aimed right at Jin, so there's really no good option here.

"Sawadee khrup, Jintara."

Jin closes her eyes tight as Bhandit says goodbye, bracing for a bullet that ends it all. This is a terrible way to go out. That's it. I'm going for it. Please, God. Don't let me die. Not yet.

Chapter 12

BMX Bhandit

I hurl my glass at Bhandit, hitting him square on the shoulder. He flinches long enough for me to help Jin down, obstructed by the desk in front of us to take cover from retaliation. Bhandit says something in Thai, probably cursing at my desperate move that has probably bought us only a few more moments together. Ignoring Seher in my peripheral vision, I look Jin in the eyes and tell her I'm sorry. It's all I can think to say.

"I'm sorry too," she whispers, as I remind myself I need to think about our next stalling move. We could take Seher hostage. Would it be unfair to use her as a human shield? I mean, she is kinda evil. But Bhandit seems to lack the compassion to respond to that type of move. And I have no weapons. I really should've brought a gun with me. Where is Jacoby?

I brace myself like a sprinter at the starting blocks to tackle Bhandit if he approaches from the side of the desk. The tinkling of shattered glass and a hard thud on the desk's wood surface add to the confusion, before Seher's ear-piercing scream really gets me wondering what could be happening out of our view. Still, I don't dare move until Seher rushes over to Bhandit, babbling in Thai. This is all very odd.

"Oh my," Jin says, rising to her feet. Against my better judgement, I stand up beside her, assuming she's understanding everything I'm not.

"Oh boy." I look down at the maple desk, where Bhandit is sprawled out, resting his head beside a growing pool of red liquid and shattered glassy shards. I glance up at the window behind and there it is, a small hole through the thick glass. It's hard to hear Jin's explanation over Seher's hysterical shrieking, as she shakes Bhandit, refusing to let him pass into whatever afterlife he believes in.

"I don't think he's waking up, ma'am."

This was the wrong choice of words. Seher snaps out of her shock and reaches for Bhandit's Uzi.

"You... This is because of you."

"Hey, Seher, I'm sorry. But the last person to point that gun at us..." I point to the corpse in front of us, by way of evidence, allowing her to draw the link. My uncharacteristic lack of sympathy only inspires rage as she thrusts her weapon at me and squeezes the trigger. I duck, hoping I'm fast enough to evade gunfire, but she's messed up somehow because nothing happens. In an instant, Jin leans back, kicking her leg high enough to make me cringe, connecting her shin with incredible force to Seher's unprotected temple. She falls hard to the ground, right next to my dropped jaw.

"What was that?" I ask Jin, as she moves our unconscious witness into a more comfortable position.

"Whoever shot Bhandit was probably about to shoot her too. She doesn't deserve to die."

"I mean, yeah, I agree with you, but what was that ninja move? Are you a Metric spy too?"

"Muay Thai is our national sport. Kickboxing. I'm not as flexible as I once was, but..."

"Enough to get the job done. That was unreal," I say, starting to look around the room for a way out. "I nearly tore a hamstring just witnessing it. Why didn't you drop that move sooner?" I do my best not to look at Bhandit's fatal head wound, as I reach into his jacket pocket for his phone to get us through the locked door.

"It's Muay Thai, not *Power Rangers*. There was a desk between us, and he had a gun!"

"Yeah, OK. But still. You probably have a move or two up your sleeve... more than I do."

"I can't believe you threw a glass."

"It worked out in the end. Jacoby, if you're out there listening, or watching, which I'm sure you are... We're fine. We'll just, I dunno, make a run for it, I guess. You have any ideas, Jin?"

"This is my first... murder scene. Should we make it look like a burglary?"

"I don't know," I say. "Whatever gets us out of here quicker sounds good to me."

"What about her, though?"

"Maybe we can make it look like she shot him?"

"Let's do that."

"But why would she be unconscious then?"

"I don't know!"

"OK. Well. I think there are enough mixed signals happening to buy us the time we need. Lead us out of here."

"You probably should lead. Being the bodyguard."

"Right. You're right."

~∞~

Apart from knowing Jin is an employee of Bhandit, Seher didn't seem to really grasp exactly who we were or where we came from. Hopefully the dots remain unconnected and we won't hear from her again. Either way, the two-day deadline Jin gave for this job is only more stringent now with a murder on the record. Leaving a witness behind certainly isn't the Metric way, but Jin and I just aren't killers. Even witnessing a death is hard enough, though it certainly didn't hit me with the gravitas of my first live fatality with Scarpino last year. Both situations involved an evil human attempting to kill me, and a last-second saviour, but this time around... maybe the empathy has been beaten out of me. It's been a long year. Maybe it's just not as shocking the second time around. Just like childbirth. I'm sure the tragedy of death and the miracle of birth each become mundane eventually. The circle of life.

"Well done... *Drake.*"

Jin's words shake me from my train of thought back into the reality of our situation. I'd fully focused on our escape route, zoning out to navigate through the party and back to safety, completely avoiding eye contact with Coppard or anyone else. We're now at the stairs, approaching the fountains and blaring pop music, soon to blend into the darkness of the vineyard's entrance and parking lot. I'll never know if Bhandit's Russian roulette station had eventuated into its full party potential.

"Yeah, we did it. We can pat ourselves on the back when we're far away from here. Where's our ride?"

"Jacoby."

"Jacoby. Hey." I look around the parking lot, trying to remember the model or even the colour of our car. "This thing is still on, yeah?" We haven't heard a peep from him since he advised us to stay away from Bhandit. I take out my Nano GEAR and inspect it, despite having no idea how it would look if it was broken.

"It's not the earpiece," she says. "It's him."

As I wait for Jin's explanation, she stands looking at me like she's still waiting for the question. I want to see her as a scientist, but I can't shake the image of her leg outstretched like Chun-Li, colliding with Seher's cranium.

"Do you think he's, like, still packing up his sniper rifle or something?"

"I don't know. But I don't think we should just stand here waiting."

"I agree. Should... Should we run?"

Jin nods and we start jogging down the long driveway, past a Buddhist shrine and sleeping dog, past a gardener working overtime, and past twenty or thirty rows of grapevines. I'm close to out of breath by the time we hit the road, illuminated by a single streetlight. I might've lost some weight through stress and a new diet over the past months, but I'm as unfit as ever.

Jin's doing just fine. I bet she works out.

"Can you ride a bike?" she asks, picking an odd time for a "get to know you" game.

"What?"

"There's a bike. Right there." She points behind me and sure enough, there's an old single speed cruiser bike leaning against the front fence of the vineyard, like God Himself had intervened to make a teenage Thai kid dump it on their way home from school.

"That's super convenient, because I don't think I could run much longer in these shoes." I loosen my tie and sit on the padded bike seat, adjusting it as much as I can without loosening any levers. Without saying a word, Jin jumps up on the handlebars and basket, resting her legs to the side of the front wheel. They say you never forget how to ride a bike, and I guess you can say the same about sitting sidesaddle on the crossbar.

"Now, which way to freedom and cashew chicken stir fries?"

"There's a town that way." Jin points hastily in the opposite direction of where we drove in, before returning her hand to balance on her awkward seat. I ask her whether the town has a BMX circuit and she misses the joke completely. Fortunately, there's a downhill slope and after a couple minutes of riding, the occasional farmhouse turns into consecutive dwellings and eventually an entire town of semi-busy shops and street stalls.

"Now what?"

"Keep going," Jin says. "We will hear from Jacoby eventually... if he's OK."

"Well, now you've got me thinking. What if he's not?"

"Then we're in trouble. We need those explosives."

"Yeah. But we could still go to the SWAN and get the data. We'd just need a new plan for the rest of it – you know what I mean?"

There's a pause and I can't see Jin's face to know if it's a contemplative silence or she just truly hates my latest suggestion.

"Jin? What do you think?"

"No offence, but I don't like our chances. We barely made it out of the vineyard without becoming dinner for those tigers."

"I thought we were a good team."

"No, not really."

Ouch. Now it's my turn to remain silent.

"It wasn't your fault, Andrew. It was a bad plan to start with."

"We improvised and the result was actually fairly decent, if you ask me."

"A bullet through a stained-glass window, blood splattered across the desk, a dead war lord and a hysterical girlfriend. It couldn't have gone much better."

"I know you're being sarcastic, but nine times out of ten, we'd probably be goners – you know what I mean?" I stop the bike, putting my foot on the ground, hoping that my panting is enough explanation for the rest. I reach out and lean against a lamp post, allowing Jin to get her feet on solid ground. I've picked a spot just outside a small convenience store with air-conditioning that looks very accommodating right this second. I watch Jin, waiting for a reaction as she stretches her back and checks the time on her phone.

"What now?"

"I don't know, but this isn't a good place to stop... unless you want to get completely saturated."

I look past her to a trio of teenagers gathered around a pipe in the ground, filling up buckets of dirty water and splashing each other as they go.

"So, this water festival thing goes day and night?"

"Songkran started two days ago and lasts three days."

"Three days. That's commitment. And that pipe water looks nasty. Why aren't they using these bottles?" I point to a rack of clear containers, stacked high outside the convenience store.

"That's petrol, you stupid."

"That's gasoline?"

Jin nods and hops back up to the handlebars, forcing me to push off and ride again. I might be unfit, but I'm not going to let the bike fall down with her on it.

"Throwing gas around would make this strange holiday a lot stranger."

"I've been to many fourth of July parties in the States, when you explode the sky. Don't act like this is so strange. *Farangs* have strange celebrations too."

"Explode the sky..." I turn the bike around the corner, aimless like a school kid taking the long way home. "That's funny. You're not wrong though. Hopefully I can see another July fourth in my lifetime."

"Don't be so sad."

"I'm not sad. Just realistic."

I think about Jacoby gathering explosives from the vineyard's hidden armoury. If he'd been caught up in a scrap, we might've heard an explosion or some kind of commotion before we left. I can't think of any explanation why he's gone quiet.

"You sound sad, Andrew. I think you'll be home for another Maven family Independence Day, free to blow things up again."

"The Maven festivities were always fairly unexplosive, to be honest."

"What is a Maven? What does it mean?"

"It's Hebrew, like an expert on something. Appropriate, right?"

"Yeah, you're an expert on lots of things. Expert on complaining, expert on fast food, expert on getting into trouble."

"I forgot how funny you are when you're not sitting completely still and saying nothing at all. What's your last name mean?" I'm not sure I could remember a single Thai name I've ever heard, given they seem to be at least four or five syllables.

"Kasetsin is to do with agriculture. My family owned farms and a mine in the Phuket area."

"Right. I bet that place has changed a lot with the tourism and everything."

"Unrecognisable. Now my family owns a business with... what do you call it? Laser cutting. For signs. Stop here, if you like."

I let the bike roll until I can put my foot down and rest by a reservoir. It's not the most picturesque or pleasant backdrop for our conversation, but it's discrete enough to satisfy Jin.

"So, your family were always farmers before that then? If it's in your name."

"For a while, I think. But last names weren't even a thing here until about one hundred years ago."

"Serious?"

"It's true. And every name is unique. There are no common last names in Thailand, so if someone has your last name, it means you are related or someone didn't do their job properly before they invented computers."

"Really? No Smiths or Joneses equivalents over here, then."

"There are many Chinese immigrants here and every family needed to change to a unique name. The new citizens couldn't duplicate any, so now you will hear sometimes a very long name, but the native Thai, they have a shorter one."

"Right. That explains a lot. I don't think I could ever learn the language, but it's a fascinating culture."

As we talk, I notice an alley cat propped up against the fence running along the reservoir. It's sitting slumped like a human eating Doritos on a beanbag, with its back to the fence and legs in front. I've never been jealous of a feral cat, but I'm close.

"There are many things you wouldn't believe if I told you," Jin says.

"You say that, but with what I've seen and heard over the past year, I would just about believe anything – you know what I mean?"

"It sounds like a difficult time."

"That's... an understatement, yes."

"But you're here to make it all right. Stay positive, yes?"

"Yeah, of course. It's just... We all have our moments."

"Moments of what?"

"You know, it just gets hard sometimes." I clear my throat, because admitting this is also very hard. "I think if I wasn't staying positive, I would've given up a long time ago."

"Well. That's good."

I feel a tiny tap on my back and turn to see a young girl waiting for my attention. She's no more than eleven years old and dressed like she crawled straight out of bed to watch cartoons.

"Hello..." I say with caution, unsure of her language abilities or motivations.

She giggles for no clear reason and tosses a folded piece of paper in my direction before running away. The paper floats to the ground in front of me, partly sinking into a shallow puddle of water. I bend down and pick it up, trying to keep track of the girl to see exactly where she's come from, until a revving motor behind us demands my attention. Jin peers over her shoulder and my concern grows as her eyes widen.

"What is it?"

"Go there!" Jin hops up to the bike handlebars, pointing to a narrow walkway between two buildings. I push off and ride with the urgency her voice demands.

"What is it?"

"It's Coppard!"

"What? How?"

"Seher sent him after us. They have guns!"

"Gotta be kidding..."

As several foreign voices yell from a red, battered pickup truck behind us, I remember Bhandit's phone resting in my pocket. Is it possible to track a phone this fast? I put it out of my mind and pedal hard, praying the locals don't step out of their homes into this walkway. The houses are crammed together like books on a shelf. I can see right into their living rooms and would feel like a voyeur if I was riding any slower.

"Move!"

A woman carrying a plate of food scurries out of our way and gasps as a couple of eggs tumble to the ground.

"Keep going," Jin shouts as we reach the end of the walkway and return to the road. "There's another path across the street."

"Good." There's no time to explain it, but sharp turning isn't easy with a grown woman sitting on the handlebars. I glance left and right to judge it's safe to cross the road, even though there's no time to brake. I hear the distant blare of a car horn and look over just in time to see the red pickup truck with two Thai men in the rear, both thrusting their weapons in the air like uprising resistance fighters. Jin wasn't kidding. I don't see Coppard, but it seems Seher has woken up, raised the alarm and sent Bhandit's crew after us. This is what we get for choosing the paragon option.

Jin yells in Thai at every critter crossing our path. The dogs are smart enough to scatter, although there's something about a speeding bike that seems to attract fat and sickly cats.

"Should we turn around? They'll be waiting ahead for us."

"They might block both sides," Jin says, her eyes locked on our path.

"What do we do?"

"Just keep going! And pray."

I follow her instructions, even though God and I have had a strained relationship lately. Then again, I have to give Him credit – I've never been in a jam He couldn't get me out of.

We reach the end of the walkway and I turn wide onto the road again. As the street ahead comes into full view, I'm faced with a dead end to the right, so I take the only natural route.

"This is... going to be interesting."

"Less talk, more pedalling."

"At the risk of sounding really unfit... my thighs are burning. And I don't know how much longer I can go."

"Fine, let's swap."

I stop the bike abruptly at the side of the road, surprised by how well the brakes work when you need them to. Jin steps down and motions for me to hurry with the changeover.

"Maybe we should just hide?" I say.

Before she can hurt my feelings, the red pickup tears around the corner and stops in front of us. It happens so fast that we can't react. My eyes focus on one of the armed men wearing a black tank top, shouting in Thai with a deranged lunacy in his eyes. He points his gun and sprays us both across the chest.

I reach down and touch my drenched white shirt in disbelief, as chills run down my spine. I can't believe it.

Chapter 13

Prodding

It's cold... so cold.

The pickup fades into the distance along with the gunmen's laughter, replaced by a low giggle beside me.

"You've got to be kidding," I say to Jin.

She's as drenched as I am, water soaking through her shirt. A single droplet reaches the end of her nose and rests there until she turns her body to face me.

"I'm so relieved."

"Did you know?"

"Did I know? I thought it was Coppard from the vineyard."

"You weren't just messing with me?"

"No!" Jin cracks up, gasping for air as she tries to defend her momentary panic.

"Why'd you say it was Coppard? Did you even see him? It's so dark out here."

"I don't know why. He scares me."

I join her with a reluctant chuckle, though my heart is still racing fast enough to stop me from truly enjoying the relief. The water dripping down my face reminds me how thirsty and dehydrated I am.

"This water festival is killing me, Jin."

"One more day. But we generally get tired of terrorising the *farangs* by day three."

"The what?"

"It's the… people like you." She wipes water from her eyes and removes her Nano GEAR to dry out her ear. "European."

"White folk?"

"Yes, white. Like, the foreigners. Westerners."

"*Farang.* OK. I heard you say it before. And I think Bhandit said it too."

"If he was talking about you, then yes. Now, is it my turn to ride or you want to keep going now that we've had some refreshment?"

I turn and spit, remembering the travel advice about ingesting the local water supply. If the KIL Unit doesn't get me, the E. coli bacteria will.

A slight crackle in my Nano GEAR interrupts before I can answer Jin's question. It's Jacoby, finally asking where we are. I tell him I'm glad he's still alive.

"*Course I'm alive. Where are you at?*"

"Um…" I look around, realising I have no idea. Jin responds in Thai, with what I assume is a detailed explanation of our surroundings or nearby signs.

"*I'm driving and I'll be there soon. Hold tight for a few minutes and I'll hustle over.*"

We do as we're told, enjoying the rest and waiting for the tropical heat to dry our sweaty water-soaked clothes, even in the moonlight. The peace is more than welcome and soothes my mind, even if we are still in danger. By this point, it just feels good to pretend we're not – to relax and imagine the worst is behind us. If Bhandit's people come for us, so be it. That's Jacoby's problem as much as it's mine.

"This is pretty weird, isn't it?" Jin asks out of nowhere, as if the reality of our situation has crystallised in her mind. It is weird. Super weird. But I don't need Jin to feel any more anxious about it.

"Weird stuff happens," I say. "I found an arm once."

"An arm?"

"Yeah. I was in middle school. I came out of a movie theatre with my friends, took a shortcut through an alley and there was an arm."

"Severed?"

"Yeah, I guess so. It was weird. They never figured it out, as far as I was ever told."

"That's messed up."

"Yeah. It was a real *Goonies* kinda moment. We talked about it for years."

"Should I watch that too?"

"Probably not."

As people walk in and out of the Chinese restaurant on the nearby corner, I have a lingering feeling there's something I'm meant to do. A family with two kids jogs my memory of the young girl handing over a paper scrap before the pickup startled us. I unfold it with care to find my soaked pocket has made the ink run a little, but it's mostly legible.

DON'T TRUST HIM BRO !! DO NOT

I can't read the last two words, but I recognise the writing and it's enough to make my heart drop.

"Change your face. Be happy. What's wrong?"

Jin has spotted the unmistakable look of panic in my eyes and I need to think quick. Can I say anything at all?

"It's nothing."

"Don't lie to me. You're a terrible liar."

"I'm not. I mean, I think I'm a decent actor."

"Sure thing, Mr Drake. What does the paper say?"

I shake my head and point to my ear, or my Nano GEAR, to be precise. Jin mouths "OK" and voice commands the devices into a hibernation mode.

"That's not going to be suspicious at all," I say with a voice laced with sarcasm.

"Well, I'm not going to spend who knows how many hours with you when I don't know what's going on."

"Look." I hand her the note and she almost immediately looks back to me for an explanation.

"It's from Mars."

"The Metric agent?"

"Former," I say, scanning the roads for any sign of Jacoby.

"Is he the husband or the son?"

"The son. It's definitely from him. Has to be."

"How do you know?" She turns the paper over, looking for some identifying feature.

"He's got to be the only adult in Thailand who would write 'bro' in what appears to be a warning message."

"You think it's a warning?"

"It's *obviously* a warning. But from what? Jacoby? I don't know. Seems... It's weird. Mars disappeared mysteriously, no warning. But this means he's gotta be nearby."

"Unless it's not him."

I ignore Jin, looking up at the nearby rooftops in a hopeless attempt to catch someone who doesn't want to be seen.

"Are you hearing me, Andrew? Why wouldn't he just approach you? You're friends, yes? He doesn't sound like the type to hide in the shadows."

"He's exactly that type. I mean, he could be five feet away from us right now and we wouldn't know."

"But why not talk to you?"

"Yeah. I don't know... Maybe he..." I click my tongue, racking my brain to figure out the next move.

"Andrew?"

"I don't know, OK? I'm sorry. Let me think for a second."

"Well..." Jin looks frustrated now. "Jacoby is going to be here in, like, two minutes. So think faster."

"I just... Let's keep the lid on for now."

"Sorry?"

"We'll stay cool. I'll... We'll go with Jacoby. I'll see if I can figure him out. I'll do some poking."

"Poking?"

"Prodding."

Jin turns her head to the side, unconvinced we're making the right move. "I mean, sure? See, I don't know who this note is from... but if it is definitely from Mars? I would not get in that car with Jacoby."

"Yeah, OK," I say, frustrated by the lack of help from her statement. "But unless he jumps out of the bushes in the next ten seconds, I don't see any other option."

Jin bites her top lip, staring into nothing and considering our options before conceding that we're not prepared for anything else.

"So... you're just going to ask him?"

"No. I have my methods." I lean against the corner of the store's brick wall, piecing together some questions that might uncover the truth. "You have to feel around the edges, you know what I mean? See how he reacts."

"You think it's that easy?"

"It won't be easy. I mean, in some ways he's a professional liar, so..."

"Who's a liar?" asks a familiar deep baritone voice behind me. My mouth curls into a cringe before I turn around to face my fate.

"Ah ha, hey, Jacoby," Jin stammers, trying and failing to cover her nerves. "You're OK?"

"Hm. Better than you two. You been swimming?"

Chapter 14

Chicken Wings

We've loaded up on strange Thai snacks and hit the potholed overcrowded road. Michael Stipe is on the radio singing about sugar cane and cinnamon in one of my top five REM tunes. It's such a long way to the SWAN research facility and I've worked up quite an appetite through the deception and fleeing. As much as I'd love to munch down on our chilli-flavoured banana chips, I need to address the elephant in the car.

"What happened to you?"

"Me?"

Jacoby is focused on driving, following directions in his ear and travelling carefully enough not to rattle the explosives in the trunk.

"You were in our Nano GEAR one minute, then nothing. Just when things got crazy."

"I told you not to sit down with that lunatic."

"Yeah, well... It was a hard situation to avoid."

"It's true," Jin pipes in from the back seat, crunching on banana chips.

"You need to be more assertive," Jacoby says.

"That's also true."

"Hey, I was in character. My *character* wouldn't stand up to his boss like that."

"And your character could've got you killed, man. Just because you're wearing the suit, you don't instantly become a badass. You can walk around holding a steering wheel, but that don't make you a car."

"I can't argue with that."

"How'd you get out of there anyway?"

I turn to Jin and she shoots me the same confused look.

"You... the sniper."

"Sniper?"

"That wasn't you?"

Jacoby bites his cheek and shakes his head. "Nuh uh. Fill me in."

"Well, I mean, Bhandit recognised me, basically, and he wanted me to work with him, but he wasn't too happy with Jin for bringing me there, so he was gonna shoot her, and then right before I could stop him... someone took him out. Right through the window, one shot. Through the stained-glass window."

"Stained glass? That's a hell of a shot. Must've had some serious gear."

"You think... Well. Who do you think it was, if it wasn't you?"

"Hard to say." Jacoby doesn't look overly fussed or alarmed by my story. I would've hoped for a little more concern, but I suppose he knows it all worked out. "That dude had no shortage of enemies. Every arms dealer in south-east Asia probably had a reason to take him out. But they would've had to take that shot from inside the vineyard grounds."

"And...?"

"And nothin'. Just... Not many people could make it in there undetected with a rig like it would've taken for that shot. That's some serious firepower."

"Like heat sensors or something?"

"Something like that." Jacoby is sounding more and more reluctant to discuss the topic. I pretend to stretch my back, turning my hips and making subtle eye contact with Jin. She nods, realising this is part of my investigation process. I have to keep digging.

"So, who could do something like that?"

"Mm. Any number of people. I don't know."

"You said not many people could make it in there."

"Yeah, but that's doesn't make it a short list. Not like I've got the names of every dude with that ability. You know what I'm saying? It's a big world out here, and Bhandit is dealing with decommissioned Metric products. Could be a competitor, an unhappy customer, disgruntled employee..."

"Maybe a rogue Metric agent."

"Out here? Nahhh. I don't see that."

"What if we're not the only ones who caught wind of this operation?"

"I mean, that is possible. But you know, there ain't that many of us left."

"What about Rust? And Mars. You know his mom is out here."

"I doubt that one. How did you get out after the gunshot?"

"We just walked out. Why do you doubt it?" I'm not letting him change the subject so easily.

"Intuition, Maven. You learn these things over time. I don't see him ditching you in Panama to go looking for his momma in Thailand. Why leave your sorry ass behind? You would've been along for the ride."

"Yeah. It's a big coincidence though. I thought you'd agree there's no coincidences out here in this world."

"Man, I would not be here today without coincidences. That's the truth. Coincidences have saved my old ass too many times to count."

"Maybe someone's looking out for you."

"Who's that, then? The African Jesus?"

"We didn't learn that one in my church."

"Man, my black ass hasn't been dragged into church for a long time... A long time."

"You talk about asses a lot."

"Let's be real for a minute."

Jacoby punctuates this statement by turning off the radio, in quite a dramatic move. If he didn't have it before, he has our full attention now.

"I know you want him to be OK. But if you think Mars is out here, running around all invisible and taking pot-shots at gun tycoons... why isn't he helping us? Hm? We're out here looking for his momma, he's doing what?"

"Yeah, I mean... I can't answer that."

"Wherever he is, I hope he's all right. He's a tough cat. But he ain't here."

I'm not really sure where to go from there. I know I'm not approaching this from a neutral standpoint and I can feel myself trying to prove my hypothesis. Telepathy would be really useful right now. Jin's so level-headed and has no bias towards Mars or Jacoby. I reach back, stick my hand into the bag of banana chips, and raise my eyebrows at Jin. She shrugs back and I know what she's saying. She's saying: "Well, we're here and there's nothing we can really do, even if we had all the facts. We're safe, we're headed for our destination. Let's play it by ear and hope things work out." It's a very descriptive shrug.

I turn the radio back on and Michael Stipe has been replaced by Shaggy. I try not to blame Jacoby.

~∞~

"I'm bored. Teach me something."

"Teach you?"

I took over the driving duties about an hour ago. A large gas station coffee has me wired enough to keep going while Jacoby catches some well-earned rest, spread out across the back seat.

"I'm a scientist," Jin says. "I like learning."

"I failed chemistry in junior year. I'm not sure what I could teach you. I'm more of a words guy, you know what I mean?"

"Teach me what you know."

"You want to learn about the history of the Detroit Pistons?"

"Hmm, no."

"Man, I still hate Bill Laimbeer," Jacoby says, half to himself as he tries to fall asleep.

"That's right. You'd have to be a Bulls guy."

"No sports," Jin interjects.

"I could tell you a lot about the late night TV wars. Letterman, Leno, Conan..."

"That's boring. What about your job?"

"What do you want to know?"

I explain my unique situation of being able to mix old and new media, with freelance writing gigs on top of the podcasting and online videos I hope to return to some day.

"I'm sure people would still listen to you," Jin says.

"Yeah, but I don't want people to listen because they think I'm a lunatic. I want people listening to hear the truth, you know what I mean?"

"We'll make them believe again."

I nod, allowing the hope to flicker but refusing to fan the flames until we're closer to our goal.

"What stories did you like writing the most?"

"I guess it was the features. Crime and politics were rewarding, but for pure enjoyment factor, it was always cool to meet athletes, musicians, actors and, you know... people I looked up to. Entertainers. They're far more interesting to me."

"Why?"

"You know..." It's been a while since I've talked about my profession without discussing conspiracy. "A lot of the time, creative and competitive pursuits are abstract. Sometimes they're quantified in dollars and cents, but more often than not... everyone had their own unique intrinsic goals and ways to measure their success. Outside of sports, I mean."

"Sure."

"Your English is great, by the way, if you understood all that. Like, I don't feel like I need to talk to you differently, at all."

"You already told me that."

"Yeah. I'm sorry. I'm not trying to be patronising. I know most people learning English are insecure about it, so I always like to encourage them. I know it's not an easy language to learn. Or so I'm told. But I guess you know that first-hand."

"Yeah." She starts giggling, making me aware that I should probably feel embarrassed by my rant. "My family sent me to live with my uncle and his American wife when I was young. They were like parents to me. They taught me English and helped send me to the States for college. So I've had a lot of practice learning the language and dealing with Americans who say the wrong thing."

"I'm sorry. I know I just said I wasn't trying to be patronising, but that was super patronising. You're a scientist. You probably know a bunch of languages."

"Actually, just Thai and English. But thanks. I do appreciate it. You have a good heart."

"That's nice. You're nice... sometimes. It's a relief from who I usually hang out with." I'm suddenly embarrassed by the discussion as I remember Jacoby is half awake behind us. I don't have long to feel awkward before Jin brings it back.

"So, tell me, what do you ask?"

"In an interview?" There's a long pause and I realise Jin thought I'd seen her nodding in response. "I mean, that depends who it is and why I'm talking to them. And what I'm trying to find out."

"What's your favourite question?"

"I do actually have a favourite question. I like to ask people where they expect to be in five years. And I almost never use that response in the story, but you can learn a lot from it, you know? It opens up an interesting dialogue."

I have no idea where I'm driving, but the Nano GEAR in my ear is providing clear instructions. I'll more or less stay on the highway for the next several hours, so my main task is to avoid the craziest of the crazy drivers flying past me. Even though it's past midnight, I'm certain I just saw a man on a Vespa with two infant children.

"So... What's your answer?" Jin asks.

"In five years?"

"Yeah."

"Wow. Lately I haven't had a chance to think a month ahead, let alone a year or... five years." I bite my lip and allow my mind to run away for a moment. "I mean, hopefully I'm back where I was.

Like we were talking about before. Get people to trust me again, or at least like me. It would be nice to work again. How about you?"

"I think I want to leave."

"Leave?"

"Thailand."

"Really? Where would you go?"

"Somewhere... far away."

"Like... Malaysia?" Jin laughs, and for once it's with me instead of at me. "Come back to America."

"No... Too much snow. Too many guns. I want to get away from the craziness."

I nod. "Sure. Like, the patriot in me wants to act insulted, but I don't blame you. How about... New Zealand? Australia?"

"Spiders!"

"Oh, come on. You have tigers and rabid monkeys jumping around here. I've never heard of anyone dying from a spider."

"OK then, it's a maybe. Or France. I'd have to learn French."

"Ah, oui. I bet someone with your talents could make a home pretty much anywhere."

"Thanks." I glance at Jin, and she's gazing down with a smile at nothing in particular. I can't imagine what she's been through with Metric and everything that's changed over the past year. My second glance in her direction snaps her out of it and she turns to the rear of the car.

"How about you? Still awake, Jacoby?"

"Mm. Maybe you two could stop talking."

"I gotta stay awake," I say. "Can't be running this thing into the jungle."

I say "jungle" but it's hard to tell exactly where we are. Sometimes we're surrounded by trees, sometimes fields and small towns. Occasionally I'll see what appears to be yellow lights blinking on a mountainside, but I really have no idea what I'm looking at. The first time, I pointed and asked Jin, "What are those, up there in the hills?"

"Just hills," she said. For a scientist, she has great comic timing, even if it's unintentional.

I repeat my previous question to Jacoby and his response is

slow to come back.

"In five years... Damn. How am I supposed to know? Come find me in five years."

If talking in hypothetical terms was a sport, Jacoby would be the Detroit Lions – quite possibly the worst franchise in history. Then again, I've been out of the loop for a year. For all I know, the Lions made the Super Bowl this year.

"I'm like Maven. I don't look too far ahead."

"So what is it?" Jin's not letting him out that easily. "Use your imagination."

"Hm. Well." Jacoby takes a breath, as if considering whether he wants to respond. " I always wanted to get my family away from Englewood. But that never happened."

"How come?"

"Couldn't follow through. Never was able to see it through. There was always another job, another mission. Or I'd... you know... get into trouble and it wasn't the right time."

"What kind of trouble?" Jin doesn't hold back. I don't know if she's brutally direct by nature or if a Thai scientist just lacks the nuance of American social etiquette.

"Just, caught up in different things. Thing is, I wasn't always with Metric. They bailed me out of a couple situations. But I'd say I more than repaid them over the years."

"What's your family doing? Big family? Why move them?"

"They do all kinds of stuff. But Englewood's just not a good place to be. It's the place you want to get out of. Think of the Khlong Toei District in Bangkok, but more violent. Lots of gun violence."

"Oh."

"And I did it. I got out. But I left everyone behind. If I could have my time over again... that's the first thing I'd change."

Jin looks curious, finally becoming reluctant to dig any deeper. I'm surprised Jacoby has even shared this much. Maybe he opens up when he's tired.

"We have an old saying here," she says. "You have to lose something to get another thing."

"Exactly."

"So what will you give up to help your family?"

"That's the question, Jin. I'm... figuring it out."

She pauses, again looking like there's something more she wants to say. After a few more moments, she turns to the back seat again.

"We have another saying: when the water rises, hurry to get some. You have to take opportunities before they expire."

"Wise," I say.

Jacoby is less taken by her advice. "That's obvious."

"So why haven't you done it yet?"

"That's enough." He rolls over mid-sentence, muffling his response. "Let me sleep."

~∞~

"He's sleeping," Jin whispers.

"You sure?"

"Yeah."

"I assumed he would sleep with his eyes open like Major Payne."

"Who?"

"It's a movie. '90s comedy."

"Is it good?"

"Um... Well, it was good in the '90s."

"Can we stop for food? I'm hungry."

"We just stopped like an hour ago."

Jin puts her hand on my shoulder and raises her eyebrows. It's a look I remember seeing when my mom had to tell my dad not to start arguments in front of visitors. No words are necessary. We'll stop for a private discussion and figure out our plan of attack.

"I don't have any idea where we are or what's going to be open."

"There's an all-night restaurant in the next town," Jin says.

"Great. Seems very American."

"It's not. Sorry. There's just lots of traffic on this road, lots of freight. It's always busy."

I'm a little disappointed. The novelty of visiting a new country wears a lot faster when you've been gone from home for so long. After more than a year in South America, I'm at the point where I really just want to walk into a Best Buy to lust after some 4K TVs, and watch college sports with a basket of hot wings and a Budweiser. But even if I had the option to feel American again,

121

there's just no time. If I don't pull this off, there's no knowing when I'll see another opportunity to clear my name. I can't see another way out. I'd have to start over, move to Sweden or something. Run a fruit stand. I really just need something to look forward to, and right now, catching up on Marvel movies and enjoying American internet speeds sounds pretty appealing.

It's just funny how things change so fast. A year ago, I wanted a scoop of a lifetime... I wanted to change the world. Now I only want normalcy. And chicken wings. I really want chicken wings.

Chapter 15

Blue Gatorade

Jacoby stirs as we pull into the empty parking lot. I tell him we're just stopping for food and he's more than happy to catch some sleep without our chatty disturbances. Despite the early hours, it's still comfortably warm outside. I toss my suit jacket on the driver's seat, squinting as the overhead lights glare down across the wide open space. The lack of customers and cars makes me wonder if it's busier during the day to justify the size, or if the land is a sign of how popular this place was in the past. We push through the glass door entrance and slide into a booth at the corner of the cafe, with photos of monarchs overlooking the empty tables and chairs. One I definitely recognise as Thailand's king – his photo is everywhere. But is he the old king or the new king? I think one is more beloved than the other. It must be hard following a popular king. It's hard enough to replace a talk show host without upsetting people – just ask Conan O'Brien.

The chef approaches us for our order and I decide one more coffee couldn't hurt. It's so late... or early. My body clock doesn't have a chance of knowing.

It turns out Jin wasn't lying about being hungry. I sit and watch as she stuffs her face with pad siew noodles, until she self-consciously covers her mouth.

"I wasn't staring at you," I lie. "I was just thinking."

"Oh, good."

"Just kidding. I was staring... You demolished those noodles in, like, five bites. It's hard to look away. Like a car crash, from inside the car. I could see it unfolding and it was horrific."

Jin throws a napkin at me and even though she's smiling, I know the fun part is over.

"We need to figure out what we're doing here, mister."

I exhale, long and slow enough to show my regret.

"It wasn't meant to be like this. I've done this before. Picking sides."

"How'd you get out of it last time?"

"Well... One side beat up the other side, then beat me up and threw us both in a prison cell, and then the two sides came together."

A young boy, around twelve years old, comes to take away Jin's plate and refill my coffee. He smiles, watching me from the corner of his eye as we wait for him to finish and leave. I wonder if his parents run this joint, or maybe he's working to help his family get by. Either way, a highway cafe is no place for a kid at this hour. Heck, it's no place for me either.

"So... we need to get Jacoby and Mars on the same page," Jin says.

"In theory. But, I dunno. We confront him? That sounds..."

"No, that sounds stupid." Unlike me, Jin doesn't mince words. "We need to see where we're landing before we jump out of the plane. We need to know for sure. We need... something."

"We need Mars."

We sit in silence for a while, probably both thinking about the futility of our situation. There are incredible obstacles still ahead of us, but I feel like we won't even get that far if we're going into battle for the wrong team.

"Maybe I could contact Alison," Jin says. "See if she's heard anything. Maybe she's talked to your friend or his father."

"You can do that?"

"Eh. Kind of. There's no guarantee the message isn't monitored. She won't be happy if I bring up this husband and son she's been keeping secret."

"I can imagine." I peer out the window, trying to see through the glare to tell if Jacoby looks asleep. "Is it just me or is every Metric woman a scientist and every man a field agent?"

Jin leans back in her seat, folding her arms and clearly not appreciating my observation.

"You're asking that question based on knowing about two women in Metric..."

"Yeah. But I met this former analyst..."

"There's women field agents. And I'm sure I've worked alongside more men than women in R&D."

"OK. I mean, yeah. Scarpino was the head of everything. I forgot that for a second."

"Don't apologise." She leans forward again, breaking into a smile. "To be honest, Metric was a very old-fashioned organisation. From what Alison's told me, it was only under Scarpino that women started to see equal opportunities."

"Right."

"And you killed her. Way to maintain the patriarchy, Andrew."

She slides my coffee mug away from me before picking it up and taking a sip.

"That wasn't me. And you know, at the time, I was more concerned about not dying, and the millions of innocent people getting lied to. Exposing evil, and so on."

"I think you're a bit defensive about this. Next you'll be saying only Asians can work in R&D."

"Hey, I didn't mention race." I bring the coffee back across the table towards me. I don't know how my beverage became the power token of this conversation.

"Relax. I'm just messing with you. It's too easy."

Is she flirting? It's hard enough to judge with an American. I can sense Jin is naturally antagonistic, but this back and forth might be playful banter. I still can't figure her out.

"What are you doing here, Jin? You know you could be anywhere. You could be working at a university, the government or anything. Is it the money?"

"Well, Metric *was* the government when I started. I don't even need the money, really. My family is taken care of. I just loved the work."

"Right."

"Honestly, there was a romantic notion of the top-secret work, the bottomless pockets of the covert research group. Metric projected an illusion of creative freedom. But, you know, eventually it became clear we were expected to work inside the boundaries of what they considered progressive. After we reached their benchmarks, there was no resources or time for anything else."

"And that was before everything changed. Before Metric bounced out of here."

"Exactly. Those were the good old days. Under Bhandit and the KIL Unit, it's been terrible. The illusion that we're working for the greater good... That's completely gone."

"And what about after this? After we're done here and we bust this thing wide open."

"Um... Well, it sounds funny to say, but I just hope working for an evil government and evil arms dealer doesn't reflect on my character."

"If you find a way to salvage your reputation, let me know. I've got a lot of work to do in that area."

"We're off-topic again. Do we have a plan?"

"We clearly have no plan. We're nowhere closer to doing anything about this, and I don't know what we can do. Can we stall?"

"No... The death of Bhandit will complicate things at the SWAN and the longer we wait, the worse it will get."

"I agree – it was an untimely murder."

"We should go," Jin says, sliding her chair back. "Just... Keep an eye out for your friend. Once we can talk to him, it'll be a lot more simple."

"Nothing is simple."

Jin leaves a generous amount of cash on the table, more than what I'd call necessary. She advises me to buy some water to stay hydrated, especially after all the coffee. I opt for a blue Gatorade instead, straight from the fridge. One of my guilty pleasures. I know it's basically pure sugar, but dammit, it tastes so good. I can't even drink it right now. I need to save it for a time when I'm relaxed, maybe as a celebratory beverage. My mouth is watering even as I daydream about that feeling of accomplishment, pumping some music in the car stereo with the windows down. Cracking open that plastic lid and filling my throat with sweet blue liquid. That ambiguous fruity flavour. Take me there.

I push the front door open and think about how this empty parking lot would be perfect for roller hockey. You could set up a few jumps and have a little BMX circuit. The possibilities are endless. I can't explain the logic of my thought patterns at this hour.

My heart rate picks up as we approach the car and it becomes clearer with every step that Jacoby isn't inside. I open the back door. Nothing. He's gone, unless he's shrunk down like Antman. I look at Jin at the opposite side of the car. She looks as freaked out as I am, until she sees something that scares her even more. I turn around in time to see a hazy shape manifest into Jacoby like he's been beamed out of the Starship Enterprise. He doesn't look impressed.

"So what's the deal? You don't want to be my friend anymore?"

"Hey? What are you doing?"

Jacoby raises an eyebrow and casually points to his ear.

"Oh. No."

"Oh yeah."

He folds his arms, allowing his bemusement to shine through. This is awkward, but if I can smooth it over, I could ask whether he thinks Jin was flirting with me.

"You were spying on us?" Deflecting his accusation is my only plan, until I come up with something better. Forgetting to disable my Nano GEAR was a rookie error. I should have learnt by now.

"It's not spying when you know we're patched into the same comms channel."

"Why'd you go all spectral then?"

"Are you seriously trying to turn this on me? You were talking about ditching me."

"We weren't!" Jin protests.

"Please. I heard enough. Is that what we're doing here, waiting for your friend to show up? I told you, man. He's not coming."

"Trust me, Jacoby, it's a misunderstanding. We're here, so can we just go? Can we drop it?"

"How about I drop you guys, if you think you're better off without me?" Jacoby sounds like a disgruntled teenager who caught his best friends gossiping behind his back. This level of emotion makes me think we've struck a nerve and there's definitely something more to the note I was given. "I've got a car trunk full of C-4 and I can do a hell of a lot of damage with or without you."

"Please, Jacoby, we need to work together," Jin pleads, walking around the car to look him in the eyes.

"I don't actually need you two. I've got the address. I've got the explosives. Step aside and I'll be on my way."

"No!" Jin sidesteps to block Jacoby's direct line to the driver's seat. Her vim and vigour never fail to impress me. "You don't know how to secure the files we need. I told you, we have to work together or this will fall apart."

"Forget it."

"You literally won't find the SWAN without me."

"Just move, lady, or I'll move you. I won't ask you again."

"Hey man, come on," I say, concerned with his aggressive tone. "Be cool."

"Be cool? Nothin' about this is cool. I busted you out of Panama, flew you halfway around the world and now you want to cut and run on me."

"That's not what's happening, I'm telling you."

"Then what?"

I grit my teeth and pull the crumbled note out of my pocket.

"What do you think this means?"

Jacoby snatches the paper from me and immediately dismisses it. I'm not even sure he read it properly. "Is this meant to mean something? Where did this come from?"

"Some kid, back in... that town."

"Some kid? You're messing around with our plans because of some kid, who was probably messing with you?"

"I thought it might be from Mars," I say, far less convinced than when I argued to Jin earlier.

"He's. *Not*. Coming. Back."

"How do you know?" I ask.

"I just know, OK?"

"No... How do you know?" Jin steps forward, posing the question in a soft, gentle voice, as if she knows something we don't.

"OK. Lady, we don't have time to stand around and... argue about this. If you'll both shut up and leave it alone, we can go. Forget about it."

"Well, yeah, that's what I was saying before, wasn't it?" I say. "Let's go."

"No."

"Jin?" Her feet are planted, refusing to allow Jacoby through to the car. She folds her arms and looks up at him, her neck almost extending as far back as comfort allows.

"I want to know how you know about Mars. That he's not coming. You're so sure."

"I told you. You just know these things."

"You can't just *know*. You're acting like you *really* know."

"I said that." As much as Jin might be onto something, Jacoby looks anything but curious about where she's going. "Keys, Maven. Hand them over."

"No... It's like you know something."

"I know we don't have time for this. Let's go."

"Hold on, let's take two minutes," I say, unsettled by how much of a turnaround he's done. "We've all got two minutes. For the sake of clarity."

Now it's Jacoby's turn to fold his arms again. "OK, so I don't know. You happy?"

"I'm happy. Let's go, everybody."

"No, I'm not happy." Jin takes a step back, allowing her to size up Jacoby, like a Shih Tzu growling at a Labrador. The sound of an approaching engine cuts through an otherwise silent and still night. I'm over this. Jin was right before – there's nothing we can do and it's almost easier to pretend everything is fine. I don't know what she's getting at now. She's obviously smarter than me, but I think she's a little lost in the weeds.

"I didn't want to assume anything when Andrew showed me that note," she says. "But if you don't tell us what you've got against Agent Mars, I don't know if I can trust you."

"I've got nothing against him. I don't know him."

"So why were you so adamant? That he's not here."

"Just playing the odds, lady. You people are good with numbers. You know how that works."

"Statistics and probability are nothing next to established facts, agent. I find it hard to believe you'd be so forceful on this topic without facts."

"Believe whatever you like. But you've got to trust your

instincts out here. Make calculated guesses based on years of experience. That's why I'm still alive and kicking." Jacoby's voice grows louder as the nearing engine, a Honda 500 motorcycle, pulls into our parking lot. "It's why my old ass is here in south-east Asia, getting eaten alive by mosquitoes, driving a car full of explosives into the middle of nowhere. You can bet your ass you'd still be sending out your SOS call and no one would've done a damn thing to help if I waited for data."

Jin finally steps to the side, unable to even respond without screaming over the purr of the bike parking behind us. I turn and see the rider, dressed top to bottom in black leather, has kept his motor running. He nods as I make eye contact, but the reflective tint of his helmet visor means I can't know for sure where he's looking.

Jacoby snatches the keys from my hand and enters the driver's seat, leaving me and Jin standing in the uncomfortable noise. The rider inexplicably revs his engine and I frown, looking away from him but making sure he could note my annoyance if he cared to take notice.

"What a jerk," I say to myself as I slide into the front seat. The revving continues, fading slightly as the bike heads for the exit, clearly not finding whatever he came looking for. "I'll never understand a motorcyclist's desire to make as much noise as possible. 'Look at me, I'm on two wheels going *really* fast.' We get it, you don't care if you live or die."

"Bikes are fun," Jacoby says, and I'm surprised to hear him enter the new conversation. "You could do with some fun."

"No thanks. Fun is overrated. That kind of fun, anyway."

"Don't you remember the airport in Panama?"

"How could I forget..."

"What do you do for fun, video games and comic books?"

"Comics, no."

Before Jacoby can make fun of me, he pumps the brakes, jolting my body forward.

"Geez, man."

"This guy." He doesn't need to point to show he's talking about the motorcyclist in black, who has stopped dead at the exit, facing towards us in some kind of confrontation.

"Just go through there, where we came in," I say, gesturing to a sign that I assume says "no exit". I check to make sure Jin is OK, but she's still grumpy from the discussion with Jacoby outside.

"This lunatic better not follow us all the way to Chiang Dao, or I'll show him what it's about..."

"He'll get bored," I say, watching the black rider watch us. As we approach the second exit, he hits the main road and floors it to cut off our path, sliding several feet and making a terrible scraping sound.

"What... That's it!"

Jacoby unclips his seatbelt and leaves the car, slamming his door behind.

"What's your problem, Honda?" I hear him scream over the engine. "You speak English?" He makes some kind of threat in Thai, but the rider is huge. In other words, he's either a foreigner, or he's the largest Thai I've ever seen. Jin leans forward from the back seat to watch the confrontation unfold.

"This doesn't look good."

"For that guy," I say. "Jacoby will mess him up."

But the black rider isn't even listening. With the engine still thundering, his head is turned towards the car, as if he has a chance of seeing through our tinted windows.

"I think... I think this guy wants me."

"Huh?"

"Hold on for a second." I unbuckle my seatbelt and ignore Jin's advice to stay in the car.

"Look, if you don't get the hell out of the way..." Jacoby reaches down to rip the keys out of the ignition, but the black rider grabs his hand and twists his arm in a circle. Using his free hand, and without standing from the bike, he slams Jacoby's skull into the front of his handlebars.

"Ho-whoa-whoa." I put my hands up, half enraged at the black rider's overreaction and half terrified of what he's going to do next, as Jacoby falls to the pavement. He's not out cold, but he's dazed enough to lose all balance. My mind rushes to think about grabbing Jacoby's gun, or whether there's a weapon in the car. It gets a lot easier to think as the black rider turns off his bike and stands up, starting to loosen his helmet. I look back through my open car door to see a concerned Jin mouthing something I haven't got a hope of understanding. I gesture for her to stay inside.

"Who are you?" I ask the black rider, hoping he can understand me. He removes the helmet, lifts his head and turns to face me.

"It's been a while, kid."

Chapter 16

Reunion

"Rust?"

His greying hair has grown out a little since I met him, but there's no mistaking that weathered face, barrel-chested physique, and scar across his eyebrow. I mean, it's him. It's Rust. I just didn't expect to see him here, even with the cryptic message from his son.

"Hm," he responds, lowering his keister to the edge of his Honda. I get about two seconds of eye contact before he returns to staring at Jacoby, struggling to gather himself a few feet away. Classic Rust. Classic anti-social, non-expressive Rust.

"It's so great to see you, man!"

I approach him for some form of embrace – hug, handshake, whatever he'll allow – but he outstretches his hand to stop me. He's dressed head to toe in black, interrupted only by a rich maroon ring around each wrist and elbow of his leather sleeves.

"We'll have time for reminiscing later," he says. "I've gotta get you outta here. Hop on the bike."

"Well, no, I'm here with Jin. We need her. Why'd you hit this guy?" I point to Jacoby, who's made it onto all fours but has yet to raise his head.

"There's a lot to cover. For now, you just have to trust me. Both of you. So come with me, she'll be fine. We'll all meet up soon."

"That doesn't make sense."

"Kid."

"Come on, Rust, give me the twenty-second explanation.

That's all I want."

He looks as unimpressed as ever.

"Twenty seconds. Please."

"Twenty seconds is ten seconds more than I want to be standing here – we need to go now!"

"Just go, Andrew," Jin chips in.

"I'm not leaving you here."

"She'll be taken care of."

"How did you find us?"

"Kid. Get on the bike."

"Was that note from Mars?"

"Andrew! Go!"

The three of us talk over each other, unable to reach a logical conclusion for our escape plan, but it's very much two against one.

"I... Just... What's going on?" I yell, cutting through the noise.

"You need to get better at taking advice, Maven."

I turn and see Jacoby has risen to his feet while we've been bickering.

"Especially from people who are smarter than you."

"X..." Rust doesn't sound very pleased to see his former colleague here.

"We're all smart in different ways," I say. "Now, can you two talk this through without beating the crap out of each other?"

"Kid, this is..."

"It's awkward, sure, but you're both Metric."

"Former Metric," Jin says, standing behind me.

"You've got the same axes to grind. Maybe you're two sides of the same coin – I don't know. But we can figure it out. We're all good guys."

"He's not..." Rust mumbles.

"He's... What?"

"Not."

"Andrew..." Jin reaches her hand to the inside of my elbow and squeezes firmly, perhaps sensing what's about to take place. I pull away, not ready to let two men I respect tear each other apart.

"So I guess I'm the bad guy then, just outta nowhere." Jacoby puts his hands on his hips and I can sense the pain in his voice. If his feelings aren't hurt, something else must be. "You even want to hear my side?"

"Your side of what, though?" I ask, genuinely interested.

"You can't trust this guy. Be smart, kid. Get on my bike, now."

"Maven, just remember we're here for the same thing. Think about it."

"Whatever he told you about coming here, it's not true." Rust's words are heavy and make my heart drop. I look at Jacoby, searching for a convincing sign of defiance, but all I see is defeat. "Get on the bike."

"He saved me, Rust."

"And what do you think I'm doing here?"

"Enough." Jacoby rubs his forehead, probably the spot Rust smacked into his motorcycle. "The cat is out of the bag and running wild. Maven, you can run and hide, or you can wait in the car. Either way, you're not leaving with this guy." Jacoby scratches his beard, starting to pace in a semi circle around us, like a shark deciding which surfer looks the tastiest.

"It's not up to you, X."

"That so? I know you, Rust. Your old ass might've forgotten, but my first mission was fixing the mess you made in Kosovo."

"Hm."

"Yeah, that's right. You remember me now. I sorted it out. I got it done. You sure as hell knew the name, but now you know the face."

"I know more than you think. I know I did the ground work with the scientist and you stepped in." He points to Jin, still standing behind me. It's hard to imagine this whole thing was Rust's plan from the start, but the way he's looking at Jacoby is enough to convince me he feels wronged in some way. "You took the lead, took the kid, claimed it as yours. It's over now. Wipe that smile off your face."

He's right. Jacoby has stopped pacing, smirking in amusement at something along the way. I don't want to believe Rust and I'm not ready to take sides.

"You're really that bothered that Jacoby pulled me out of Panama before you could?"

Rust grits his teeth, probably remembering how frustrating I can be. "You think Mars just got sick of your jokes and hit the road?"

"What?"

"Ask your friend what happened to him."

I look at Jacoby again and his smirk is gone, replaced with a vacant look, staring past me at nothing in particular. I'm not going to let him off that easily.

"What's he talking about, Jacoby?"

"He won't say it. This guy knows exactly why Mars disappeared on you."

"What?"

"It's true, kid. Ask him."

Jacoby's lack of eye contact doesn't do anything to suggest otherwise, but I need to give him another chance to explain.

"Tell me something."

"I've got... a lot of reasons for the things I do." He finally looks up, biting his cheek and meeting my incredulous gaze. "I've done far worse things than lie to you. But I don't feel bad about any of them. You have to believe me. It's all been for the mission."

"This isn't a mission. It's my life, man. That's my friend we're talking about. What did you do?"

"I did what I had to. You wouldn't get it."

"Then tell me."

"I really don't want to."

"But I'm asking you nicely."

"Maven... I'm sorry, man."

"But you like dogs. Bad guys don't like dogs. Rust... He really likes dogs."

"That's enough, kid." Rust snaps his wrist in a violent gesture, signalling the time for conversation is over. "Now, are you walking away, X, or do we have a problem?"

"I've made that clear. I've come too far to roll over for you or for anyone."

"Then we've got a problem."

"One hundred per cent. But out of respect for who you are and what you've done, I'm not going to kill you. Not today, man. This is not the day."

"Wait, did he just say kill?" Jin nods in response and I let out an embarrassing wheeze. The blood must be rushing to my head. I can't believe this is escalating so quickly.

"But you can't stop me," Jacoby continues. "And your best

call is to be the one who walks away."

"Not happening." Rust grits his teeth and cracks his knuckles the way tough guys have been known to when they're about to throw down – a classic move from a classic guy. I'm just not sure it's going to intimidate Jacoby. I can't imagine a magician is overly impressed watching his rival go through their whole routine before a big trick.

"When you're picking your teeth off the pavement, don't say I didn't warn you, old Fox."

"You talk too much." Rust reaches to a holster at his back and pulls out his trusty Custom M1911. "You might not want to kill me, X... but you haven't earned the same respect from me. And I've run out of patience."

"You always were a grumpy bastard."

Before his last word is out, Jacoby disappears into spectre mode. I try to track the blurry shape of his movement, but it's amazing how quickly the translucent apparition tricks your eye. Rust is caught off guard and knocked to the ground, probably wishing he'd spent less time cracking his knuckles and more time pulling his trigger. I know Rust's motorcycle leathers can't perform the same function, but I'll have to wait until this is over to ask why he brought a knife to a gunfight... or a biker outfit to a spy fight. He was probably counting on a quick exit with me on his bike, so there's a tiny chance this is my fault. He should know I can't leap before I look.

Jacoby phases back into view and picks Rust up to his feet, only to throw a fist into his gut and toss him headfirst into the motorcycle. It tumbles to the ground under Rust's weight and I cringe at both the damage to his limbs and the scratches to the gas tank. Jin steps forward to help Rust, until Jacoby thrusts his hand directly in front of her.

"Don't."

"Agent!"

Jacoby ignores her, picking up Rust again. This time he generously spreads out his punches – one to the face and one to the kidneys, just to mix it up a little.

"C'mon, Rust!" I yell.

"Yeah, c'mon, Rust," Jacoby chips in. "Put up a fight."

"Andrew, don't just stand there."

"What do you want me to do, Jin? I can't kickbox him in the head." We shudder and cringe in unison as Jacoby grabs Rust by the hip and shoulder, rolling him across the asphalt.

"Let's just... Both at once!" she says, pulling me by the wrist as Jacoby approaches Rust again.

I take a deep breath and run forward, grabbing hold of Jacoby's forearm just as it rears to punch a struggling Rust on all fours. He turns to me with a look of disgust and rips out of my grip, like I'm a mere child, before turning his fist into an accusing finger point in my direction.

"You run up on me again, I'm goin' in your mouth."

"What?"

"You ain't about this life, man. Just stay back."

Before I can figure out exactly what this means, Rust has seized an opportunity to rise up and throw a punch of his own, right in the back of Jacoby's skull. I don't care how tough you are, that's going to knock you down.

"What happened to 'both at once'?" I ask Jin. She doesn't respond.

With blood trickling from his nostril, Rust leers over Jacoby's body, catching his breath and monitoring any movement.

"You OK?"

Rust turns to me, without making eye contact, and grunts in response.

"That's a 'yes', if you're wondering," I tell Jin, as Rust spits out a swab of red saliva.

"He's pretty good."

"Yeah. He got you real bad, Rust. You're going to want some ointment on that." I reach over to point out his bruised cheek and he flinches slightly, then something else catches my eye. "He's gone. Jacoby."

Rust turns back to see Jacoby has gone into spectre mode again and slipped away.

"Ugh. You're killin' me, kid."

"I was just checking on you!"

Reaching to the ground for his pistol, Rust starts circling, hunched over, looking for any sign of Jacoby.

"X!"

"It's like in *Predator*."

"X!"

"I think he's gone," Jin whispers to me. "What did he mean about 'going in your mouth'? What is that?"

"I don't know. He's from Englewood."

"What does that mean?"

"It means I'm white, so you're asking the wrong guy."

"Where is he?" Rust snarls through gritted teeth. "Hurry up…"

"I think he's gone."

"Not him…" Rust says.

"Who else are you expecting?"

The sound of quick footsteps lead Rust to turn around just in time to get spear tackled to the ground. He overpowers Jacoby, rolling on top of his veiled form, driving manic punches into what I assume is his midsection.

"This is so weird," Jin says, and I realise she's probably never seen her Spectral Suit in true action.

The sound of gurgling snaps me into alert and I bend down to pry Jacoby's hands reaching up around Rust's throat. I wouldn't have tried to help if I didn't think it was possible, but breaking Jacoby's grip is like turning a rusty bolt without a wrench.

"Stop it!" Jin shouts.

The balance of power shifts as Jacoby rolls Rust onto his back, pulling away from my grasp on his strained fingers.

"Stop! You're killing him!"

With Jin's voice ringing in my ears, I pull at Jacoby's arm. Nothing. I shove him, trying anything to break his choke hold. He said he wouldn't kill Rust, but his instincts could be getting the best of him. I take a few steps back and charge into Jacoby with my head down, hoping for the best. This time, my momentum is enough to knock him to the asphalt and reintroduce Rust's windpipe to the oxygen it craves. Jin helps him to his feet as he catches his breath.

"You good?" I call out. "You're good, yeah?"

"Look out!"

I follow Jin's outstretched arm to see Jacoby recovering on all fours, fully visible beside me. I don't fully understand the tech, but the way he fell looks to have messed with the Spectral Suit's circuits or power. It's possible he just ran out of juice, like Mars' suit did months ago.

Either way, it's finally a fair fight.

"Hurry the hell up and get the scientist," Rust says in between panting breaths.

"She's fine," I say, knowing Jin is right there in his peripheral vision.

"I've got the kid."

"Are you talking to us?"

Rust punches down, striking Jacoby right across the jaw.

"No more tricks," he tells his fellow agent.

"No more tricks," Jacoby echoes, spitting blood onto the concrete inches from his face. Before another punch is thrown, Jacoby weaves his legs through Rust's and trips him to the ground. I'm not sure if this counts as a trick or not, but it's effective. Jacoby lifts Rust, throwing him into the motorbike again. I can see why he likes this move. It's very effective.

Rust trips hard, breaking his fall with his hands, which snap to a sickening angle as they connect with the hard bike frame. Before I can express any concern, Jacoby is hounding him again, wrenching his ankle across the bike until I'm afraid it'll snap.

I run up to them, waving my hands and yelling to stop. Jacoby's squinting eyes dart over to me with a look that threatens to beat me if I even dare to lay a finger on him. Finally, Rust frees his foot, but the onslaught continues as Jacoby leaps the Honda and rams his fist into Rust's face, right when he starts rising to his feet. Kneeling above his bleeding head, Jacoby drives punch after punch into his jaw.

"Holy crap."

With every connection, I feel like I'm seeing a little life drain from Rust's eyes. Panic starts tugging at the thought of Jin and I being left alone here with a vengeful Jacoby. While I'm wavering about approaching him again, Jin squeezes my shoulder and points to Rust's handgun, wedged underneath the motorbike.

"Should I get it?" I ask, hoping she's suggesting something else.

"I think so."

"Do you want to get in there with that kickboxing?"

She shakes her head. I don't blame her. Where is Mars when you need him? If Rust is like Batman, brutal and cerebral, Mars is Spider-Man, acrobatic and agile, with the quips to match. That's the DC-Marvel crossover I really think we need to see right now.

I take a deep breathe and duck down, reaching under the bike for Rust's pistol. If I can take over this situation, perhaps I can calm everyone down. As my fingers grasp the grip, Jacoby yanks Rust by the jacket and drops him on top of the bike, pinning my hand to the ground. I crank my neck around to see Jacoby glaring at me as he beats Rust with repeated strikes. One of Rust's eyes has closed over, and he's gasping for breath as blood pours out of his mouth.

It's disgusting.

"Come on, man," I beg, softening my tone into an earnest plead. "Look at him."

"Stop!" Jin shouts.

"You said you wouldn't kill him."

Jacoby pauses for a moment, as if he's a cyborg computing the binary logic behind our pleas for peace. Rust is motionless, aside from his attempts to breathe, resting against the flattened motorbike just inches away from me. Jacoby picks him up to his feet, supporting him for a moment before releasing his grip and allowing Rust to crumble to the ground.

"Aren't you going to clap?"

His question catches me off-guard and all I can do is say: "No." Jacoby laughs, but he's clearly not amused. "You backed this guy. Really?"

I don't respond, staring blankly at the man who saved me from imprisonment only a few days ago. I pull my hand free from under the motorbike, holding the pistol but having no reason to use it now. Jacoby looks down at my scuffed hand grasping the weapon and scoffs. "Pathetic, man. All of this. Don't even come after me."

I finally wake to the reality that we're in public and notice a small group of bystanders at the restaurant entrance, as well as the roar of another motorcycle approaching.

"Jacoby..."

"Don't. Trust me. You don't want to see me again."

He slaps his shoulder and disappears into stealth mode again, leaving me to wonder if that was the last time we'd see each other.

"Call an ambulance!" Jin hands over her phone as she opens Rust's jacket, presumably freeing him from any breathing restrictions. I can't bring myself to look at his multi-coloured face.

The reds and purples... They're unnatural.

"Are you sure?" I ask, cautious of exposing Rust to authorities without knowing his preference.

"He could die."

"But, but an ambulance, are you sure? I don't want him waking up and choking me out for putting him in a hospital."

"Andrew! He might not wake up at all if we don't get him there."

"OK, I'm sorry! What's the number?"

She stands up frustrated, snatching the phone and telling me to put pressure on Rust's bleeding head wound.

"I don't know what..."

"You have to do it," she yells over the sound of the motorbike rolling up behind us.

I wince, grit my teeth and kneel down in front Rust, wondering if he can see me through his blurred vision and swollen eye. This is just wrong. My stomach is turning, not because of the gruesome injuries but what they represent. Rust has always been like Superman to me – unstoppable, unwavering, just... unrelenting. This here is like watching Apollo Creed's body go limp after his Drago fight in *Rocky IV*.

"You got this, Rust. You got this."

He grunts – possibly in response, possibly involuntarily.

"You got this. It's all right. You got this."

"Bro!"

I recognise that commanding voice. I look over my shoulder to see Mars rushing from a motorcycle towards Rust. Despite the mystery surrounding his disappearance and the relief of seeing him again, there's absolutely no time for the kind of reunion our friendship deserves. Right now, we have to focus on his father.

"This is my fault," he says, kneeling down beside me, straightening his old man's neck. I haven't seen this before. He looks distressed. Just like Fox Senior, Fox Junior is dressed for the road in a black leather jacket and grey jeans. A thick yellow stripe runs down his right arm, with five black stars in an emblem across the shoulder. He still looks like a GQ model, with a fresh fade, a solid hair part, and week of scratchy stubble. But even his slick appearance can't hide the painful angst on his face.

"How could it be your fault?"

"I took too long. I just..." His eyes well up with tears as he feels for breath from Rust's mouth. "I took too long. I'm sorry, Dad."

Eyes closed, Rust clutches my hand and chokes out a single word before his grip loosens and he's gone again.

"Alison..."

Chapter 17

Waiting

I might need another coffee. It's been a long morning – the longest morning, even. Leaving Bhandit's party, getting no sleep and driving all night, followed by a brutal fistfight and everything that's happened in the hours since. Mars took off on his motorbike, keeping up with the ambulance. I did my best not to fall behind, with a stunned Jin in the passenger seat giving occasional directions to the closest hospital.

I've heard good things about Thai healthcare. The regional hospital itself is small, three-storeys high, but surprisingly clean. The emergency waiting room looks like it was built in the '80s and furnished in the '90s. The speckled linoleum stinks of ammonia and liquid soap, the way all hospitals do. *National Geographic* is the only English magazine available to read, but they have yesterday's *Bangkok Post* if you feel like learning about the Songkran road-death toll or latest gold prices. It's not the best place to finally catch up with Mars or figure out exactly what's been going on, but we don't have much choice as we wait for doctors to stabilise Rust's condition.

"Didn't think we'd ever be here, did we?" Mars says, handing me a cold aluminium can and a vending machine snack.

"But here we are," I say, because it feels like the only way to respond. "What's this... Five-hour energy drink?"

"You look super tired, bro. There's also some... weird pretzel stick things."

"Thanks. You know, I spent two days in an airplane, had one solid night's sleep, and at least three coffees to get me this far. So yes, tired is the word to describe me. If I fall asleep mid-conversation, don't take it personal."

Jin is trying her best to sleep across several chairs beside us. I know she needs a break from the drama after what we've been through in the past twenty-four hours.

"So what happened back there?" Mars asks.

"I just realised, I could hear Rust talking to you on the Nano GEAR. I think he wanted you to take Jin away so he could take care of me."

"You don't say," Mars mumbles, knowing exactly what the plan was.

"But I think I messed it up by not, you know, just going along with him from the start. I'm sorry, man."

"It's all right."

"It was just, so crazy... and I wasn't expecting to see him or, like, any of the stuff he told me."

"Bro, don't blame yourself. We didn't expect to catch you so soon, but when you pulled into that cafe we knew we had to take the chance. I was just too far away to help. That's on us."

"How did you know where we were?" I crack open the energy drink and pour its sweet, gross, synthetic caffeine down my throat. I'd inject it through an IV line if the nurses would help me, but I doubt that's a request they could grant. "And at Bhandit's, that was you, right, with the sniper? And the note from the kid?"

"The sniper was Rust, but yeah, that was all Team Fox. We've been tracking you since you hit Bangkok." He points to the Nano GEAR tucked inside his ear.

"But how?"

"I don't know exactly, but we just picked up a signal."

"But... how?" Maybe he didn't hear me the first time.

"I just said, I don't know. Rust found these Nano units when he raided Metric HQ last year. Right after we left Kansas."

"Oh, man."

"They weren't designated to any specific agents, so he figured by now they were safe to use without being tracked."

"Right. Well, that makes sense." I lean back, looking at Jin and wishing I could get her to explain her technology. My eyes widen as I piece the past couple of days together and I realise it's only been one full day in Thailand. We've crammed a lot in.

"Yeah. OK, I got it. Because Jin gave us this new model, and yours must be compatible. You know what I mean?"

"That's what I was thinking. We were searching for a signal that might connect to the SWAN, and then suddenly I'm listening to you talk about Modesto and drugged-up tigers."

"Ha, yeah. That was me. Dang, man. If I had the manual for this thing, we would've been talking this whole time."

Mars explains the good fortune of scoping out Bhandit's place for information on the SWAN when they found us there. Now seems as good a time as any to clear up what happened in Panama, but Mars is just as clueless as I am. After leaving our place, he woke up in an American embassy in Mexico City. He doesn't know why or how, but it was clear he was being delivered back to the US authorities, which is where I must've been inbound before Jacoby rescued me.

"And that's where Rust came in?" I ask.

"Yeah, he busted me out. Said he'd been contacting this Thai research facility," Mars says, nodding at a sleeping Jin. "And he had a lead on tracking down Mom."

"I knew it!" I say, punching the air and splashing a drop of energy drink onto the floor. Being right is the only victory I get to taste since I've reluctantly lost all touch with sports fandom. Rust uttering Alison's name this morning makes total sense now. "She's alive. That's so awesome, man."

He smiles at me briefly, before his face is taken over by the sobering reality that we're in a hospital waiting to see if his father has survived the beating of a lifetime. As sweet as it would be to find his mother, you can't imagine this is how he wanted to do it.

"But we lost contact with Jin. It was like she'd switched comms channels for no reason."

"It sounds like Jacoby cut your lunch. Beat you to the punch."

"I know, bro. It explains a lot. We waited at our meeting place like a couple of jabronis – she never showed up."

"Man." Jacoby's lies and betrayal hit me hard. I've been focusing on the mixed emotions of finding Mars and Rust, only to watch the latter get beaten to a pulp. I haven't even had a chance to process Jacoby's motivations or his treacherous turn.

"I can't believe he did this."

"He's bad news, bro. But you couldn't have known."

"I... guess he is. But he just doesn't seem like it. He likes dogs, you know?"

"So did Hitler. He painted them. It doesn't mean a damn thing."

"I know, that's just where my mind goes. There was so much more. He opened up to me. His intentions, his actions, they all seemed noble. Right up until he was crushing the cartilage in your old man's nose. He's never getting his lucky tracer round back, I can tell you that."

I pull it from my pocket and show it to Mars, wondering if it means anything to him. It doesn't, or at least it doesn't elicit a reaction that suggests as much.

"I've got some other cool stuff," I say, putting the bullet away, hoping to impress my pal. "See this tie? It's made from graphene microfibres. Strongest light material known to man, or so I'm told."

"That sounds made-up."

"This is some James Bond stuff, right here. Your mom probably worked on it, you know."

"Sounds like someone got bored in the lab."

Mars' eyes light up as the door opposite us beeps and slides open. A janitor pushes a cleaning trolley into the emergency waiting room, followed by a nurse walking towards the hospital exit. Neither looks to be offering us any news so we continue to wait, unsure if it'll be five minutes or five hours until Rust is awake and ready for visitors.

"So anyway. We figured what you were doing. Rust took out Bhandit to help you out of there, and we were going to hijack your explosives once we could take X out of the scenario."

"OK," I say, struggling to keep up in my tired state. "Here's where you gotta fill me in. Do you have any idea why he's doing this? Why we can't all work together."

"He's one of *them*, bro."

"Them?"

"Metric. The Order. NWO. Whatever you want to call it."

"Do you know that for a fact, or you're just guessing?"

"It's pretty clear, isn't it?"

I explain to Mars that nothing is clear. Jacoby has said enough to make me sceptical of his incentive to stay loyal to a group that has done nothing but lie to him and steal years off his life. That is, unless literally everything he told me was made-up. Englewood. His family. That can't be possible... can it? Even with my proclivity to suspicions and conspiracies, this theory doesn't ring alarm bells.

"Trust me, bro. He played you. That's what we learnt in Metric. We impersonate and infiltrate. He got inside your head – he's here to stop us and nothing else."

"So why not just kill us all? Once he had Jin and me in the car, that could've been the end of it. Plus, you weren't there – he said explicitly that he wouldn't kill Rust. And he definitely had a chance, so I'm pretty sure he meant it."

Mars doesn't realise I'm withholding the fact Jacoby might've very well ended Rust if Jin and I hadn't intervened, but that doesn't play into my theory. I feel like I've developed a pretty good lie detector over the years as a political reporter. I know I'm not at the espionage level, but I have no doubt the majority of what Jacoby told me was true. I can't imagine a reason to lie about almost all of it. Deep down, I knew he was hiding something about Mars – I just assumed it was to protect me, in one way or another.

"That might be true," Mars admits. "All I know is he intercepted Rust's intel and instead of contacting him, he took it and he ran. There were so many chances to explain himself. You're sitting here, you think you know him. What's your theory?"

I open my mouth, but instead of words forming an explanation, I wheeze out a noise of hopelessness. I've got nothing. "Maybe I'll get a chance to ask him."

"Bro. If I see that bastard, I won't be taking it easy. He'll need more than a Spectral Suit."

I sip my drink and nod silently, not knowing exactly what Mars would do, but believing it would be suitably violent. It always is.

I start imagining how I could get through the hospital doors if they say they'll only allow family to see Rust. I could sneak in. Or I could pose as a representative from the American embassy. I can pull that off, unless they'd expect me to speak Thai. That's not going to work.

"You know we've got a car full of explosives out there on the street?" I remember out loud, but not too loud.

"You sure do."

"Do you think it's safe?"

"Who knows. You want to stay out there and watch it? Maybe the lady could. Backseat would be more comfy than those chairs."

"Jin."

"Yeah. She seems..." Mars looks over at her, making sure she's definitely asleep. "She's nice. Pretty too. You into her?"

"C'mon, man," I say through gritted teeth. "We're literally at the hospital and you're asking me that."

"She cool though?"

"Yeah, she's cool. She's super smart. And she kickboxed Bhandit's lady friend right in the face. It was awesome."

"Sounds emasculating."

I shake my head, not in the mood to ascertain whether Mars is being sexist or just making fun of me. "No more than every time you got me out of a jam. She just looked a lot better doing it."

"OK. That's hard to believe."

"Well, you better believe it. You know she works with your mom. That's what we're here for."

I mention the data we're hunting and explain how it'll back-up our entire story. Like the good friend he is, Mars responds with enough enthusiasm to perk me up.

"You'll get your life back. You'll get to write that book you talked about. It's perfect. I've got a good feeling about this."

"We'll see. You're very optimistic for someone who just lost his partner."

"Rust will be fine. *You're* my partner. He's my dad. Don't forget what we've pulled off over the last year."

I nod, wondering if he's talking about exposing Metric and the New World Order, or the mere act of surviving on the run since then. As much as I hesitate to go up against the KIL Squad on their own turf, we've got something they don't – a former Metric agent. Maybe two, if Rust recovers in time, but that's seeming less likely the more we wait. Every minute we sit here is another ticking towards Jin's deadline to avoid the encryption reset on the SWAN computer system. If we lose our digital paper trail, we lose our original reason for coming here. As much as I love family reunions, bringing the Foxes back together won't help with my problems.

"How much longer do you think this is going to be?" I ask Mars. He expresses some eagerness to leave in time to beat Jacoby to our destination, but I explain he apparently won't be able to find it without Jin's help. Mars sighs, clearly conflicted between his sense of duty and his new-found relationship with his father. A year ago they were more or less estranged, literally throwing punches on opposite sides of Metric's plot. A rogue spy and a loyal patriot asked to take down his own son. I'm not saying I'm responsible for bringing them together, but Mars has certainly indicated it wouldn't have happened without me. Is that enough to make all of this worth it? Perhaps, from a philosophical point of view. I don't know. My perspective changes depending on my state of mind. Sometimes I regret the whole thing. But the more positive view is easier to take. It's easier to live with. It keeps me going. When everything else is crumbling around me, that still, small voice inside comforts me and tells me this is my purpose. This is the valley of darkness and it's only by faith that I'll be able to climb out. The road is long and the night is dark, but after what I've been through... I can't stop. I just can't. And I keep saying there's no other choice, but the reality here is that the other choices are unacceptable to me.

"You're the son of Bryan Fox?"

An unfamiliar female voice speaking Rust's actual name shakes me out of my contemplative state and I notice a doctor has approached Mars, clipboard in hand.

"Yeah, how's he doing?" Mars stands up to shake her hand. The Chinese doctor is older than both of us and has an earnest disposition. A stethoscope over her shoulders is the only indication of her clinical background, as she's otherwise dressed the same as Jin with a grey button-up shirt and jeans.

"He's stable, but needs rest. At his age, I think he's lucky to be alive."

"So he's OK?"

Mars' interpretation of the news clearly catches the doctor off guard.

"Sir, your father is in bad shape. Minor blood loss, abrasions to his neck, a broken nose, and some severe contusions. There are several lacerations around his temple and I suspect a mild concussion. We'll run a CT scan as soon as the machine is available."

"But only minor blood loss," I say, looking on the bright side. "I'd call that a win."

"I haven't finished," she says. "Our greatest concern is his zygomatic and orbit fracture, meaning his cheekbone and eye socket."

"Oh."

"Now with the jaw, it could be a complex fracture, so we're trying to book a dental x-ray. That CT scan will tell us more, so I wouldn't say he's out of the woods yet, but in a few weeks I'm optimistic he could experience a full recovery. But only if he's treated right."

"Right."

"Obviously we would recommend surgery to reduce the risk of infection... but in his current state of mind he's refusing consent."

"Sounds about right," Mars says, folding his arms. "But when it boils down... Broken nose, some bruises and a few scratches is what I'm hearing."

"Well, no. At this stage, technically..."

"Is he awake?" I ask, before immediately regretting interrupting her.

"Yes."

"Sorry if he's been difficult," Mars says.

"It's OK. He has been trying to leave for the past ten minutes..."

"That's what I meant. He's as tough as nails. I've heard he's broken his neck twice, and the second time was in the middle of the Nairobi Desert. I bet they didn't have a hospital like this."

"Tough or not, I'd advise it will take a long period of rest until he's pain-free. The wounds are clean now, but he's heavily medicated and will need a day or two on a ward before the swelling goes down and he's cleared for discharge."

"I can tell you now, he's not going to be in that bed all day."

"I'm afraid he just won't have a choice, sir," the doctor says, moving back towards the emergency room entry. "I'll come and let you know when he's ready for visitors."

"Thanks, doc."

Mars sits beside me again, with a slight grin on his face. I'm relating a lot more to the doctor's reaction than his, especially since I witnessed all the brutality, while Mars showed up after Jacoby had rearranged Rust's facial features.

"That... really... doesn't sound good."

"Relax, bro. It's fine. As long as he can stand."

"It's fine?"

"It's fine. We need to start planning our approach from here. We've got a car stacked with C-4, a couple spies on the inside..." He points to Jin, who's still asleep and unable to speak reason into our situation like usual. "And we've got that head of yours."

"I don't really know that I'm much of an asset here."

"Don't talk like that. You're the glue, bro. None of this happens without you around."

The doors of the emergency room beep and swing open again, this time revealing Rust lumbering out of the hallway towards us, clutching a plastic bag. His leather jacket is gone, leaving a tight black T-shirt to hide the blood stains.

"Let's go."

"Rust! You..." He looks like crap. That's what I want to say. He looks terrible. As he limps closer to us, I can see his eyes are dark with bruising, like De Niro in *Raging Bull*, with one almost completely closed over. What I can see of his nose is displaced half an inch to the side, and the rest is padded with as much tape as a Fed Ex parcel. One side of his face is caked in brown antiseptic and his clothes are covered with dried blood.

"Are you sure this is..."

"Good to go?" Mars bounces to his feet, eager to leave and motioning for me to wake up Jin.

"We need to move," Rust says, probably referring to the nurses he expects to come looking for him any second. "I take it your car's outside?"

"Yeah. What about your motorbikes?"

"They were rentals, bro."

"What's in the bag, Rust? Did you steal drugs? You know, your eye is completely red."

"Relax, kid. It's fine. Can't you see I'm standing?"

Like father, like son. The Fox boys are back.

Chapter 18

Road Trip

According to Jin, it's only a few more hours to the SWAN research facility. She's far less concerned than I am about Rust's health and mobility, having slept through the doctor's diagnosis. Mars is practically beaming as he turns our car onto the familiar major road, even if no one else has the energy to match.

"Look at us, Maven. After all those nights in Panama, road trippin' out in the open. Life is a highway, bro."

"Yeah."

I'm sure tracking down his mother is playing a part in his excitement, but I'm finding it hard to muster the enthusiasm. Don't get me wrong. I'm all in. But I'm also completely unprepared to go into this situation. Jin is more or less a double agent, so she'll be safe. Mars can take care of himself. My usual enforcer, Rust, is hobbled and not in a position to put my safety ahead of anyone if things turn south. What I'm saying is, I've got a bad feeling about this.

"Antibiotics, Rust. You need some?" Mars asks, watching his father slumping in the rear vision mirror.

"I'm good for now," he says, shaking his plastic bag of pills. "The painkillers will get me through the day."

"Sure. We'll get you some proper treatment tomorrow. And we'll stop to get you some yoghurt soon. No pretzel sticks for you. What do you like, strawberry?"

"Mm."

"I actually remember you as more of a vanilla guy."

"Mm. Don't care."

"Vanilla it is." Mars looks over to me, pausing before revealing his inner monologue. "What's up? You're quiet. You're never this quiet."

"He's tired," Jin chips in from the back seat. "We drove all night, remember."

"True," I say mid-yawn. "And I only had three coffees."

"Well, get some sleep," Mars tells me. "I can handle this. Rust probably shouldn't be dozing off with that concussion, so there's no use everyone staying awake."

"I don't know if I can sleep with everything going on. But I'll try."

"I know your body, bro. If you haven't slept for twenty-four hours, you'll be snoozing in five minutes."

Jin shoots me a sideways glance and raised eyebrow. "Sounds like you two really got very close in Panama."

"Separate beds."

"Sure."

~∞~

I wake up abruptly, as our two-tonne vehicle jolts like a shopping trolley jumping a curb.

"Sorry. Couldn't avoid that one," Mars says.

"I felt that." I look over to see Rust wincing and holding his ribs.

"We'll slow down and walk you over the next pothole."

"Smartass."

I stretch my neck and rub my eyes until I can peer out the window at our colourful surroundings.

"Wow."

"It's beautiful, isn't it?" Jin smiles at me, enjoying my sense of awe at the green landscape surrounding us. It's easy to take your home environment for granted, but seeing it through new eyes can remind you to appreciate what's always been right in front of you.

"This is incredible."

Past the trees lining the road, I can see a wide vista stretching for twenty or thirty miles, scattered with distant lush mountains.

We must have climbed quite high, although the wall of green on the other side suggests we still have some driving to do if we're on our way to the top.

"Welcome to the Chiang Dao district."

"What is this road? It's like a sidewalk."

"There's not much traffic up here."

The road is barely wide enough for our car and looks like a solid slab of concrete. If we meet any oncoming traffic, we're going to have to go off-road just to squeeze past.

From the driver's seat, Mars asks about our timeline and Jin explains it's not far until we go off-road.

"We're walking – through all this stuff?" I ask, surveying the mountains and trees.

"Don't be like a baby."

"Jin. I don't know if you realise this, but we have a lot of explosives in this car."

"Yes, I know," she says. "Don't patronise me."

"Well, did you realise we've got a guy here who's meant to be in hospital right now?"

"I'm fine, kid." Rust's insistence is in stark contrast to his quiet voice stumbling through tired lips.

"Andrew, what do you want me to say?" Jin says, leaning forward without a hint of compromise. "You want to drive in like normal and hope they don't notice the extra bodies in here? We can't just park the car in a loading bay. It's not one of your Wendy's drive-thrus."

"OK."

"I know this place. You need to listen to me. That's why I'm here."

"OK!" I throw my hands up in defeat, knowing I'm in the wrong but still feeling justified in my concern. "I said OK. I'm sorry."

"No, it's fine. I'm sorry," Jin says, calming down. "I don't know. I'm a bit nervous. We can probably drive slowly along this back road, for the most part. It'll be fine."

"You guys can both relax a little, all right?" Mars interjects, like a bus-driving teacher directing his overexcited students on a field trip. "You both make some good points. We can't just rock up. But we do have to think about these explosives. What did X manage to find at Bhandit's storeroom, exactly?"

"I don't know, exactly. We didn't really talk about it. He was looking for C-4. I remember that because it rhymes with see-saw, and I kept imagining what it would be like if Jacoby ended up stealing a see-saw."

"C-4..." Rust repeats, ignoring my hilarious remark. "Miss, you better know the layout of this place like the back of your hand."

"My name is Jin. I know it well enough."

"Mm. I don't know if you get it. We're gonna need to hit every key structure support, or C-4 won't do a damn thing towards wiping this place off the face of the earth. That's the idea, right?"

"Yeah."

"So are we talking steel structure?"

"I think so."

"You better know so. If we're cutting through steel, we need a shaped charge with shock waves fast enough to get it done. C-4... That's about ninety per cent pure explosive, but ten pounds of it will only take out one eight-inch square steel beam. I'm guessing we don't have that much of it."

"We have nanothermite."

"What?" Rust sounds equal parts impressed and confused.

"There's not much of it, but we could divide it. I know where it's stored at the SWAN."

"What is that?" I ask Jin.

"It's basically regular thermite with the constituents mixed more completely, which means..."

"It'll melt steel faster," Mars interrupts.

"Mm. But it's a metastable intermolecular composite," Rust says, as if we all know his implication.

"Right, the finer powder is more reactive," Jin says, making it clear I'm the only one who doesn't follow.

Rust goes on to say something I can't follow about vapour pressure, Henry's law, and PETN. They might as well be talking about World Cup soccer because I have no idea what's going on. I'll probably never know who Henry is.

"You're really smart at this, Rust."

"Wait a second," Jin says, as if feeling challenged to out-science Rust. "Thermite releases energy in the form of heat and light. But that's it. They won't move an object, even with nanothermite. If you want the structures to move, we need to combine it with a high explosive we can safely detonate at a distance."

"The C-4," the Foxes say in unison, with Rust's mumbled baritone harmonising against his son's enthusiasm. Jin's face cracks into a wide grin.

"That was cute. Alison will be so happy to see you again. I can't wait for that."

They both smile in response – that is, Mars smiles and Rust's frown levels out into a neutral expression, his equivalent of smiling.

"Rust, you must be..." I stop to conceive of a word that describes how he would feel right now – one that's not too emotional for him to admit. "Pleased? To see her again?"

"Mm. Very."

"Wow. *Very*. I don't know if I'm prepared for such a show of emotion from you."

"Laugh it up, funny man. I've been working towards this every day for the past year. While you were hiding in South America, I was digging through archives, shaking down informants, and–"

"Rust, I'm happy for you. Plus, I can't wait to meet the woman who inspired you into oil painting. Yeah, I didn't forget about that. Jin, this guy used to do landscapes. She was his muse."

"Really? That's so sweet."

"Still life..." Rust mumbles under his breath.

"It's OK, we know you're still a badass," I reassure him. "Great shot back with Bhandit, by the way. Thanks for opening up his skull right in front of us."

"You're welcome."

"It was disgusting. You couldn't take him through the heart or something?"

"Yeah, it was a great shot."

Jin interrupts to ask Mars to slow the car. This is the spot, apparently. She leans forward to look through the windshield with a careful eye, as if the SWAN is going to manifest in the jungle. "That tree. That one there."

"Stop there?"

"No. If we want to save time, there's a walking track we can drive down until we can't drive anymore."

"How far is that?"

"I don't know. I've never actually been here."

"You don't know?" Mars and I both ask at once.

Jin explains she's far too busy to wander around the jungle outside the SWAN by herself, comparing walking tracks. However, she did find time to consult some locals and fly a drone over to make sure the path was clear.

"What are you saying?"

"If you drive off-road with that tree to your left, and you're going fast enough... you'll hit the walking path."

"Through that bush? Off the edge?" Mars asks, seeking clear instruction.

"Yep."

"Through that bush? Off the *edge?*" I ask, hoping there's a misunderstanding.

"It's only a few feet down."

"Should we get out and have a look? I would prefer to–"

It doesn't matter what I would prefer. Mars puts his foot on the gas and his faith in Jin's research. I sit back, holding my breath as we skid over the turf and ram through ten feet of shrubs, before launching into the air. It feels like forever, but it's probably less than half a second until we thud into the ground below, arriving at a clearing slightly narrower than the car. If we proceed slowly, it looks like we could push through the bushes much faster than on foot.

"Why is there even a track here?" I ask Jin. "You guys do a lot of BMX riding?"

"Elephants actually."

"Oh sure. And I heard they ride kangaroos in Australia." She doesn't really acknowledge my disbelief so I move onto my second burning question. "How did the C-4 not go off? When we hit the ground. Was that not enough impact?"

"It's not nitro," Rust scoffs, like I'm supposed to know the difference.

"You need a certain level of shock wave to detonate C-4," Mars says, with a much more helpful answer. "Or temperature. You can't even shoot it. Hopefully your friend pinched a remote detonator as well."

"He's not my friend. I bet he doesn't even really like dogs."

"I don't understand what happened," Jin says, watching the trees drop to the side of the car, cracking beneath our tyres.

"Which part?"

"Jacoby... He had the same goal as us. He wanted to take down the SWAN and clear your name."

"That's what he said. But–"

"It just doesn't add up. That's all. If he was lying about that, why's he really here?"

"I'm telling you, he's a Metric pawn," Mars says. I feel like the driver carries the most authority in this situation, which I know is the psychological result of my parents always claiming the driver was in charge of the radio selection.

"We talked about this at the hospital when you were sleeping," I say.

"That's right. He's a pawn, Jin. A pawn."

"But Metric is disbanded," she responds. "There's nothing to gain from staying loyal to something that doesn't exist. It's not logical."

That's classic Jin, bringing logic into an emotional discussion.

"But the New World Order is still pulling the strings," Mars says.

"And if they're not, what are we all doing here?" I ask, hoping she'll actually answer me because sometimes even I can lose track.

"I'm not an expert on the New World Order," Jin says. "I've seen your video. I know enough about these things to know we can't stop the forces in play. They are too powerful. You've sown the seeds of doubt and maybe that's as much as we can do."

"Jin, I know this. Trust me, I've come to terms with it."

"Just let me finish, please. What I do know is Metric. And Metric is long gone. The principles and direction of that organisation are non-existent now, for better and worse. The surface level, peacekeeping and intelligence work..." She gives a thumbs up. "And the shady, underlying manipulating puppetry." I watch her thumb turn upside-down, then point with her other hand to Rust and Mars. "You two are proof of this. You've been working outside Metric for a long time and I'm guessing you haven't seen a trace of them. In official capacity."

"Metric?" Mars considers the question for a moment as Rust merely grunts in the affirmative. "We've been dealing with all kinds of people sent after us, from Kansas down to South America. Some military. And CIA mostly. But not Metric."

"Exactly. It's gone. All that's left is the infrastructure of the SWAN. I don't see the Order, as a faceless group, finding Agent Jacoby and asking him to come here on their behalf. He has no reason to co-operate when they've done nothing but pull strings for so long. I don't see him as a man motivated by money or success."

"C'mon," Mars says. "One way or another, for these people, it always comes down to power."

"No. She's right," Rust mutters. "It's something else. It's personal."

"Why?"

"Yeah, why? How do you know?" Mars is as confused as I am.

"Well..." Rust reaches up to his bruised nose and smooths down his bandage with great care. If I had to guess, he's recalling the beating Jacoby gave him several hours ago. I don't know what goes through your mind in those moments, but it wouldn't surprise me if Rust has been through enough of them to pick up on smaller details others would miss. "I know because that's exactly why I'm here. And I wouldn't step foot on this continent if my wife wasn't involved. Him and me... Us. We're just on opposite sides of the coin."

I try to remember what Jacoby told me about his personal life as I start to respond, but Rust cuts me off.

"Trust me," he says, a phrase we all seem to use a lot. "There's something more to this. It really hurts to say it..." I wonder if he means literally or figuratively, because the angle of his nose and the colour around his eyes mean either is possible. "That bastard could have killed me on the spot. Had me beat, no question. I thought my time was up. But he let me go. I know I underestimated him and he kicked my ass."

"He had the Spectral Suit."

"Yeah. Didn't say it was a fair fight. But the way he fought... I saw somethin' in his eyes that was a lot more than following orders. He was fighting for his life."

"Yeah. But still..." Mars says, uttering the three words that take any losing argument up to a tie.

I wonder out loud what Jacoby is doing right now, how far he's made it. Mars is the only one to response, but isn't willing to offer a guess.

"You're not concerned?" I ask him, expecting he would know what a former Metric agent is capable of.

"It doesn't sound like he knew how to get here without some help, any more than we did."

"Yeah, but, I dunno. What if he's following us, or tracking us somehow? That seems like something a spy would do."

"If he wants a piece of us, I will tear him apart. He'd have to be crazy to show up again, even if he knew where we were."

"You still say that after what he did?"

"You know me, bro. Never underestimate the blind certainty of a competitive man. Isn't that what you say about sports – every team needs an 'irrational confidence' guy?"

I hear a noise come out of Rust that isn't his usual sigh or groan – it's the involuntary sound your grandpa makes without realising when he has to stand out of his recliner. I can't help wonder what he's expecting from the next few hours. I'd usually look to him for leadership in this situation, but his injury and our lack of intel make for a lot of unknown factors. That's nothing new, and frankly, I feel like planning ahead for these things makes it worse when our ideas inevitably falls apart. The past year is proof of that.

Expectations versus reality – this concept is as sobering as the sun beating down, finding its way through the tall trees and car windows on my pale burning skin. I really expected to change the world. I thought the secrets I uncovered would be enough to shake the cage and force authorities to ask questions of their superiors. When you let the cat out of the bag, you don't expect it to look around, lick itself, and crawl back inside again. But that's exactly what happened. If our efforts had any influence at all, I didn't hear about it. I'm disappointed in America, to be honest, but I shouldn't have been surprised. I thought people would want the secrets revealed, but it turned out to be more than they could handle. I tried to open the gateway to a world of inconvenient truths, but the door was closed instantly.

And now? Now we have another shot. Some might say, one

shot and one opportunity. I have absolutely nothing to lose. If I don't use my last breath to shout the truth, I might as well move to New Zealand with my parents for the rest of my life. I like Middle-Earth as much as the next guy, but I know I'm meant for more than that. At least, I think I am. It's time to find out.

"This is a problem," Rust mumbles.

"Yeah. We can't drive through that."

I lean forward from the back seat to see a giant round, dark object blocking our narrow path through the jungle shrub. "Is that a boulder?"

"That's no boulder."

Jin mutters something under her breath in Thai, just loud enough for Mars to hear.

"My thoughts exactly. But you didn't mention this was an elephant trail."

"I did, though. I literally did."

Chapter 19

Trekking

The elephant isn't getting up, deciding it would prefer to block our path like a sleeping Snorlax. Just like humans, these things retread the same paths through the scrub until they become walking tracks – only this monster is taking a break from its trek and doesn't seem interested in getting up.

I take off my jacket and throw it into the car, hoping to avoid turning into a sweaty mess after ten seconds in the sun. Leaving Rust to regain his strength, the rest of us get out of the car to see the elephant up close.

"I really don't want to punch an elephant in the mouth," Mars says. "But I'll go there if I have to."

"You'll do no such thing," Jin scowls back at him. "If you wake it, we don't know how it could react."

"Is this thing wild?" I ask, my voice hushed to avoid disturbing the beast.

"She looks wild. I don't know what a mahout would be doing out here."

"A ma-what?"

"Elephant keeper. Training and riding," Jin says. "This is very rare. We only know there's about one thousand five hundred in the wild here."

"Cool." The elephant is impressive, and seeing it is a treat, but it's hard to express my enthusiasm when it's so hot. I'd love to complain about the heat, if only it wouldn't make me look so weak. Jin hasn't even broken a sweat.

"It's amazing," she says, gazing at our new friend. "But also, very frustrating. I'm sorry... I should have planned for this."

She furrows her brow into an angry pout. I squint, trying to make out details of the elephant from our distance.

"You sure we can't wake her?" I ask.

Jin explains a startled elephant could ram our car, or even attack us. It's hard to imagine such violence from such a peaceful and docile sleeper. What's she thinking? What occupies the mind of a wild elephant? I'm a little jealous as I realise she gets to just sit here, regardless of what drama might be going on around her. Surviving is all that matters. There's no reputation at stake or truth to uncover. She's just an untamed beast, living her simple life in an isolated environment, surrounded by food sources. What a place to be.

"Can we drive around? We can't really, can we?"

"No, it's too dangerous with the C-4. Worst case scenario, this big bag of meat destroys the car and gets blown into a million pieces." Mars puts his hands on his hips, looking along the green path beyond us. He sighs and I notice his right hand shift to the Mk 23 pistol in his holster. Surely he wouldn't. Surely.

"You're not shooting this thing. Mars."

"I know! Geez, bro."

"Good."

"Keep it down, OK. You'll wake her. And c'mon, it wouldn't be any easier moving the dead carcass if I did. Is it much further, Jin?"

She shakes her head. A couple of kilometres, she says. I think that's just over a mile, but I don't want to ask. Mars pauses briefly at the front of the car to check on Rust, or so it seems. His eyes are closed, but he's clearly breathing. Hopefully getting some much-needed sleep. We examine the trunk of the car to figure out how we can move the C-4 from here to the SWAN. It's the first time I've seen what Jacoby managed to collect from Bhandit and it appears to be at least ten bricks of plastic explosives.

"Each of these is probably four pounds of C-4. That's enough to take down a baseball stadium."

"Really?" I ask, thinking about my last visit to Wrigley.

"If you're smart about it, probably. But it's got to be more than enough for the SWAN. We'll just have to take as much as we can carry. Or we could always blow up the elephant with this much C-4.”

“Not smart so close to the SWAN,” Jin says, missing the joke entirely. “I have two backpacks in the car, and your sports bag, Mars. We just have to prepare wisely.”

“If I can't take my blue Gatorade, I'll cry.”

~∞~

After ten minutes of careful packing, we wake Rust and begin our trek through the jungle. It's fair to say he's slowing us down, although he's managing reasonably well for a man who's been through so much trauma only hours ago. Despite the muggy humidity, I decided bringing my suit jacket would help keep my disguise believable once we arrive.

“Do your guards wear the tie?” I ask Jin, hoping I can ditch at least part of my sweat-soaked ensemble.

“They all wear the tie.”

“Ugh. This thing is so restrictive. I've never liked ties.”

“Remember, it's a special material,” she says. “Graphene fibres. I'm very proud of that. It's revolutionary.”

“It's going in my pocket, is what it is.”

The elephant's tired eyes track us with suspicion, like a house cat making sure nobody takes away her food, even though she's well past hungry.

“Rest up, Nelly. You have your own dramas going on, I'm sure.”

I imagine what it would be like to walk through here at night. Pitch black, lit only by the moon and the brightest stars. We're so far from man-made pollution and lights. This could be the deepest into nature, the furthest from society I've ever been. In some ways, it takes me back to that brief peaceful moment in Hawaii, but there is a pending sense of uncertain fate taking away from the serenity of this setting. Still, I try to focus on the beauty of our surroundings and not the hot stickiness it evokes, or the fact that this black jacket stinks with sweat from wiping my brow.

“Beautiful out here, isn't it?”

Rust is the last person I expected to break the silence, let alone with this kind of remark. It's like he read my mind.

“Are you feeling all right?”

"The jungle. It's nice."

"It is. Just didn't expect to hear it from you."

"What kind of weapons are coming out of this place, Jin?" Mars asks, changing the topic, as if he too is shaken by Rust's sudden fondness for nature.

"We make some really cool stuff," Jin says. "I bet you would have loved to see it in full force. Electro-magnetic research. Quantum particles."

"Sci-fi stuff," I say.

"It sounds impressive, but they're mostly modifications to pre-existing weapons. Guns you don't have to reload. Heat-seeking bullets. I spent six months figuring out how to apply the Spectral Suit tech to claymore mines. With a solar battery."

"Sounds tedious," Mars says.

"That was my job."

"Was?" I ask, picking up on the past tense.

"I guess I've already moved on."

"Clearly. Why do you think she wants to blow up this place?"

I don't answer Mars, choosing to save my energy for this hike instead. As I think over Jin's words, she must be doing the same because only a few quiet moments pass before she resumes her line of thinking.

"That's not entirely true. I feel pretty awful about it, to be honest."

"You're having second thoughts?" I ask.

"No. Not at all. But it's that bittersweet feeling like…"

"Like finishing school… or moving house."

"Yes. All at once."

"Except you're blowing it all up."

"Exactly. We're about to destroy the place I've been working for most of my adult life."

"Yeah, but… for Metric," Mars says, with an obvious implication. "And a damn militia group."

"No, you don't get it. It's not like that," she responds, with a tinge of annoyance. "Those Metric years were incredibly fulfilling. My time there was transformative. I learnt so much. I helped develop cutting-edge technology. When we discovered Metric was an instrument of evil, when you all came forward last year... Ugh. It was so obviously true, but we didn't want to believe it."

"No one did," I grumble, showing the wound is still raw. "You know what, I realised people really don't know what they want. They think they do. And usually you can show them. Like when *Seinfeld* debuted, America's biggest TV sitcom was *Alf*. This alien puppet with goofy hair. People were lapping it up and had no idea the world of comedy was about to change forever, and that's what I was expecting when we dropped that truth bomb."

"You were expecting *Seinfeld*?" Mars clarifies.

"I was! Honestly. But it was more like an *Arrested Development* where no one notices it and it's gone way too soon."

"I'm sure that's a great analogy to you, but let me finish, please."

"Sorry." I feel terrible as I realise I've interrupted Jin's therapy with a bunch of references that mean nothing to her.

"We were killing ourselves for this work, knowing it had the power to change the world, save lives, improve society. That's always the goal. Some of us are more cynical and we admit there are grey areas, but you can't do this work the way I've done it if you don't believe it's for the greater good."

"Makes sense," Mars says.

"So, to realise the good you've been doing for so long is being used to bolster a force of evil... That made so many us feel like..."

"Puppets," Rust says, eyes on the ground in front of him. I watch him for a moment, noticing he's taking care with every step while also avoiding eye contact during a rare solemn display of emotion. I can see how Jin's story would resonate with him after the difficulty he had accepting the same reality a year ago.

"But you didn't leave when you found out," Mars states. "How come? You and Mom could've cleared out well before Bhandit and the KIL Unit moved in."

"Look around us. We couldn't just walk out of here, run through the jungle," Jin says, probably unaware she's quoting Creedence Clearwater Revival. "A couple of people tried. Maybe they made it, but we never heard from them. And also, many people refused to believe it until it was too late."

"And you probably had the KIL Unit here breathing down your neck pretty fast too," I say.

"Exactly. They were running our security and after two or three days Metric had washed its hands of the SWAN altogether, leaving us alone out here. That was when Alison started planning. This operation is a year in the making."

"A year? I feel like we've done a lot of winging it for twelve months of prep work. "

"You can thank Agent X for that," Mars says, stomping a fallen tree's branch flat for us to step over.

"We knew we had to take our time," Jin says. "And find the right people to liberate the SWAN. I just wish I had known it was her husband and son we were waiting for. I would have been a lot more patient."

"I'd say you took the news a lot better than Rust did. He punched me in the face. Almost broke my glasses."

"I'm not surprised. I can see the appeal of that."

Rust grunts, joining Jin with his version of laughter. "Can't say I didn't enjoy it. Glad I got to do it at least once."

"At least?"

"Gotta keep you on your toes."

"Trust me, I'm on my toes," I say, squatting underneath a leafy branch at head height. "There's no part of me relaxed right now. That five-hour energy drink is still wearing off. Believe I should have an hour or so to go."

"Andrew."

"Yeah?"

"We can walk faster if you stop talking. Drink some more water."

I don't even respond to Jin, taking her rebuke to heart. I know I can be a little too chatty when I'm nervous, but I need the levity to get by. It's possible our coping mechanisms are at odds with each other, or she just doesn't like me as much as I thought. That's very possible. I'm self-aware enough to know I'm not as likeable as I think I am.

After another twenty minutes, now in total silence, we cross a shallow stream and a few dozen yards of soggy turf before meeting a solid dead rock-shaped end, like the base of a mountain or cliff, covered in brown vines. If I could see beyond the trees around us, I'd know exactly what our obstacle was, but we're completely at the mercy of our tour guide.

"This is it," Jin says.

"Are we climbing the rest of the way?" I ask. "Didn't bring my carabiner."

"This is the fire exit to the SWAN. We're gonna sneak right in."

"Ohh. Cool." I still can't see any door or stairs, but I've expressed enough confusion and Mars doesn't seem to be concerned. Jin reaches down behind a bush until the vines begin to shake. To my surprise, the rock wall in front of us parts in two like an elevator, revealing a concrete stairwell with steel steps running up several storeys.

"Rock on."

Chapter 20

Big Tom

I rap my knuckles against the sliding door, realising it's probably just fibreglass – like those fake rocks used to surround tiki-themed swimming pools at hotel resorts. I can feel the heat emanating from the three walls as we step inside, like an asphalt oven as the door closes behind us. With my quads burning, I ask for an update on our plan.

"We can't split up if we don't know our way around," I say.

"We have numerous options," Jin says loud enough for everyone to hear over our clanging on each steel step. "We can stay together, but a group of four looks very suspicious. If we can find Alison first, she can lead one group through with the explosives while I work with the other to secure the data you need."

"Actually, we'll probably need both groups planting explosives," Mars says.

Rust grunts in affirmation as Jin takes a moment to think it over. "What if Rust and Mars wait here, Andrew and I will bring back Alison and we'll figure it out together."

"What?"

"Yeah, what?" I echo, unsure about leaving my safety nets

behind.

"You want us to leave this guy out there with you?"

"He's wearing the uniform," Jin says in my defence. "There's no reason for anyone to see this as anything suspicious."

"To be fair," I say. "We could've said that at Bhandit's, but that didn't work out super well."

"Just hurry," Rust says, surprisingly putting up no resistance. "I could do with the rest, to be honest."

"You'll be OK here in this concrete sweatbox?" I ask.

"It's not so bad," Mars says with a sigh, which is the only consent needed to go along with the plan. "We still have water. Just, take a gun this time, bro. You remember how to use this thing?"

Mars pulls out his Mk 23 and hands it to me. I eject the magazine and slide it back, the way I've seen him do many times.

"You know it."

"Why'd you do that?"

"Just, to show you how I remember."

"You don't need to do that. It didn't look as cool as you think."

"I dunno, it looked pretty cool to me." I aim the gun at the wall opposite me, looking down its sights.

"Agree to disagree. Just hurry up. Go find Mom and get back here."

"No worries, pal. I've got this."

"Hey." Mars grabs my arm as I try to leave. "Take off the backpack."

"You got it. Don't drink my Gatorade though."

I lean the bag of C-4 against the wall and open the door in front of us. Before I can look both ways, an air-conditioned breeze hits my sweaty face like a kiss from God. I could just bask in it, but there's a job to do. After looking down the corridor, Jin tells the Fox boys they're safe to come inside and hide in the storage closet nearby. It's a little cramped, but at least it's not ninety-five degrees. She says Alison will most likely be sleeping or reading in her quarters around this time.

"Do you need some water, Andrew?"

"I think I'm OK."

"You *farangs* get dehydrated so quick."

"It's true, we do. Can't you call Alison or something? How do you normally communicate in here?"

"There's a comms system, but it's monitored by security," Jin says, striding through the curved corridor. We're hustling just fast enough that I can't really tell what's inside each of the rooms, but they all seem to be unattended, holding storage or supply crates.

"What about the Nano GEAR?"

"Well... Yeah. We could have set that up."

"But what?"

"But I didn't think of it."

"Oh. That's unlike you."

"There are jammers on the outside to protect our comms being intercepted here, so it wouldn't have worked until we arrived. I guess it slipped my mind. But seriously, it will only be five minutes."

"That's good, because I really don't want to bring back Drake – you know what I mean?"

"Drake? Oh, your... character from before. You're right, we don't want him back."

"I prefer 'alter ego'. And I'm ready if I have to be."

I adjust my tie, wondering if it will ever fulfil its high-tech potential as we stop at an elevator and wait in silence. I take a moment to look around, trying to get a sense of the SWAN's layout. It's hard to picture without seeing its exterior, aside from the greenery growing off the rocky cliff.

"It's amazing that this whole thing is inside a mountain. This is the bottom level?"

Jin nods.

"And this is going to be covered in C-4 soon."

She nods again, this time dismissively.

"Are you sure you're OK with all this? It was your suggestion to blow this place up, remember?"

"Yeah. It's fine. I just don't want anyone to get hurt."

"Yeah. I mean, I get that. But you don't need to worry. We'll get everyone outta here. I'm sure."

"I hope so."

"Maybe we can, you know, evacuate by doing, like, a fire drill. Or a mini explosion first or something."

"Yeah. That might work."

Jin eventually selects the top floor of the elevator, which has a rear wall lined with three laser-printed posters. One is in Thai script, one seems to be some kind of scientific process update notification, and the other is describing the evacuation protocol with a top-down map. It jogs my memory of how Jin explained the SWAN as a cylindrical main structure, with rooms shooting out from each corridor on all three levels. The circular rooms in the centre of levels two and three are research and development, while the rest are storage, admin and personal quarters respectively.

"So the files we need are on the second floor?"

"Correct. We'll take Alison down to the Foxes and go from there."

The elevator stops short at level two and Jin shoots me a nervous look that says: "This is not good, but it's not terrible – just relax and we'll be fine." It's a very specific look, but this is a very specific situation and we've been in basically the same position together already at Bhandit's party.

The doors open to reveal a well-built Thai man dressed the same as me – black jacket, white shirt and red tie. He grins politely, steps inside and faces the door. I nod at Jin, doing my best to tell her: "Hey, I think we are getting away with this." It's another specific expression, but whether or not the message is conveyed, it's only a short ride up until we're all exiting the elevator together. I wait for Jin to walk ahead, but it seems like we're going the same direction as the buff Thai guy.

"This place is so clean. Who cleans it?"

"We just keep it clean," Jin tells me with a hushed tone.

"Nah, you must have janitors."

"No janitors."

"I don't believe you."

"Believe what you want."

Opposite the doors leading to their personal quarters, there's a window running the length of the corridor into an open space. I peer down and can see the entire circular room below on the second level – a huge room, half divided by cubicles and desks, with the remainder opened up to a variety of equipment in use, as the worker bees move around below. This is where the magic happens. I bet that's the entire research and development department right in front of me. As much as the room is busy with activity, it's a smaller space than I imagined for the amount of work that comes out of this place. It's not the "sitting and typing at a keyboard" kind of research I usually picture. I ask Jin if anyone is working on our floor, but she says at this hour most people are in the central lab, and the rooms along the corridor are soundproofed for rest or research.

The chap we'll call "Buff Thai Guy" is still a good few paces ahead of us and I can see it's bothering Jin. I catch her attention and she whisper-hisses back at me.

"What?"

"Is everything cool?"

"This guy. Do you think you can distract him?"

"Me? Can't you?"

"You don't know where we're going."

"Ugh. Maybe. But why?"

"Two of you patrolling the same area is going to seem weird. There are cameras everywhere. You need to get him out of here."

"Like how? You..."

I stop talking as Buff Thai Guy half glances over his shoulder. I don't think he can hear us, but it's better to be safe than sorry.

"You know this place better than I do. What would be a good excuse?"

"I... I don't know. I'm not good with this thing."

"OK. What's his name?"

"I don't know. I think he's new."

"Hm. Go on ahead, maybe."

Jin picks up her stride and overtakes Buff Thai Guy. I need to get him away from Alison altogether if this approach is going to work.

"Excuse me," I call out. "Hey. I think we've been given the same task. Someone messed up."

"It's my patrol," he says with the self-assurance of someone who knows their role, even if he is the new guy around here.

"Oh, I checked it just before I came here. You would've missed the changes?"

"And who's authorised that?" he asks in what appears to be a cockney British accent, leaving me feeling as confused as he is. Even if I didn't need to talk to him, I'd be curious to keep the conversation going just to hear that voice come out of his mouth.

"It was John," I say, with assured certainty. In my attempt to answer every question with pure confidence, I've chosen something far too specific for this situation. Why didn't I just say "the boss"?

"John?" Cockney Buff Thai Guy is clearly not buying it. I need to salvage this. "I don't know John."

"Who's John?" I ask, feigning confusion. I actually can't believe there's not a single John here.

"You said John," he says, pointing at me and expecting an answer.

"I said *Tom*. Sorry, I meant Tom."

"Oh. Which one?"

"Which Tom do you think? C'mon." I roll my eyes, hoping he'll fill in the gaps.

"Big Tom," Cockney Buff Thai Guy says, cracking a wide grin.

"Exactly. I wouldn't worry about listening to that other Tom – you know what I mean?"

"I thought Big Tom was on the mid shift this week."

"Yeah. He was. That's the thing. He had to stay behind, just a bit longer. But long enough it's messed up the whole roster from here on out, so that's why we've switched and I'm meant to be here now, when you should be relaxing somewhere." If there's one general bone of contention you can assume for a workplace with 24/7 shifts, it's rostering. "He wasn't happy about it either. You know how Big Tom gets when he's held up."

"Damn. Running through that checklist again, without a doubt."

"Yeah. Exactly," I nod enthusiastically, just happy this nonsense is actually working. "That... checklist. What a waste of time."

"It's getting worse lately too."

"It is what it is."

"True. True."

"So anyway, I'm happy to take this one. You can take a break, but come find me if you feel like it."

"I mean, same to you. Thanks for letting me know..." He extends a hand.

"Drake."

"Drake. I'm Tae. It's nice to meet a *farang* working here with some good sense, *khrup*."

"I know what you mean. Just don't say that around Big Tom."

We share a good laugh and go our separate ways. Tae seems like a nice young man. It would be a shame if this building caved in on him today, but it's a possibility. I get the sense he learnt English from watching *Monty Python's Flying Circus,* and that's a story I'd love to hear one day.

Jin reappears from the room she ducked into, beckoning me to follow her again.

"Did you see that?"

"I heard bits and pieces."

"Drake is here. The transformation is complete."

"You didn't take off your glasses this time."

"True. I forgot. But perhaps that was the missing ingredient last time. Did you hear that guy's accent?"

"This is it." Jin stops short at a door numbered forty-two. She takes a deep breath and knocks, giving me a nervous smile.

"Let's do it." The door swings open and... there's Alison, with half a dozen rollers in her greying brown hair. The clear resemblance to Mars is enough to confirm it's her.

"Well, the kids came through," she says, sizing us up. "Took you long enough."

Chapter 21

Shaft

"Alison, this is Andrew."

"It's nice to meet you." Alison shakes my hand and smirks ever-so-slightly, as if she expected me to be taller. Her grip is firm with direct eye contact to match. Maybe it's confirmation bias, but I can already sense her similarities to the Fox boys. Even after two sentences, I'm getting vibes of Rust's no-nonsense attitude and Mars' sense of humour, voiced through a slight Midwestern drawl – somewhere around Nebraska or Missouri if I had to guess.

"It's good to meet you too. I've heard... a few things, I guess. And I'm sorry I'm not Rust or Mars, but they are here, I promise. Downstairs. And they can't wait to see you."

Having turned slightly away from me to prepare her exit, Alison pauses and breaks into a wide grin at this news. She has a kind face, marked with the expressive lines of a woman who smiles far more than she frowns. It's a nice moment, seeing the relief wash over her before she fades into her quarters, moving room to room, throwing clothes and items into a khaki backpack.

"Why didn't you say these agents were your family?" Jin asks her.

"I'm sorry. You know I trust you. But... Jintara, I've trained myself to keep it private, even during the Metric years. It was frowned upon, it was complicated... Bryan was always in danger."

"Makes sense," I say, just trying to be part of the conversation. "If he's at risk, it puts you there by association."

"Correct. Call it decades of habit."

"I understand," Jin says with a nod, accepting the explanation but maybe still wishing things had been different. "It just would've made the operation smoother. You know we almost brought a different agent here altogether?"

"You did?" Alison stops her packing for a moment, showing concern until she's reassured.

"It's a long story," I say. "But basically, it ended with Rust getting hospitalised. He's OK now though. Mostly. Depends who you ask."

"Oh my. This is my fault."

"It's really not."

"What happened?"

I explain Jacoby's role in this escapade and how we still don't know his motivation. Alison sighs, with the same frown I've seen from Mars many times. But she doesn't let it linger. She shakes it off and zips up her backpack. "Well, let's go find my boys."

"Are you going to...? Or are they...?" I point to the rollers in her hair, then rub my own short hair to remind her she might want to look in the mirror before we leave for good.

"Oh. Bless your socks, Andrew. One more minute."

"Sure. I thought they could be some kind of high-tech support item, but..."

"Well, no. They're to curl my hair."

"Of course. I'm sure it'll look great."

~∞~

As we return to the corridor, Alison takes charge ahead of us, heading directly for the elevator. I get the sense the power dynamic has shifted and Jin looks to Alison for leadership. I'm taking this as a sign of the respect the veteran scientist earned in her time with Metric, as well as the way she carries herself. She's not on the intimidating level, but she definitely doesn't strike me as someone you want to disappoint. Like Jin, Alison is free of any jewellery, dressed in a lightweight blue button-up shirt. She looks a little younger than Rust, probably early fifties, with her curled grey and brown hair tied back into a ponytail and an outgrown fringe swept to one side. She's also rocking a pair of white sneakers with her denim jeans in classic mom fashion – function over fashion.

As we step off the elevator, I start imagining how Rust and Mars will react to their family reunion. It's taken a long time, a lot of heartache, and a lot of bloodshed to find her. I think Rust knew all along, but Mars certainly spent a lot of late nights wondering whether his mom was still out there somewhere, whether her eyes were still open. The way she disappeared left so many questions unanswered. The mystery is starting to fade and soon we'll know everything we need to tie the bow on these misadventures.

And finally.

This is the moment when a normal family would burst into tears, but the Foxes are far from typical, so I don't know what to expect. Jin pulls the final door open and I hold it for Alison to walk in before me.

"Bryan? David!"

"Hey Mom."

Mars' bear hug lifts her off the ground as her laughter fills the storage room. Jin and I can't help smiling as they embrace, with Rust quietly waiting in the background. He looks relieved more than happy, like a dying man receiving some mildly good news. As Mars releases his mother, she spots Rust and covers her mouth in surprise.

"Al... I'm sorry."

"Come here. Don't be a nitwit, Bryan." She nestles her head into his chest and wraps her arms around his wide chest as he holds her close. "I don't even know what you could be sorry for."

"I just... I've missed you. And I should've found you already."

"It's OK. We did it."

Rust cups the back of her head and kisses her on the temple, continuing their long hug. I'd be lying if I said I wasn't fighting back a tear or two, thinking of my own parents and wishing I could see them again.

"I'm so proud of what you two have done. That video... We all saw it. You did so well. Both of you." Alison pulls Mars by the arm for a group hug. It's the first time I've seen Rust physically embrace his son, but it's not awkward. It's like Alison is the liaison for affection and there's just too much joy in the room for anything else. It won't last, so I'm going to ride out the positive vibes and let our operation stay on hold.

"How much time do we have?" I whisper to Jin, knowing we have a job to do, even with the family reunion in full swing.

"It's best we stay in here until double staff time is over," she says. "The new guards just changed earlier, so right now is the busiest hour of the evening. We have time to plan."

"You finally got a nose job?" Alison says, lightly touching the bandage on Rust's face. He smirks and I wonder if it's possible these two have their own in-jokes. Obviously it's more than possible, but I find it hard to wrap my head around Rust having a sense of humour beyond smirking at my emasculating failures.

"They really got to you. Look at your eye. I haven't seen you like this since Turkey."

"Turkey?" I ask, failing in my attempt to stay out of the family reunion.

"She says he fell down the stairs. He thinks she bumped him," Mars says, as if he's heard the story constantly growing up.

"That's gotta be at least thirty years ago..."

"You've got a bit more padding nowadays, hon."

Jin and I shoot each other raised eyebrows. She called him 'hon' *and* she made fun of his body. This is fantastic. I'd be in a wheelchair if I tried that. It's even weirder that he goes on to respond with a compliment, telling Alison she's as beautiful as the day they first met.

"That's sweet. But seriously, they really got to you."

"Would you believe it was one guy? I might be getting too old for this."

"We all are. But I know what it's taken to get this far. You're an old dog, Bryan, but you've got some good tricks."

"Mm. You know, I feel like I've run dry. With Metric done, there's no reason to keep running around. Especially when I look back and see how much I've been running in circles."

"You're too harsh on yourself, with everything you've done. Jumping out of planes. Raiding bunkers. You've seen your share of crusades. And so have I."

"Well, this is my last."

"I hope so. But not for the reasons you're saying. You've got some dancing left in you."

"I'll save the last for you. But I've got to be honest, Al. I can't see right. Hurts to talk. My face is numb and every time I stop moving, I think I'm going to pass out. I'm not useless, but I'm getting close to it."

"I know you," Alison says, placing a gentle hand to Rust's face. Hearing him admit his own vulnerability is as endearing as it is concerning. "You will get through this. You will push your body past the limits of what's humanly possible to get this job done. And then you'll never have to do it again."

"I wish I was old enough to retire," Mars says, probably growing uncomfortable with the genuine sentimentality.

"Oh." Alison cracks a smile, not letting him ruin the mood. "You don't know how proud it makes me to see my Fox boys working together."

"Kid's actually a hell of an agent. And a good man. You've done well."

"We have," she says, correcting him.

"No. You know what I'm saying. It was all you. And I'm sorry I wasn't there more. You know, I just..."

Alison waits for him to continue, probably curious whether or not he can finish the sentence.

"It's OK," she says, letting him off the hook. "I know. You did what you had to. If I needed you... Well. It doesn't matter now. He's got the best qualities of both of us."

After another minute or two of catching up, Mars reluctantly turns his attention back to me. It's probably weirding him out to see his parents together, let alone cuddling. To have all these moments happening in front of me and Jin feels a little voyeuristic, but we can't exactly risk waiting in the hallway.

"So, you're all right to take it from here, Maven?"

"Hey?"

"We just came for Mom, so, you know… You're on your own now."

"Yeah, right." I lean against the wall behind me, accidentally knocking a broom to the floor. "There's no way you'd pass the chance to blow something up. We didn't bring all that C-4 here to light a birthday cake for you guys."

"I didn't expect you to have such a smart mouth." Alison folds her arms, sizing me up a second time. "But you're right, he always had a thing for exploding junk. Boys will be boys. Have you been blessed or cursed with children, Andrew?"

"Me? No. That would require a woman to withstand my company for some period of time."

"We were basically roommates in Panama and I think I've heard about every one of his romantic misadventures," Mars adds. "So I can confirm, there's definitely no ladies waiting back home."

"Panama. Sounds romantic. Maybe you can take me there, Bry?"

"Mom, gross."

"I have to say 'thank you', Andrew." Alison's sincere gratitude catches me off guard and makes me a little uncomfortable. There haven't been many compliments to accept over the past year or so.

"For what?"

"I know you were instrumental in opening these floodgates. And believe me, the world will know your name when this is done. We might not be able to stop the New World Order, but we can tell the world about Metric and stem the blood flow. I think the world is hurting and we're the best chance it has."

"Thank you. I couldn't have said it better."

"Only chance," Mars adds to his mom's statement, and I wonder if that's true. Even if others have looked into Metric and the New World Order, we're the only ones here right now and we're the only people who know exactly what we know. I've always been a big believer in taking opportunities that present themselves. The windows of destiny and providence open and close for a reason.

"Enough of this," Rust says, attaching a suppressor to his pistol. "We can't change the world from a janitor's closet."

"No janitors here, believe it or not," I say.

"Hm. Noted."

"It might not mean anything to you now, but wait 'til you see how clean this place is and you'll appreciate knowing that."

We spend a short time discussing the plan of attack, landing on an outcome that puts us in two groups again. Jin will lead me and what's left of Rust to find the intel and plant C-4 at key points, while Alison takes Mars through the rest of the SWAN with C-4 and clear out the staff, as much as possible. Rust was reluctant to leave his wife, but Mars made the convincing argument that Rust plus Maven equals one fully capable secret agent man, in theory, and Jin needs to stay with me to secure the Metric data.

"Jintara," Alison says, securing Jin's full attention. "Security has been especially high today. I heard something happened with Bhandit Kaypradee. He might be coming here."

"No. He's dead," I state as a matter of fact.

"He's dead?"

"And that was us," Mars adds, avoiding taking full credit for the .308 calibre love letter he sent to the KIL Unit leader's skull.

"Oh. Well. Good riddance, I suppose."

"Jin kickboxed his girlfriend in the face," I say.

"You love saying that, don't you?" Jin folds her arms, I suspect secretly enjoying the recognition more every time.

"It's a cool story."

"All right. Let's go," Mars says as he approaches the door, one hand on his mother's shoulder. "Don't be scared to use that gun, Maven. Good luck."

"Thanks. I don't believe in luck, so... all the best."

Mars stops and turns his head ninety degrees, his face solemn as he delivers his reply. "I *am* the best."

"No." I shake my head. "That's not a good line. Sorry."

"Bro. It was good."

"Agree to disagree."

~∞~

I haven't used a computer for about eight months. Can you believe that? Me. I haven't read a news article, watched a YouTube video, liked a Facebook status – nothing. I'm a little excited at the idea of getting my fingertips on a keyboard to find this data. Oh, this sweet, sweet data. It's my ticket out of this mess. This data is gonna set me free. It's the smoking gun I was missing a year ago. The testimony from Rust and Mars will be seen in a new light, especially if Alison and Jin will support it along with the digital records. Revealing the paper trail, emails, financial reports, work orders, and Metric product designs should be more than enough to be taken seriously – at least by the people already suspicious and open to hearing the truth. People have a funny habit of ignoring the facts that conflict with their worldview – call it cognitive dissonance, call it confirmation bias, call it what you will. My plan is to present enough evidence this time that no one can stand against us.

We're placing C-4 at five points throughout the SWAN, including two on the second level where the database is stored. There's apparently a server room full of power generators, which we'll hit to trigger a chain reaction and set off the rest of the C-4. To be honest, I have no idea how it works, but it sounds like the power source is meant to ignite the explosive and the chemical-filled laboratory is the final nail in the coffin.

"What do we say if we run into someone?" I ask. "Or when. Rust doesn't exactly fit in. He'd be more incognito on a hospital gurney. Even with a black T-shirt, those blood stains are a bit of a red flag."

"Don't worry about me," Rust says, eyes closed as he leans against the wall and waits for the elevator. "I'll be hidden until it's clear."

"I was going to ask 'how', but I forgot who I was talking to. The stealth gene and all that."

"Mmhmm."

"You ever been inside an elevator shaft?" I ask Rust, stepping inside the opening doors.

"One time."

"Sounds like a story."

"Another day."

Once we reach the second floor, we peer out to see not two but three security guards loitering nearby, including my friend Tae, the cockney buff Thai guy.

Oh boy. I open my mouth to say something, but decide casually ignoring them would be more natural. I follow Jin down the hallway, turning to see how Rust is travelling. And he's gone. I search for him, hoping he isn't back in the elevator, but there he is slinking in the shadows. He's good.

"Hey, Drake."

That's me. I spin around to see Tae and his friends watching us with curious eyes. This could be where our flaky plan falls apart. Each of them has a short buzz cut like me, which makes me feel more at ease. Maybe I can fit in after all. Then again, it's been a few weeks since I had access to a razor, so yeah, my anxiety level is back where it started.

"Aren't you meant to be on the third floor?"

"Shift's over," I say. "Big Tom. You know."

"What's he doing?" Tae's smaller Thai friend asks. I follow his line of sight and sure enough he's looking right at Rust.

"That guy?" I need to think of something fast. "He's just here to... sell some of these fine leather jackets. I was, you know, I was gonna take him to..." The three guards begin approaching us slowly, eyes fixed on Rust. "I was just... Jin?"

"Drake is trying to be funny. This is another new guy. He took a tumble outside so we're making sure he gets to the med bay."

"Yeah, your face is messed up something shocking," the third guard says, with what has to be an Australian or New Zealand accent. I can't tell them apart. "Let me take a look at you, big fella."

Rust grunts and Jin steps in to tell them that's unnecessary. They should get back to work, she says.

"We're off duty," the Aussie/Kiwi replies.

"Then you can leave it to me. I've got this," I say, turning my back. This could be against my better judgement, but my hope is that walking away is the most natural response and they'll decide to let us go. I look at Rust, still propped up against the wall, conserving his energy as he reads the situation. The tension rises as the three guards inch closer, now just a few feet away from us, breathing down my neck. I look to Jin and she's already started to walk away, hoping we will follow. But Rust hasn't moved, as if he knows something we don't.

"Time to dance."

"Dance?" My lips curl into a horrified smirk as my realisation turns to action. I take a fast, long step to clear space between Rust and the three guards, watching the former Metric agent reach for his gun.

"Get down!"

I watch Jin scoot along and I follow behind with my head down as the commotion escalates behind me. Glancing back just in time, I see Rust's M1911 jab the Aussie/Kiwi in the eye, then connect with his face, sending his pistol flying across the corridor. Rusty kicks Tae in the knee, sending him staggering to the floor. This all takes place in about two seconds flat, but with Rust's element of surprise gone, he catches a fist in the face from the tiny Thai. The left hook lands square on his jaw, luckily the opposite side of his major bruising. Rust barely flinches, as much as it's got to hurt.

I slide my hand into my jacket, resting my fingers on my Mk23 just in case I need to help out. My heart accelerates as the Tiny Thai draws his weapon and I visualise myself shouting orders across the room. Before I can act, Rust shoves his M1911 into the guard's thigh, pulling the trigger twice. The shots are quieter than I expected, even with the suppressor. Maybe it's just drowned out by the Thai's surprisingly high-pitched scream, which pierces our ears until Rust's free hand muffles him with a punch right in the mouth. I think he's done.

"You want to get in there?" I ask Jin, keen to see a kickboxing comeback.

"He's doing fine."

The Aussie/Kiwi, now recovering on all fours, sweeps his leg to trip Rust, but he somehow spots it a mile away through his swollen eyes. Rust stomps hard on the Aussie/Kiwi's ankle, then shoots him twice in the chest.

"Geez, Rust." For all the ass-kicking I've witnessed from Rust, I've never seen him shoot someone dead. His battered condition has left no other option in these high stakes.

"Look out!" Jin shouts, pointing to Tae across the room, reaching for the Aussie/Kiwi's gun. Just as I build up enough courage to wrap my fingers around the grip of my Mk 23, Rust fires two shots through Tae's head.

"OK," I say, hoping it's all over. Bang. One more shot, this one putting an end to Tiny Thai writhing around on the floor.

"Rust. Was that necessary?"

"Bad guys," he says, gesturing to the bodies with a lack of sympathy to rival Darth Vader blowing up Alderaan. "You're welcome."

"Yeah, well... I kinda liked that bad guy." I point at Tae, deliberately not looking at the pool of blood growing around his body. It's sickening, but I'm not as disturbed as I would have expected. Perhaps I've become more than slightly desensitised after inspecting the inside of Bhandit's skull back at the vineyard.

"He's right," Jin says. "They would've killed us."

"Would they really though?"

"Yes. Or worse."

"What's worse?"

"You don't want to know. There's more than one reason we're blowing this place up."

"What does that mean?"

"We should go before anyone finds us. The data room is on the other side."

"What's going on up there?" Mars chimes in through our earpieces. *"Is that what I think it is?"*

"You should see this mess. I think they might need to rethink the janitor situation."

"Why are you so obsessed with janitors all of a sudden?"

"I have no answer for that. It just keeps popping into my head."

"Well, stop it."

"I agree with him," Jin tells me, and I don't need to hear what Rust has to say about it.

~∞~

The data room is full of terminal screens I don't understand. It reminds me of visiting the main AT&T telecommunications hub in Grand Rapids. Wires and cords everywhere, dated systems too complicated to replace with something recognisable by modern standards. I'm not saying that's what we're looking at here, but it's just as overwhelming.

"This one," Jin says, making a beeline for a small monitor and keyboard in the corner beside a six-foot cabinet. The adjacent wall is lined with circuits boards and industrial fans cooling the room's equipment.

"Rust, there are guards everywhere down here." Mars sounds genuinely alarmed. *"I don't think I can get to the lab without causing a stir."*

"So stir it up."

"What am I meant to do with Mom?"

"Hm. Wait."

With Rust finessing the plastic explosive into the space between the circuits and fans, I realise this room is also powering the entire SWAN facility.

"This room's a structural point?"

"We don't have a detonator."

"What do you mean? I didn't quite follow all that."

"We have to detonate the explosive somehow. The best we can do is–"

"Shush," Jin catches our attention, waving her hands around and crouching to the floor. "Someone's coming... Get down."

Rust draws his gun, leans backs onto a computer server casing and slides down into a squat, as I huddle down behind cover. I can hear a male and female voice approaching from the corridor, but they seem to stop right at the entry to our room.

"There's something about drinking from the tit of another animal that's unnatural to me. People think that's weird to say, but I don't know. I think everyone else is weird."

"It's teat," the woman responds.

"What is?"

"You said 'drinking from the tit'. But it's teat."

"It is from the tit though. They're the same thing. You're just thinking about it from a sexual viewpoint."

"No, I'm not. It's about linguistics. If you're talking about a cow, it's teat."

"Well, my point is... no milk in my coffee, thank you. Just two sugars."

One set of footsteps grows distant as the other draws near. Rust raises his gun to his chest, drawing long breaths. He closes his eyes and stands to his feet.

Chapter 22

Three Times

"Stanley! You need to go."

The young server technician looks like a stunned deer in the middle of a highway, glancing from Jin to Rust's messed up face to the M1911 pointed towards him. He doesn't ask any questions.

"You need to stay calm and listen, OK? Go find as many people as you can and prepare to abandon the SWAN."

"I... What's the..."

"We're getting everyone out of here, OK? There will be plenty of time to leave. But you won't want to stay."

"There will be *some* time," Rust chips in with the appropriate level of sternness. "Don't you go blabbing this around, kid. Be discrete or you'll blow this for everyone."

Stanley nods and backs out of the room, probably wondering what he's meant to tell people without sounding like a lunatic. That's what I'd be thinking.

"Uh, the... The new password." Stanley takes a second as he lingers near the door, struggling to find his words. "The password is on the bottom of that coffee mug."

"I know. Thank you, Stanley."

He disappears through the door and we resume our espionage activities.

"Seems like a good guy."

"He's OK," Jin says, returning to the computer terminal where she's already logged in and navigating several windows in an operating system I've never seen before.

"So what's this about the detonator, Rust? I tuned out earlier, so explain it like I'm a child."

"We've got a bunch of blasting caps, but most are electric. This limits the places we can use them because what we don't have are the blasting machines or wires to deliver the burst of electric current."

"Sounds complicated."

"It's fine. We're improvising. The circuits will spark the C-4 to explode, which should ripple through to other power boards. It all helps weaken the structure."

"Right. Like removing blocks from a Jenga tower."

"So that's four points taken care of," Rust says, ignoring my great analogy. "But then there's one more."

"The lab," Jin says as she types at the computer.

"Right. The final blasting cap is a more traditional fuse ignited by a flame source. That shouldn't be hard to find. And Alison says if we can hit the lab, the whole place will go down."

"OK. So..."

"So we'll improvise. I'll meet Mars down there when we're done."

"That should be soon," Jin says, and I step up to the terminal to see the data she's brought us here to copy.

"What's happening over here? You've got this?"

"Yeah, take a look. All of this. That's your ticket to freedom, Andrew."

I look over her shoulder at the monitor to see one open window transferring the data to an external drive.

"What is it?"

"It's everything. You wouldn't believe what we have access to. Once Metric shut down we found a way into the master server and I'm told it's a complete record of everything up to that point. Emails, government certifications, research development grants from DARPA, staff records, analysis and intel, operational briefs and debriefs."

"Everything," I repeat, hypnotised by the flashing file names flicking through the file transfer window. "You're right. This is it. This is my exoneration. Even the US government couldn't turn a blind eye to this."

"Don't jinx it, Andrew."

"No, I mean, I know the New World Order has its tentacles everywhere, but this amount of information has to shake the cages. What do you think?"

"I think America is ready for this. And if they're not, it should be enough to grant you some asylum somewhere friendly."

"True. Enough to get me out into a First World country – no offence. Japan. Australia. New Zealand. This is the proof to get the public back on my side."

"It's solid proof, Andrew. That's what it is." Jin rests her hand on my wrist. I know she's aiming to put me at ease, but she's actually making my pulse accelerate. "Let yourself be hopeful. This is what you've been searching for."

An involuntary smile splashes across my face and for just a second, my eyes well up. I realise I've forgotten Rust is standing a mere dozen feet away, which makes me fall back to reality. "Yeah. I mean, thanks. We can celebrate when we're out of here."

"We'll split that Gatorade."

"Hm, we can talk about that."

Rust asks how much longer the transfer will take, leaning on the wall as if he's conserving every bit of energy for when it's needed. Jin suggests there's only a few minutes remaining until we're ready to move.

"It's mostly documents. There's some video footage, but I'm told it's compressed. Probably CCTV."

"Hey, maybe we're on there, Rust. Our antics with Kent Moriarty at the Manhattan Club. I wouldn't mind seeing that footage."

"Maybe." Rust inspects his C-4 handiwork, pressing the malleable plastic further into the groove between the fuse box and the wall. "Mars..."

"Yeah?"

"If it's clear, you should see about detonating the first two of your charges. We're on a separate circuit up here."

"Absolutely. A few rounds into this distribution board will set them both off. One of the circuits is already sparking."

"Let me guess," Jin says, briefly looking away from the computer monitor. "The one in the armoury?"

"Do you even have to ask?" Alison responds. *"It's the same problem we talked about a month ago."*

"Those idiots. It's so dangerous."

"Well, it's going to play in our favour today," Mars says. *"I'll detonate the storage room fuse and the armoury will go boom, shake the room. Stand by."*

Before I can stand by anything, the floor shakes with a tremor and an alarm begins blaring through a PA system I hadn't even noticed until now.

"That worked," I say.

"You felt it?"

"Uh, yeah." I eye off our C-4 charge and blasting cap, ready to blow like the homemade fireworks at my cousin Ronnie's sixteenth birthday party.

"Alison." Rust clears his throat, eyeing the ceiling, perhaps waiting to speak between the rhythm of the blaring alarm. "How inflammable is the storage lab on level one?"

"Oh. Well... Remember what happened at that warhead disposal facility you told me about?"

"Aleutian Islands. Of course."

"Relative to size, you could expect the same result."

"Right." Rust closes his eyes and takes a deep breath. I can't tell if he's doing maths calculations or solving some logistic issue, but he doesn't look thrilled about it, either way. "We have options."

"This is done." Jin does something I've never considered being necessary, "safely" ejecting the portable hard drive from the computer with a couple of mouse clicks. She hands it over with a kind grin, knowing exactly how much this means to me. I grip it tightly and consider its power to change, the way missionaries carry their holy text. I have a good feeling about this, or at least I'm finally allowing myself to latch onto the hope that's been missing until now. I slide the hard drive into my bag and pull the zipper closed, making sure there's no way for it to escape.

Rust points to the door, telling us to make for the elevator. We're about to go boom. He follows us to the exit, stops to line up his shot and pops a single bullet into the fuse box. We keep our heads down and run for cover, while physics and gravity do the rest of the work. The sound is deafening as sparks fly and detonate the C-4, collapsing the room behind the walls behind us. Smoke and dust begin to fill the hallway as the sprinklers shower water across the floors. I can hear shouting in the distance, but there's no one around. The evacuation has been swift.

We call the elevator and Rust catches up, looking ready for a nap.

"You good?"

"I wouldn't go that far," he admits.

"Can you take a break?"

"We literally can't," Jin says with regret. The floor shakes yet again and we wait for Mars and Alison to check in.

"That's two, bro."

"Nice one. Rust just detonated the server room, so we've only got the one left, right? I can't believe this is working."

"Alison, can you take Mars through the hatch exit to the roof?" Jin asks. "We'll find you after the final detonation."

"We're closer. We can do it," she yells back, trying to make up for a nearby loud speaker blaring the siren.

"We've got more C-4," Jin says, seemingly formulating a plot that wasn't discussed when we were all together. "We can't risk this one not working. Plant yours around the pressure point, leave the blasting cap and we'll finish it off with everything we've got."

"No, I..."

Alison begins to interject but stops, with a long pause. Rust has frozen still, now peering down as he listens carefully for a response from his family. I can see he wants to carry this burden himself, whether through a sense of duty or protection over Alison and Mars.

"It's OK, Mom."

"OK," Alison finally says after another pause.

"We'll be fine," Jin says. She looks to Rust who nods in confirmation before our elevator arrives. He points his M1911 towards the sliding doors.

"It's clear."

I don't know how this place isn't swarming with guards. I know things aren't like in the movies, but still I find my preconceptions of this world are constantly challenged. In reality, the security guys have been smart enough to jump off this sinking ship before the sharks drag them out. I'm sure it's a great gig when everything is quiet, but no job is worth dying for, when you think about it. So yeah, I would be a terrible bodyguard.

It feels like we're only halfway back to the ground floor when the elevator jams, as if blocked by a giant below.

"Someone's unhappy with us," Rust says – one of his classic understatements.

"There's a guy out here giving us hell," Mars interjects. *"It's a bit of a stand-off. How far are you?"*

"We're close," Rust says, shoving the wall of the elevator as if it could free us – the equivalent of banging on a vending machine that won't release your Twix. "Keep Alison safe. We'll be there soon. We're just... stuck."

"You're what?"

"Close yet far," I say.

"Bro, with the amount of firepower this guy has, we're both stuck. Handlebar-moustached goon is loaded to the hilt."

"Coppard?" I look at Jin and she's thinking the same thing. Bhandit's number one man might've followed us from the vineyard, or he could just be here to take over. Either way, he's not someone you want to deal with in a narrow corridor.

"I think he has a Gatling gun."

"Seriously?"

"Seriously. Looks like an XM556."

"You're kidding." Even Rust seems impressed.

"Whatever it is, it's pumping out 5.56mm clips like you wouldn't believe."

"Can't be. Those things burn through six thousand rounds a minute."

"Do I not sound concerned enough, Rust?"

"Where did he even find a Gatling gun?" I wonder out loud. Maybe we could get one."

"This is the *SWAN*, Andrew. 'Special Weapons and Nanotech', remember?"

"Special, indeed."

"Lady," Rust says firmly. "Does this thing have a way out?"

"I've never heard of this happening," Jin says ignoring the unwanted hailname as she senses Rust's urgency. "It must be part of the alarm system. Alison, can you make it through level one? That's where we came in."

"It's behind us. That just means..."

"You have to escape on foot. Mars can lead you back to our car. It's not too far, but it will be dark."

"Sounds like the lesser of two evils, with this mean mug blasting his way around the lab. We might not even need to detonate it, the way he's going."

I don't understand Coppard's intentions, and they don't seem clear to Mars or Alison either. They tell us Mars escaped a shoot-out with him and he's been going room to room ever since, shooting up any hiding spots that could be housing one of us.

"Avoid him or take him by surprise," Mars says. "I'd stay and help but I need to get Mom safe. We'll be out of here in a few minutes."

"There are jammers outside the SWAN," Alison reminds us." The Nano GEAR won't work from inside to outside, so we'll meet you at Chang Mai."

"Take care of yourself. And each other. Please."

This is the only goodbye Rust offers, and I can understand a man like him holding a policy against public sentimentality. Still, it leaves me a little unsettled after the emotional unbottling that took place only an hour ago.

"Life's too short to play it cool, Rust," is what I want to say. But part of me wonders if he doesn't want to acknowledge the risk involved, if that only makes it more difficult for a soldier to go to work.

"Up here. I'll boost you," he says, gesturing to the elevator roof.

"Up there?" Sure enough, there's the typical hatch you'd expect to find when one must escape an elevator, only it's missing any obvious access points.

"There's no handle. Does it open inwards or outwards?"

"C'mon, there's one way to find out."

"And then what? Because I don't know if you've seen this movie *Speed,* but it doesn't end well for the guys in the elevator shaft."

I know I'm just stalling while I work up the courage, but before I can suck it up, Jin steps forward and takes the boost up through the hatch, leaving me in a natural state of shame and inadequacy.

"I was... going to do that. I was."

"You don't get points for good intentions, kid. You see anything up there?"

Jin's voice echoes up and back to us with uncertainty, explaining there's nothing visibly blocking our way from the top.

"Hm. Must've been that guy."

"You think Coppard's waiting for us?"

"Seems like it. Your turn, get up there."

As much as I'd prefer to know why, I just do as I'm told and let Rust boost me into the dark chamber, hoping Jin doesn't make fun of me for lacking her bravery.

I reach down and pull up Rust, with Jin's help. He groans as he reaches the surface, rolling over instead of standing. In all the commotion, I'd forgotten about the effects of his concussion, broken ribs, and mashed up face.

"What now?"

"We wait."

"Until?"

"Until we move again. Then we've got the jump on this guy."

"Oh yeah. Literally."

"Exactly."

"The blaring siren is a lot quieter in here. Might disorientate Coppard."

Jin remains silent, preoccupied with her thoughts. She's clearly going through something in all this, and as much as I want to be the one to help her, I just can't find the words. Instead of trying, I sit down and rest my backpack in front of me.

A few minutes pass and the sound of gunfire grows distant after Mars confirms they've escaped to the exit unscathed, right before our communications cut out.

"I think it's gonna work out, Jin."

This is all I can think to say as we wait in silence, uncomfortably perched against steel surfaces not designed for leaning or sitting.

"I can't see how this can end with everyone escaping unharmed," she says.

"We know what we're doing. Mostly."

"Not us. My friends here."

"Oh." I should have realised this. There are no confirmed deaths, but I can see why she thinks collateral damage will be a factor after the commotion we've caused. We weren't able to warn any of the brilliant minds working here about our plans to liberate the facility, or even gain a consensus that this was the best plan of action. We've made that decision for them – or Alison and Jin have, at least. There are too many explosions and bullets flying around to assume no one will be caught up in the mess and I don't have what it takes to pretend I know any better.

"We're doing the right thing," is my compromise. "This is what's best. It's the way to get everyone out of here, and whether they want to leave or not, the work happening here can't keep up. You didn't make this call without thinking it through."

"I know. You're right. I think."

"Rust?"

"I hope so." Not the back-up I was hoping for. "I really do, kid. For your sake. I know what this means to you... to get out of this and have it be everything you've wanted."

I look down and squeeze my backpack, checking it still holds the hard drive of freedom inside.

"But here's the thing." Rust clears his throat, ready to dish out some rare advice. "Whether you're leaving here and walking back home to a ticker tape parade, or just doing enough to get Uncle Sam to let you return home, this thing is going to follow you around forever... one way or another. I've seen it before."

"That's... Yeah, I mean, that's part of it. And that's what I've been prepared for since Kansas and shooting that video with you."

"Right. But changing the world... saving the world... whatever it is you've been trying to do – these things tend to go different to whatever you plan. You might be holding a full house, but you can't know if there's a royal flush about to kick your ass sideways all over again."

"That's like anything though." I'm not sure what Rust's point is, but there's something he's trying to convey. I'm just not ready to outright ask him. He leans back against the wall of the elevator shaft, folding his arms with one foot rested on the crosshead bar. I can't tell if he's uncomfortable or holding his ribs, but he looks uneasy for someone who always seems so confident in his own ideas and decisions.

"Rust, you know better than anyone by this point, we can't stop the New World Order. But we can prove they exist and we can chip away at their stronghold. That's all this is. A single spark can start a spectral fire – you know what I mean?"

"We've been down this road. Maybe it helps. Maybe it doesn't. But let's be honest about this – I'm here for my family, and you're here to get your life back. There's nothing wrong with that. The sooner you know the score, the more time you've got to make your play. I've been chasing demons for decades, not realising they were chasing me too. By the time I realised that, it was too late. I'd already hurt so many people who deserved better than that."

"I mean, yeah, that's a black and white way to look at it. But the things you've done for Metric, you didn't know any better. Following orders is different to–"

"I'm not talking about assassination targets. I'm talking about her. And him." Rust stares down at his feet and lets out a long, exhausted breath. He's always been a curmudgeon, but right now he just seems tired. I don't mean that he needs to rest – he just seems worn out, like an old farm dog that doesn't know any different, so doing anything other than rounding up the herd is never an option. "I wasn't there when it counted. I sacrificed my place in their lives for something that turned out to be far less noble than my pride would allow me to realise."

"But like I said, you didn't know any better. Your intentions are the–"

"I appreciate what you're trying to say, kid. I really do. But good intentions don't mean a damn thing at the end of the day."

"What does any of this have to do with me?" It feels rude to be so frank, but if Rust isn't going to listen to me, he can at least try to explain the value of this conversation.

"My point is... I don't know my point. But I don't want to see you waste your life away chasing after this... recognition.”

“I don't need recognition. I just want my life back and I want people to hear what we're telling them, Rust. There's a reason this has consumed our lives for a year – it's important, man. We wouldn't have given up everything if it wasn't.”

“That's not what I'm saying. Even if the plan works, there will always be a part of you wanting more. More awareness, more changes, more action, more justice. But it's a white whale because it's never enough.”

“Where's all this coming from?”

“Aren't you listening to me?”

“He's just saying there are similarities with what he's done and missed out on,” Jin says, trying to act as a voice of reason. “I get it. Whatever happens after this, you could let it control your life and consume you, because it will always be there. Or you could let it be whatever it is, and just live with it. Good or bad.”

I don't know if she's more eloquent or if I'm less defensive towards her, but it's starting to sound like genuine advice when it comes from Jin. I look to Rust and he nods in agreement with her summary.

“If that's what you're saying, then I appreciate it. I have to be optimistic though. I wouldn't have lasted this long if I didn't think there was a chance for a significant outcome. Modern history is full of these stories. Deepthroat, Snowden, Serpico...”

Rust almost smirks, like he's amused or borderline frustrated by what he's perceiving as incredible naivete on my part.

“You talk about Snowden a lot, but this is a different time. The Snowden Effect is working against you. The distrust in the government has spread to a distrust in media agencies and authority in general. But whether people believe you or not, this thing is going to chase you around the rest of your life – if you let it. That's what I'm trying to say.”

“So what am I supposed to do?”

“Whatever you gotta do. Just find your place in this world. But as long as your name is attached to this thing, there will be people trying to take you down. Don't get me wrong. I think what you've endured is remarkable. Through all of this, you still have hope. Most people would've given up months ago. But there's a fine line to walk – I just want you to know what that line is.

Resistance makes you weak, kid. It's the persistence that makes you strong.

The weight of these words must show on my dimly lit face because Rust is fast to follow-up with some consolation.

"I'm sorry you've got to deal with this. But after everything we've learnt about these people, you always knew it wasn't going to just... go away like that."

"If you shine a light on evil, it hides or dies," Jin says.

"Sometimes. But don't be so sure it's that simple."

They're both right. I know the right thing to do. I just don't know if it's enough. Even in the darkest night, light is only an instant away, but that light needs to be bright enough for people to notice it.

"Honestly, while we talk about it..." I start, before fading as I reflect on how I truly feel. "It's getting hard to know what's motivating me anymore – illuminating the truth so people can see it, or doing it to clear my name."

Jin slides down the wall to sit next to me, placing a hand on my shoulder. She seems a little awkward about it, but that makes it even more genuine to me.

"There is more to life than whatever it is that you're afraid of losing."

She's right. Perhaps I've taken Rust's advice the wrong way. I'm swinging between hope and dread on a bi-polar emotional pendulum, which is par for the course over the past twelve months. I nod to acknowledge Jin's words, chewing the side of my mouth as I wonder how we got this deep into conversation while waiting for a psychopath to show up with a Gatling gun.

"I know all that, really. It's just easy to forget. I've always known though. I still hold true to, you know, my belief that this is why I'm here. It's no accident."

"That's a good way to be."

Without warning, the elevator drops back into it's slow descent and Rust snaps to attention, pointing his gun into the open hatch.

"What should we do?" I ask, remembering I have a pistol of my own.

"Stay quiet."

Jin and I crouch against the wall, with a view to the inside of the elevator, while Rust positions himself where he can watch the doors open. We slow to a stop and the sound of a ding initiates a brief moment of silence before gunfire echoes through the shaft. Rust's face lights up with each round, shooting five times before he lunges for cover. It's Coppard's turn to fire back and hope a lucky ricochet gets the job done. He's too smart to walk into an empty elevator with an open hatch, and too dumb to shoot directly through the roof. Jin and I fall into a near-fetal squat, holding each other tight as the bullets fly, too many to count. I know most of them are flying well above us, but I can feel the vibration of bullets dropping around us.

I look up at Rust, crouching on the opposite side, knowing he's not well enough to last through another fist fight. He makes eye contact with me, pointing to my gun and yelling to get ready. Sure enough, the gunfire stops and I see Coppard's shadow disappear from inside the elevator.

"He's reloading?" I ask.

"He'll have another gun. Follow me – now! Do it!"

Without giving me a chance to ask questions, Rust drops down and lunges out of sight. I say a quick mental prayer and follow him, landing awkwardly. I brace myself with my right hand to keep balance, dropping my weapon in the process. The sound of a struggle draws my attention as I scramble to recover, looking up to see Coppard overpowering Rust in the hallway. Rust is unarmed with his gun knocked away, as Coppard's huge biceps wrap tighter around his neck. He flexes, wrenching Rust's neck. Twice, three times. It's kind of amazing how much detail I can observe and process in just a moment, as I fumble for my gun. I see Coppard's white shirt damn near bursting at the sleeves as he keeps grip of his own handgun through his vice grip headlock. I notice the Gatling gun dumped on the floor, surrounded by bullet casings, with the stench of gunpowder still in the air. Rust's red face is turning redder as he throws punches into Coppard's sternum to little effect, with a wound around his eyebrow reopened and pouring with blood.

"Drop him!" I shout, pointing the Mk 23 at Coppard.

He adjusts his headlock to use Rust as a human shield and suddenly I'm out of options. Rust is struggling to breathe with the toll of his facial injuries adding to his exertion.

"I said 'drop him'," I repeat, hoping for a change of heart. "I won't tell you again."

Coppard smirks, seeing through my bluff. He knows I'm not Drake, KIL Unit bodyguard. He knows I'm Andrew Maven, former reporter. Former podcaster. Whistle-blower. I have to make it more than a threat. As Rust struggles, he turns his body just enough for me to fire a bullet towards Coppard's lower body. I know I'm taking the risk that I'll hit my friend instead, but it seems like a risk Rust would want me to take.

Coppard's leg buckles and he howls as the bullet throbs inside his thigh, giving Rust the opening he needs to break free and drive his fist into the thug's face. Twice, three times, and he puts him down.

Rust picks up Coppard by his underarms, knees him in the groin, and throws him shoulder-first into the corridor wall with every remaining ounce of strength.

"Let's go. C'mon." Out of breath, Rust motions for us to take off down the hallway, wherever it is we're meant to go. Jin drops down the elevator shaft holding my backpack and covers her mouth in shock as she sees Rust's bleeding face.

"Head to the final detonation point," he says, grabbing Coppard's firearm from the floor. He points it at our attacker's temple, as he slowly rises to his feet, leaning heavily against the very wall he was thrown into. From five feet away, there's no way Rust will miss. "Sorry, pal."

I turn away as Rust pulls the trigger, but a quiet click replaces the gunfire I expected. It's a moment of carelessness that could only result from the beating Rust has endured over the past day. Time slows down. He curses with disgust, his eyes widen and he swings the butt of the gun towards Coppard's face.

But it's too late.

Rust falls to his knees and wheezes, with a single .45 bullet shredding through his chest. Jin screams and Coppard begins to turn the M1911 towards us. Without thinking, I raise my pistol and squeeze the trigger.

Twice, three times. I put him down for good.

Chapter 23

Free-falling

Shot with his own gun. Rust can't go out like this.

I rush to help him as Jin makes sure Coppard is well and truly gone. What am I supposed to tell Mars and Alison? He opens his eyes, squinting from the fluorescent bulbs directly above us.

"Just a flesh wound."

"I thought he got you in the chest." There's so much blood on his upper body that it's hard to distinguish the fresh wound from the stains of older ones.

"Guess I got lucky."

"First time I've heard someone call it lucky to get a bullet through the shoulder."

"Oh, thank God," Jin says, joining me by his side. "Rust. You scared the daylight out of me."

"Hm. We're not out of the woods yet. Nice shots, by the way."

"Is there a med bay, Jin? Infirmary or something?" I don't respond to Rust's compliment, choosing to ignore the fact that I quite likely just killed a man a few moments ago. You hear about all kinds of coping mechanisms, but I've come from the "pretend it never happened" school of trauma management.

"Don't be stupid," Rust says, sitting upright. "We're so close to being done."

"Yeah, but... you just got shot, man. C'mon. You're tough, but that's not exactly–"

"Not so bad compared to the rest," he interrupts, shaking off a limp to walk down the corridor. "Look at my face. I can barely breath through these broken ribs."

"Yeah, I was getting ready to make a tourniquet out of my tie, but I'm guessing that's probably not even the right way to go."

"Mm."

"Just let us get you treated in Chang Mai, please. When this is all done."

"Whatever you say, kid."

Jin looks at me and shrugs, taking off after Rust and leading the way to the final detonation.

~∞~

I continue to be surprised at the emptiness of the hallways, but the droning siren and remnants of Coppard's shooting rampage go a long way to explaining why no one would want to stick around.

"What is this?" I ask, following Jin into a room with more hazard warning signs on the door than sponsor logos on a NASCAR driving suit.

"It's our chemical storage room," Jin says. "If our plans are correct, it's the point that will cause an implosion of the entire SWAN facility. The chemical properties also make it highly flammable in the right conditions."

"Well, that sounds perfect for a giant explosion."

"Implosion."

The room is lined with shelves of marked gas tanks and pallets of white plastic containers, while chemical drums are stacked halfway up to the roof. I don't know if we're looking at powders, pills or liquids, but I imagine there's a good amount of all three.

Rust trails behind us and wastes no time placing the final piece of C-4 alongside the blasting cap and C-4 that Mars and Alison left behind. He's so meticulous with the placement, taking great care to shape it and adjust the detonator.

"OK. This is it."

"Done? All right, let's bounce out of here. Well done, everybody."

The blaring alarm finally stops, leaving an eerie silence as Rust lowers his head, still facing the wall.

"This is it for me. You need to leave. I need to stay."

205

"What are you even talking about?"

"The detonation."

Jin mutters what I assume is a Thai curse word under her breath as she realises we've overlooked the escape plan. I can't help wonder, did we forget to come up with a plan or did we push the inevitable problem out of our mind until it came time to face it?

"Can't we set a timer?"

"How would we do that?" Rust asks.

"I'm sure if we put our minds together..." I can see the wheels turning in Jin's scientific mind as her eyes dart around the room, calculating mathematical equations of chemical combinations and reactions. "How about a cigarette and some string? I've seen that somewhere before."

"The longer we wait," Rust speaks loud enough to stop us talking over him. "The less chance of Alison and Mars meeting up safely with you two, and everything working out in the end." He finally turns around from the wall with a strange look on his battered face, one I don't recognise. "Trust me. I've thought this through."

Rust holds up a single tracer round between his thumb and forefinger, making sure I see it before loading it into his M1911. I pat down my pocket and realise Jacoby's lucky incendiary bullet is out of my possession. I want to ask how he knew about it and how he ended up with it, but none of that matters next to the fact that he's planning to use it to detonate the final C-4.

"Hell no. I'm not leaving. Let's just forget about blowing the SWAN altogether. We have the data."

"If we don't shut it down," Jin protests, "it's just going to keep going, whether Bhandit's gone or not. Even without Metric."

"I've seen it before," Rust says. "You cut off one head and another grows back."

"I'm sorry, Jin, but is it really our problem? I mean... I'm sorry. I get these are your people. But let's put together another plan. We can come back. I promise. We can't just leave Rust here. We're talking about a man's life."

"Look at me, kid." Rust pauses, stares into my eyes and exhales with his usual impatient candour. That unfamiliar look on his face is actually a true sadness peeking from behind his weathered mask. For the first time, when I hear his sigh, I sense defeat instead of the usual frustration that comes from his own stubborn determination. "Even if I get out of here, if the internal bleeding doesn't get me, if the infection doesn't get me, I'm only gonna be messed up bad enough to make my final days miserable. There's no happy ending for me after this."

"I can see what's happening, Rust, but I'm not letting you become a martyr for this. Just because you've made some mistakes in your life, doesn't mean you can throw it away. We can get you help."

"Kid. You have no idea what's been running through my head. I'm doing this."

"What about Alison?"

"She'll understand. I'm doing this for her. I got her boy back to her again. I got to say goodbye. Got to say I'm sorry. Truth be told, they're better without me."

"That's garbage, Rust." I'm livid, and I can tell Rust is taken aback by my strong reaction. He's finally got me fired up. "You have a chance to be together. It's a fresh start."

"It's too late. You might have a normal life ahead of you, but it's not what I want. It feels like I've either been wounded or wounding someone my whole life. So just let me do this. Let me die feeling like a hero."

"This isn't heroic, it's stupid!"

"Sometimes there's not much difference, Maven. It's like I told you. There are no true heroes. No one's clean. Anyone who lasts this long has blood on their hands. So let me do this one thing. Let me hope it will redeem my mistakes. There are worse places to die."

I look to Jin for support, but instead I see a defeat in her eyes that hits me hard. There's an acceptance or knowledge that there's no other way. My anger melts into sadness as I realise we can't dissuade Rust from this decision, and even if we could, there's no better option. Is this endeavour worth dying for? I can't say it is. It's impossible to know whether this will change the world or leave no great consequence.

"And what am I supposed to tell your wife, your son?"

"Tell them... I always fought for what I believed in. But now it's time to stop fighting."

Rust holds up his M1911, signifying he's preparing to detonate the C-4 as his way of telling us it's time to leave.

"I'll wait ten minutes," he says.

I nod and step up to him, pulling down his arm to bring the gun to his side. I'm surprised he lets me do it, and I can't tell if he's lost enough strength that he can't stop me, or he's open to whatever gesture I'm about to make. Both possibilities seem unlikely, yet here we are. I take Rust by each shoulder, making the effort to look into his eyes, as hard as it is.

"I know you aren't into this, but you gotta let me say something. You *are* a hero to me. I don't care about your past. You've always had my back. You've saved me more times than I can remember. You've taught me so much."

"That's..."

"I'll miss you. Just promise me you'll say a prayer before you go. You've done so much already, I know, but do that for me. That's the only way I can leave you."

"Mm... OK. I could do that."

"I don't know if you mean it. But thank you."

I rest my head against Rust's barrel of a chest and squeeze his body with a gentle firmness, knowing his resistance to affection as well as his multiple injuries. I turn and head for the corridor, unable to draw out my goodbye any further. I hear Rust and Jin converse briefly in Thai before she catches up to me. I try not to think about the fact that I'll never see this man again.

Even after surviving Coppard's bullet wound, it turns out he's still going out with a shot from his own gun. It seems kind of appropriate to end things on his own terms, but I know this strange version of closure will haunt my memory for the rest of my life. Part of me wonders what life would be like as free men, able to reflect on the madness we've been through and the crazier stories of his younger years. I really value the friendship I've built with Mars, and it's led me to fantasise about the amazing conversations I wish I could have with his father, if only we had the chance. I know in reality, Rust would've wanted little to do with me in the real world, despite what we've been through, but now the whole hypothetical scenario can never take place.

"Andrew."

Jin is hustling to keep up with my pace, but I'm too upset to slow down and interact with her.

"Where are you going?"

"I don't know. Where are we going?"

"We can reach the rooftop exit and take a gyrocopter. That's the fastest way out."

"OK." I don't quite know what a gyrocopter is, and I'd normally have a dozen questions about this kind of plan, but I just can't do it right now. I feel numb. I feel nothing. As much as I can pretend like shooting Coppard never happened, there's no escaping the reality of leaving Rust to his inevitable death. The next few minutes are a blur as I let my mind run away with the lingering anxiety of one man's sacrifice.

Before I know it, we're climbing a ladder and pushing through a hatch into the warm night. I shuffle along the concrete with a full moon and dim sensor lights illuminating the path through dark vegetation until we reach a small clearing. I can see two of the gyrocopters remaining in a port clearly designed for at least a dozen. Surrounded by tall trees blowing in the wind, I imagine this would be the perfect hidden rooftop for a facility like the SWAN, undetectable from the sky. The entire place is built into the mountain, with foliage and presumably fake trees and rocks designed to cover or shield the numerous exhaust fans, transformers and satellites from any outside surveillance. I can just make out the edge of the mountain, with nothing but darkness beyond it, obscuring what I can only imagine is an amazing view of the jungle below us.

"You can fly this thing?" The army camo gyrocopter looks incredibly flimsy by design. If I'm being generous, it's a poor man's helicopter, but if I'm honest, it's more like a glorified bobsled with rotor blades to keep it airborne. It's like a chopper designed by whoever invented the Thai tuk-tuk taxis.

"I can fly it." Jin sounds confident.

"Can you land it?"

"Sure, I can land it." Jin sounds less confident. Without a better option available, I slide onto the rear of the gyrocopter and anticipate the pending sound of C-4 detonation. I wonder if we'll be able to feel the SWAN implode below us or there will just be a slight shake to signify a mission accomplished.

"Is it OK to fly in the dark?"

"It's not ideal, no," Jin admits. "We will land near the road and see if we can meet with the others. They won't be too far along."

"Are they in Nano GEAR range?" I ask, knowing they would've responded by now if they could hear us.

"No. The jammers, remember."

"I thought they might've been destroyed by now."

"I'm not sure how that works to be honest. Now, are you ready?"

I take off my backpack, gripping it in my lap so I can fully lean into my padded seat. Once again, I press my hands into it to make sure the hard drive is still inside, like a concert ticket I can't afford to leave behind before a road trip.

"I'm as ready as I could be."

The second she starts up the engine, I feel a gentle metallic poke into the back of my head.

"Ow. What is that?"

"What?"

A familiar voice chimes in from behind, frightening us both. "Together again. Just in time."

Ah, nuts. Was it too much to ask for things to work out this time?

"Take off!" I mutter to Jin with haste, subtly dropping the backpack to my floor space before raising my hands in the air. "You're too late, Jacoby. It's all been done."

"How about you guys step off this thing and we can figure out where we're at?"

"We found Alison. We blew up the SWAN. We copied the hard drives. I'm sorry for whatever's made you go crazy here, but there's nothing left to do."

"I don't agree with that at all. Now, step off. Both of you."

"Why did you do it? You know you've essentially killed Rust? And for what? Why did you do it?"

"I know he's an old bastard, but I left him a long way from dying. I'm not gonna tell you again – step off."

I feel the ground tremble and turn to see Jacoby in his Spectral Suit, caught off guard by the distant explosion below us. With the pent up anger from his role in killing Rust, fuelled by the morbid detonation taking place below us, I let the rage flow through my arms and launch myself at Jacoby. His gun tumbles to the ground and I'm suddenly energised as if Rust's spirit has possessed my body into action.

With Jacoby off balance, this is my best chance to overpower him, so I lower my head and spear my shoulder into his sternum. It feels like running into a lamp post, but he does indeed fall. I quickly return to the gyrocopter, taking care to hunch down clear of the spinning rotor, and repeat my instruction to Jin.

"C'mon, c'mon!" I look over my shoulder as Jacoby rises to his feet and I wonder if I have any chance at beating the man who broke Rust.

"We'll be up in a minute," she yells over the whirring blades. "We can't go straight up, we have to move forward."

"Even if you leave without me, you have to go, OK?" I spit out, fast enough that I worry she might not understand me. "The backpack is right here, Jin. You've got this."

Jacoby is now chasing as we hook along the runway, only a few feet behind us the gyrocopter gaining enough speed to lift off. I make the mistake of reaching out to kick him away. He catches my ankle and pulls it. The force combined with our movement yanks me from my seat into an awkward position, but I grip onto the side of the gyrocopter, hanging on for life as we continue to rise. I can feel his grip inching closer, like he's climbing a rope, and I'm now supporting Jacoby's full body weight as he dangles below us, preventing the gyrocopter from a buttery smooth flight. After a few seconds, I realise I'll either lose my grasp or the commotion will crash this damn thing. And so I submit, hoping Jacoby breaks my fall.

As I plunge towards the hard ground, even if it's only a second of free-falling, it's surprisingly not the pending physical impact or subsequent back injury flashing through my mind. All I can think about is how I was wrong about myself. Was all my self-doubt unfounded? If I only cared about returning to my normal life, I'd still be up in that ascending aircraft, fighting for my life instead of sacrificing my well-being to send Jin home with the revelations that live on the hard drive.

I land with my hands outstretched, allowing my knee and hip to take the rest of the major impact.

Everything hurts. I don't even know. I probably hit my head.

I probably broke my neck. I could be dead. I don't know. My whole body hurts and everything sucks.

I turn my head, seeing Jacoby rise to his feet and turn to the sky.

"Hey. Hey."

He reveals a second gun from a holster at his shoulder, ignoring my attempts at distraction. I can't tell which stars above are real and which are the result of knocking my head, but I can see Jacoby is attempting to shoot down the gyrocopter.

It's too dark. She's too far away. He turns his attention back to me, standing over my crumpled body with dimly lit disdain across his face.

"What are you thinking?"

"What?"

Jacoby turns to the jungle and releases a frustrated yell from deep inside his lungs.

"Tarzan..." I mumble.

"You..." He picks me up to my feet. I can hear him breathing heavily in seething anger as he drags me along in the dark. "Do you have any idea what you just did?"

"Um... Yes. But also, no. Because you won't talk to me, Jacoby. I wanted to talk all of this out, but you said it was too late and you ditched us."

"You picked your side, man. You screwed me."

"I don't know what your side is. All I know is these guys have had my back, always, and they want the exact same thing that I want. So if that's not your side, then... we're... I'm sorry, my head really hurts. Can we slow down?"

Jacoby lets go of my wrist and turns back to face me.

"You're right. I'm doing what I've gotta do. You're doing what you've gotta do. That puts us on different sides. But that doesn't mean I have to like it."

"Uh, well... Yeah."

"Can you walk? Keep walking."

"I don't... OK." I realise there's no point arguing. If I wanted to escape, I couldn't. For starters, I wouldn't know where to go, and I wouldn't be able to outrun him, even if I was uninjured.

"How did you find us?"

"It was easy enough to track you to the area. Then I just

waited. I've been up here since everybody started deserting the SWAN."

"Oh, right."

"The fleeing gyrocopters made it easy to pinpoint. Now, there's a cabin in the trees over here. We'll be camping until your friends come back for you."

"What do you even want?"

"You know what I want. The data."

"We can just make a copy."

"I don't want a copy, Maven. I want to destroy it."

Chapter 24

Canteen

Jacoby pushes me into a green and brown camouflaged door. Everything but the entrance to the cabin is covered by fake shrubs or shaded by nearby trees, making it resemble a hidden fallout bunker. There's little of note inside this aluminium box – a sink and bar fridge, a booth with a table covered in old newspapers and dental floss, and a small messy bed down the other end. The whole place stinks like body odour, which is no doubt aggravated by the muggy heat. There are two motionless cooling fans, rendered useless after our explosive exploits in the SWAN cut off the power supply.

"I need water," I say.

"Help yourself. There's a refrigerator full of canteens right there."

"No bottled water?"

"Sorry, princess. But you'll be fine. Probably rainwater."

"Well, I guess I'm just thirsty enough to risk the diarrhoea."

I open the creaky fridge door and to my surprise, no moths fly out. I take one of the canteens and seat myself inside the booth. I instinctively pick up a newspaper before realising I have no interest in old Thai news and there's a story far more mysterious to uncover.

"I think it's time for you to reveal your evil plan, Jacoby."

"It ain't like that, man." He leans back against the sink and fridge, folding his arms in a defensive stance.

"What is it like then? Don't you want me to understand why

you're doing all this?"

"You wouldn't get it."

"I'm sure you can explain it to me. We've got a lot of time here."

"I could make the time pass pretty fast for you," he says, raising his eyebrows with an obvious violent implication.

"Let me guess – you want to sell the data back to someone in the NWO and retire in the Maldives."

"Psh. You're way off base. Trust me on that."

"Jamaica, then."

"All right. OK." He takes a seat opposite me in the booth, with either a change of heart or the realisation that I won't give up. "You want to know?"

"I do."

"You really want to know?"

I give him a blank look, unscrewing the canteen and taking a swig of water without breaking eye contact. I'm not going to repeat myself again. He knows who I am.

"When I joined Metric, it was a big deal. First black agent, you know?"

"Right."

"But I couldn't tell my family about it. I couldn't tell no one. All they knew was that they couldn't find me anymore. That wasn't easy, but I felt it was important. World changing, world saving. You know the Metric story by now." Jacoby peels down the blinds of the cabin to peer into the darkness outside.

It's strange. Despite what he's done, I still want to hear some justification to make sense of his actions. I feel like I'm a good judge of character and I'm certainly not used to being so wrong.

"But then everything changed. Mars and Rust showed up on the internet, talking about New World Orders, Metric spies and lies. Vatican, Wall Street, dudes in dark rooms filled with smoke... all these things that never mattered to me, but now they're defining the past decade of my life. You know how that feels?"

"No, but... I know how it feels to have your world turned upside-down. The NWO changed my perception of everything I thought I knew."

"Right, but this is *my* personal story getting flipped upside-down," Jacoby says, leaning in to emphasise his strong feelings on the topic I already know so well. "The twist is that I'm the bad guy here. After everything I did, leaving everyone behind for a greater cause... This wasn't some revelation I'm reading about in a newspaper. This is my whole life. My history, my success, my achievements – all just dirty dishes in a kitchen sink full of filth and piss."

"Yeah. Like, I get that it's a lot to wrap your head around... but that doesn't explain why you're here. These other guys went through all the same stuff. Mars and Alison and..."

My voice trails off thinking about Rust's lifeless body, crushed by rubble and chemically burned several storeys below the exact spot we're sitting and chatting. I know it's what he wanted, but it's so morbid that I can't speak his name with such casual reference.

"I'm not talking about them. This is my story," Jacoby says, making it clear that comparing his actions to others won't draw any guilt or regret. "Once I learnt the truth about Metric, all I wanted to do was get what was mine and get back to my family. Get them out of Englewood to give them the life they deserve. They were so damn proud when I became a marine and I wanted them to feel that again. It's been so long since I've seen them. I just needed to turn up with enough finances to make a difference. End the hustle."

"So this is about money."

"Hell no, man. Let me finish." I thought I'd caught him out, but my assumption has been denied again. "I sent back money whenever I could, but it was never enough to get them outta there. It would bail one of them outta jail, pay off a car loan, even put kids through school for the year... but there were too many people, too many needs and I couldn't help from a distance. There's good people on the ground in Chicago, and it's hard enough for them to make a difference, so hustling around the world with Metric, I didn't have much hope of seeing things change the way they needed to... And then your video comes out and changes everything."

"Twenty million views, baby."

"Good for you. So once I deal with the identity crisis, I realise, hey. Maybe I can make this work. I spent months waiting for clearance on the funds after I transferred everything from my

Metric bank account, and just as I had it all at my fingertips, I find out the beans are about to spill. You're still out there and you haven't given up on your little quest to tell the world every little thing about Metric."

"That's when you tracked me down."

"I don't need to go into every detail, but I knew I had to find you. I couldn't let the world know about my work with Metric. I need to stay under the radar to keep any chance at a normal life with my family. A better life. That's always been my goal, even when I was 'saving the world' and running black ops. I did it all for them."

"Wow."

I'm hearing words from Jacoby that have come out of my own lips. He wants a normal life too. I know he's talked about his family before and even then I sensed a level of guardedness in his Englewood pride. There was an unwillingness to explain why he hadn't returned. I assumed he had outgrown the community or there were some family issues. Dynamics I wouldn't understand. I was way off, again, but he hasn't exactly been forthcoming with personal truths.

"So you get it now." He slides out from his seat, walking over to the refrigerator to grab his own canteen water. "We both want the same thing, Maven. But it's gonna take exact opposite outcomes to get us there."

"Then it's either I tell the world the truth to get my normal life back, or we keep it silenced so you can get the white picket fence and liberate your brothers and sisters in suburbia?"

"Don't you undermine this," Jacoby says, sharpening his tone after misreading mine. "This is my life we're talking about."

"I'm not. That's my genuine assessment. You see it like it's either you or me. But here's the question, what happens if the truth gets out? What are you afraid of? You never did anything but follow orders. You couldn't have known better. Surely, it won't be easy, but you can get out of this and do it the right way."

"You really think that's how they're going to spin this?" Jacoby grins, incredulous with my naivete. "Let me tell you something, small fry – and that's what you are in all of this, never forget. We're all small fries. That bank account I've been securing is going to disappear, first of all. Proceeds of international illegal espionage. Secondly, even if they don't throw me in prison, you can forget about living a quiet life with my family. I don't want them dealing with any of that. I don't want them to see what I've done."

"Is it really that bad though? You could just disappear and they wouldn't know any different."

"Man, I've got sources and contacts from here to Easter Island. If I wanted to disappear, I'd be gone tomorrow and you'd never see me again. But it's not about that. Let me tell you – I've fought in Somalia, Zanzibar, Syria, the Philippines, Malaysia, Afghanistan and Iraq. After everything I've seen, my mind still drifts back to my people in Englewood. My own flesh and blood are caught in a cycle of violence and crime, getting ripped off by a system and government that doesn't care about them and is built to work against them. Teenagers shot over sneakers in a neighbourhood where poverty gives birth to violence. Closing schools and clinics, pushing up rent while the cycle continues. Nothing anyone does is enough to truly help the vulnerable. Nothing. Hell, Englewood might as well be Jupiter, as far as anyone in a suit is concerned. They don't care, man. They don't care. But I do. I'm doing something about it. I'm getting my people out of there."

"Sure, I get that, but–"

"Let me explain this. When my pop moved to the south side, there was a hundred thousand people in Englewood. It was crowded, he tells me. I can't even imagine. And then the gun violence starts and people start dropping. They're either dying, they're getting locked up, or they're gettin' the hell outta there. My friends are hustling just to survive. If they're light-skinned like me, they're asking to pump gas. If they're rough looking, it's shooting dice or slinging dope. By the time I was old enough to join the service, people were bustin' to move on out and now it's just twenty-five-thousand souls struggling to survive there in one of America's so-called greatest cities."

I nod, understanding the passion Jacoby has for this cause. It always escalates when family is involved. I know that's why Rust was so willing to put his body and his life on the line, and it appears Jacoby is the same way.

"There's good people there. Real good. Seriously, the only difference between you and them is where you were born. And even those hustling on the streets are there 'cause they don't see any other way. They don't know any other life. No opportunities, no future. You reporters like stats, right?"

"Right."

"I got some stats for you." Jacoby wipes the side of his nose, a sign of emotion as he warms up to drop some knowledge he's been sitting on for a long time. "This is a ninety-five per cent black community, just left alone and cast aside like yesterday's newspaper. We're talking thirty-five per cent unemployment and an average household income of $20,000 a year. You can't improve your situation on $400 a week and it's not getting any better. So you gotta see this, man. I can't leave my people in a forgotten place, hustlin' 'til they die."

"I understand this is important to you, Jacoby. And I understand that–"

"You don't understand nothin', man. You wanna know how bad I want this? I'm in Thailand, man." He laughs to himself, looking down at his fist inside his palm. "For real. Thailand. Do you think I wanna be here getting eaten alive by mosquitoes? I wouldn't be here. No one wants to get Zika."

"What about doing the right thing, and dealing with the consequences?"

Jacoby shakes his head, as if he's heard or at least considered this argument many times before. "Screw it. Look where that's got us. How do you even think this is going to end well for you, after you put the truth out there? Some people will believe you, sure, but you know what happens to whistle-blowers, right? They get into 'car crashes', freak accidents or they disappear in the night."

"Yeah, well. That's a risk I'm going to deal with. Better than living a lie or living in the shadows."

"Then you're dumber than I thought. Watch me, living in the shadows the rest of my life with a smile on my face. I'll be the guy not in prison, not six feet under, not being harassed by media and nutjobs."

"We'll see."

"Yeah, we'll see."

Jacoby sits down on the bed at the other end of the cabin.

I guess this means I'm sleeping on the floor.

"I don't know what your friends are doing. I don't know if our comms are still jammed, but they better get their asses back out here with that data or I'll be hunting them down myself."

"You think staying here overnight is a good idea?" I ask, changing the topic to avoid acknowledging the prospect of a manhunt. I honestly don't know if Mars and Jin will come back for me or go ahead with the mission. It's hard to imagine them leaving me behind, but coming back isn't going to be easy. "You've got me thinking about Zika now."

"It's the yellow fever you want to be worried about. But I'm sure you'll survive."

"I hate you so much, Jacoby."

"I don't care," he spits back, resting his head and rolling over on the bed. He certainly doesn't appear to care. But...

"I think you do."

"Ha. You know how many people have tried to kill me in my life? And I'm supposed to care that you're pissed at me."

"But I don't hate anyone else. Just you. That's gotta count for something."

"I don't care. And you don't mean it anyway."

Dammit, he's right. After everything, I still want to see Jacoby come around. I hate what he's done. I hate that he's the reason Rust is gone and I'm not ready to forgive that. But I'm not ready to completely write him off as a villain. I feel like he could've put a bullet into my head the second he spotted me and Jin, but he didn't. Even Darth Vader had a bit of good left in him, enough to make the difference, and he'd blown up a whole planet before he came around.

Come to think of it, we were in this position with Rust not long ago. Back in Kansas, he beat the crap out of me and Mars, turning us into Metric when we first found out about the New World Order. He basically signed our death warrants before he saw the light. He went from killing us to saving us, so if I try hard, I can imagine Jacoby going through the same transformation. It's unlikely, but it's possible, and that's enough for me to hold out hope.

Rust not only turned a corner that day – he changed my life. Every time I've done something brave, it was as if Rust was pressuring me into it. I'm no action hero, but as an ordinary man, overcoming a rational fear of danger could only happen with the pressure from a veteran badass like Rust, even when I've had no other option. I felt like knowing he was there or imagining him watching had inspired and pushed me to be bolder. It started like a father throwing his kid into the deep end of pool for a swimming lesson. In the end, it was more like a high school football player pushing himself when he knew the old man was watching from the bleachers. These are strange analogies for a guy in his mid-thirties to admit about a man he hardly knew, but I can't overstate the power of meeting Rust at the point in my life when everything turned upside-down, and realising that he and Mars were the only human anchors I had to get through it. I had to be bold. I had to be brave. There was no other choice. I need to remember that as I sit here in this sweltering cabin with no certainty over my fate. This time tomorrow I'll likely be dead or flying home to America with my exonerating disk drive. Either way, for better or worse, it's all because of Rust.

Chapter 25

Fight-or-flight

"Rise and shine."

"I barely slept."

Jacoby is leaning over me, using a scary knife to cut the zip ties he wrapped around my ankles. He was kind enough to throw a pillow on the floor, but I'd be surprised if more than a handful of hours had passed. There's a dim light peeking through the windows with the glow of an early dawn.

"That's a good thing," Jacoby says, pushing open the door to let a stream of sunshine fill the cabin. "You probably had a concussion last night, so sleep is your enemy."

"Uhh, but I still slept. That's not good, is it?"

"You're still here."

"I think I should get to a hospital. If you let me go, I promise I'll come back."

"Nice try. You hear that sound?" Jacoby turns back to me, pointing to the skies outside. "That's your friends coming to save your ass."

"I can't hear anything." I help myself to another canteen from the fridge, focusing more on avoiding dehydration than the mind games Jacoby is playing.

"You'll see. You might think there ain't no way to avoid one of us being the loser in all of this, but I'd mark it down in the 'win' column if we're all breathing at the end of the day."

"I'd call it a win if you can switch sides and we can stick to the plan we agreed to when you flew me out to this country."

"Ha. You can forget about that. Now, get out here. C'mon."

I take a deep breath, closing my eyes to refocus and recentre myself. I need to remember who am I and why I'm here.

"What are you doing?"

"Can't a guy say a quick prayer before he's thrown into a hostage swap situation?"

Jacoby leans through the door, and places a hand on each side of the frame. "It must be pretty cool to be you. Sustained by holy faith."

"It's not doing much for me right now, to be honest."

"You think believing in God has made your life turn out any differently? Look where you are, man. This is not the life you want. A God who throws you into this mess, you gotta wonder if that's worth believing in."

"I don't expect you to understand it," I say, stepping towards the exit. "I never questioned whether or not I should believe. But sometimes I wonder if God believes in me."

"Poetic. Are you done?"

"Why are you like this?"

"I think we've covered that already."

Satisfied with his response, I follow Jacoby outside, squinting into the rising sun. Once my eyes adjust, I can't help but marvel at the breathtaking view before us. The daylight reveals we're far above the treetops of the jungle I trekked through yesterday, with an artificial flattened clearance to make this space the main entry into the now collapsed SWAN. I half expected the mountain to cave in entirely once Rust detonated the facility, but that doesn't seem to be how this works. If you removed the trees and foliage, both real and fake, it would look like an airport tarmac. Different vehicles and sheds litter the brown concrete surface, each designed and disguised to remain hidden from above and afar.

"I think He does, by the way."

"What?"

"Believe in me. God."

"That's nice."

"You underestimate what I can do. That's the beauty of a higher power. I don't need to be that strong."

"We'll see."

I follow Jacoby's gaze to the sky and spot a distant speck approaching. I can make out two figures, presumably Jin returning with Mars. If there's a way for us to get out of this, he'll know it. At the very least, he'll put up a good fight. As tough as Rust was, Mars has the moves like Jagger. I've seen him kick a goon in the face before they even knew he was in the room. It's hard to keep up when he's flying around the room, like Bruce Lee moving too fast for frames to catch.

I toss my jacket into the cabin and step fully into the light, shielding my eyes to watch the gyrocopter's descent.

"Sit your ass down," Jacoby barks, pointing to a camping chair resting against the cabin.

"Always with the 'ass' stuff," I say.

"Do it."

Again, I obey and sit, confused as Jacoby zip ties my wrists to the chair's arms. I guess he doesn't want me getting in the way if it comes to throwing fists. It doesn't really matter. I have nowhere to go, but I know even if I freaked out and tried to bail, I wouldn't get far tied to the chair. Jacoby looks down at me, loading his gun in what could only be an attempt at intimidation.

"If you move, I'll put a bullet in you. If you talk, I'll put a bullet in you. If you even raise an eyebrow..."

"Bullet. In me. Got it. Seems excessive, but... Got it."

I look past Jacoby to watch the gyrocopter touch down at the runway across the clearance. It manoeuvres into a wobbly landing that matches Jin's self-assessment. Jacoby watches them taxi towards us, holding the gun at his hip. If he's nervous at all, he's hiding it.

To my surprise, Mars leaps from the gyrocopter before it stops, then watches it pick up speed again and take off, brushing the trees as it flies over our heads. Mars is walking our way with an incredible calm, now dressed only in his Spectral Suit. If I didn't know any better, I could be convinced this whole thing was his idea.

It's only now that I realise Mars' potential to come here with an emotional reaction. C-4 detonations aside, Jacoby is the reason Rust is gone. I can only assume Jin has broken the news to Mars and he's had to deal with it in a very short time before returning to face the man who put his father in hospital a day earlier. As I inspect his face for signs of rage, all I see is a sense of purpose and determination. It's as if Mars is filling the void of his father with a new level of grit. Maybe it's the remnants of my concussion or his face being silhouetted by the light, but as I look at David Fox in front of me, for a split second I can only see his father Bryan.

"Hirano," he says, coming to a halt about a dozen feet from us.

"Fox."

"Or do you prefer X?"

"Jacoby is fine."

"All right. You cool, Maven?"

I nod back to Mars in response, remembering the "bullet in my head" threat.

"Let's make this quick," Jacoby says. "I want the data. That's it. You give it to me and your friend is free to leave."

"That's it, huh?"

"I know there's been a lot for everybody to deal with already, from what I hear, so there's no need to add to the body count."

"It's funny you should say that, Jacoby. As you can see, I don't have the hard drive with me. In fact, it's flying around that gyro-copter up there. I could tell you it's all yours once you let Maven go. I could give you a dummy hard drive and let you believe it's what you're after, as we make our escape..."

Yes, these are all great ideas. But please tell me you have an even better one.

"But I respect you enough to know you're not going to believe any of that without proof. And I don't have any proof, because I don't intend to give you a damn thing, bro."

I feel Jacoby's gun raised to my temple before I can even process what Mars is saying.

"You better change your tune fast, Fox."

"You might've been able to take my old man down, but I'll bet dollars to doughnuts you haven't got the balls to face a younger man in an even match."

Please tell me you didn't just challenge this dude to a fist fight, Mars. Please tell me you didn't just say "dollars to doughnuts".

"Dollars to doughnuts, huh?"

Yep.

Mars shrugs, still yet to pull a weapon. I remember he gave me his Mk 23 yesterday, but I suspect he has more firepower up his sleeve. It's actually alarming how calm he is with a gun pointed at my head. I appreciate the confidence, but it would be great if he could show a little sense of urgency. It's killing me that I can't say a damn thing about any of this and that my silence isn't unnerving Mars, if he knows me as well as I think he does.

"I can see you're underestimating how much I want that data, if you think I'm putting this gun anywhere but inside your friend's neck."

"Do you really want to risk it though? The way I see it, if you pull that trigger, it's all over. If you kill both of us, the world keeps spinning. We become martyrs for truth and justice, you become the new face of the conspiracy."

"Again, you're underestimating my ability to get what I want."

Neither of these guys are giving an inch. There's a metagame of chicken taking place below the surface and the first one to show a slight glimmer of insecurity is going to lose.

"You're out of your depth on this one, Jacoby. Our friend flying around us will be long gone before you have a chance to wipe the sweat off your brow. That data will be in inboxes everywhere."

"So what's my best-case scenario, from your perspective? Even if we throw down, I take you out. I'm still standing here with a disgraced journalist waiting for what I came for."

Disgraced seems a little hurtful, but I hide my reaction, still conscious of my orders to sit here like a sweaty mannequin.

"I get the feeling Jin's a lot more fond of this guy than I am," Mars says.

Again. Hurtful. It's got to be a bluff, because I don't even think Jin likes me that much.

"So if you take me out, there's a good chance she'll bargain with you in a way that I'm not willing to. But you'll have to take my word for it. Until then, let's do this the right way. A gun in every hand leaves the whole world wounded. You had enough respect for my father not to kill him in that parking lot – what's changed since then?"

"I don't respect you so much," Jacoby says. "That was un-planned. Things are a lot more dire now."

"Look, enough talking. You can put me down like a rabid dog or you can fight me like a man with honour. Make your Bushido ancestors proud. The choice is yours, old man."

Even from my view in the chair, I can see this remark has rattled the typically unshakeable Jacoby. If the stereotypical allusion to his Japanese roots doesn't offend him, calling him "old" might. Jacoby seems to clearly identify as a black man and I haven't gathered any sense of his connection to his Japanese heritage, but it's got to mean something to a man so well-travelled.

Either way, it's a bold strategy. I trust Mars has played enough mind games to know what works and what doesn't. He's like Woody Harrelson pushing buttons in *White Men Can't Jump*, pin-pointing the teammates who play better basketball when they're angry or which opponents will go off the rails once they're riled up.

Jacoby moves his gun from my temple to my jaw, pressing harder. I take a deep breath and close my eyes, praying to God for a miracle.

"All right." The cold steel eases off my skin and I breathe. Maybe this means I can talk again, but I'll wait until the gun is gone before I take my chances.

"Then we're doing this."

"I took it easy on your father. I won't be so kind with you."

Jacoby slides his weapon into a hip holster, cracking his neck left and right like an Olympic wrestler about to hit the mat for a gold medal bout. Mars spaces out his feet to shoulder width, then slides one back into a relaxed but action-ready stance.

The two former Metric agents are dressed identically, each wearing nothing but their Spectral Suit. This is something I would have quipped about by now if I were allowed to speak, but as I sit here holding in my observations, I realise there are times when it's better to keep these things bottled up.

"Took it easy? You beat him within an inch of his life. Sure, you didn't kill him. But make no mistake, he's dead because of you."

Jacoby fabricates a nonchalant sniff, unwilling to acknowledge or deny the statement.

"And yet, Mr Hirano, if it wasn't for your stealth camo, I bet he'd still be here."

"Excuses." Jacoby pouts, clearly without the moral high ground needed to object. "You won't have any this time."

I take this as a confession that his Spectral Suit has also run out of charge, much like Rust's had in their last battle. So this is it.

Two fierce beasts fighting for my life. It seems so primal, archaic, and weird, but we're in the jungle and this is all we have. No witnesses. No laws. No barriers. No holds barred. Just two gladiators and a steep drop to the forest below.

Mars slides his front leg forward even more, mirroring Jacoby's posture and furrowing his brow. He finally looks ready to throw down.

"I know this is insane," he says, raising his fists into a martial arts stance. He once told me marines were taught a fighting style that combined Ju Jitsu with Judo and boxing, but as a former CIA agent he's thrown in a self-defence called Krav Maga and incorporated the most athletic variant of Capoeira. "Two grown men throwing fists instead of talking. But this is where we're at. And for the fight that determines the final chapter in Metric's long story, I feel like this is the only way it should be."

"You know what, Fox..." Jacoby begins circling Mars with slow precise steps. Mars mirrors him again, inching closer together until there's only six feet between them. "You're absolutely right. Metric is dead, but we're not free. This push and pull between us... We're prisoners to it. All of us. And there's no other way out than this right here."

"Good. We finally agree on something."

"Oh, don't you worry. I still see you, trying to take everything I've worked for. One way or another, this is the end. Now, show me what you've got!"

Mars and Jacoby lock up, grabbing each other by the shoulder and neck, continuing to circle as they struggle to gain an upper hand in a stubborn battle of strength. Jacoby exerts himself and pushes his hold into a forceful thrust that sends Mars to the ground. He bounces back up and attacks with a straight punch. Jacoby catches it and uses it to throw Mars to the ground a second time. Rather than attack his downed victim, he takes a step back and waits for him to rise to his feet. They square up and circle once more. Mars throws another punch, which Jacoby predictably catches again and counters into a quick hip toss... again.

C'mon Mars, you can't be trying the same move twice.

This time Jacoby leans forward and punches down towards his face, attempting to sandwich it between the ground and his fist. Mars rolls out the way and spins his legs to springboard back to his feet. Undeterred by his failures, he approaches with a sweep kick, which Jacoby leaps, but he's not fast enough to avoid the follow-up roundhouse kick that connects to his back. The force sends Jacoby staggering forward until he regains his composure. He faces up to Mars before any more attacks are made, taking a moment to smirk and update the scouting report inside his head.

"Nice shot."

"Thanks."

Jacoby steps forward as the aggressor, throwing a flurry of quick hooks, each caught by alternating forearms, until he lands a hard uppercut to Mars' chin.

Mars swallows the punch, shaking it off to catch a follow-up lunge, which he counters into a hammerlock. Despite the pressure on his arm and neck, Jacoby smashes his elbow backwards into Mars's sternum with two quick pumps to loosen the grip. Mars doesn't take kindly to this and throws an elbow into the back of Jacoby's head.

He goes down but kicks backwards to shoo away Mars' attempt to start a chokehold, then rolls out of harm's way. He rises to his feet, catching his breath and attempting to avoid looking panicked.

"You're pretty good, young blood."

"I'm the best."

"We'll see."

They lock up again, but this time Jacoby gains the clear upper hand and pushes Mars into a headlock. Several quick punches into Mars' chest are interrupted as he runs blindly in my direction, pulling Jacoby along with the headlock still in place.

"Look out!" I shout, breaking my silence.

Jacoby takes the opportunity to throw Mars into the cabin behind me, adding to his running momentum with significant force. Instead of trying to avoid a collision, Mars appears to voluntarily run into the cabin, running up the exterior with two steps, then flipping backwards to land on his feet behind Jacoby.

"What in the..."

A swift sweep kick drops Jacoby to one knee and a punch to the back of the head puts him on the ground. He leans down and strikes Jacoby hard across the cheek with a stiff hook. As if that wasn't enough, he does it again, catching his chin and cutting it open. This should be it.

Before I realise what's happening, Mars has used the break in the action to cut my hands free, using a knife from one of his many holsters.

"You good, bro? Get out when you get a chance. Wait 'til it's clear and Jin will pick you up."

"I can help you."

"This is my fight."

"Dude."

I can see it happening in slow motion, but even still I don't have time to properly warn Mars. Jacoby yanks both his ankles to trip him, using the momentum to rise to one knee.

"You must be crazy to turn your back in a fight," he says, wrapping his hands around Mars' throat and beating his head to the ground.

I stand up from my chair and kick Jacoby straight in the face like a mule, sending him staggering backwards. When he recovers, he stares at me with a look that could burn a hole right through me, but quickly turns his attention back to an approaching Mars.

"Stay out of this, Maven!"

"Get back."

With both warning me to step aside, I edge away to the side as an awkward spectator. Jacoby bats away a spinning kick from Mars, but then takes a straight punch to the chest and a side kick close to his throat. He manages to take the next kick to the side of his body with little contact and returns it with a punch. Mars blocks the first, then a second, but gets caught by a third to the side of his neck and a fourth to his abdomen.

"C'mon, man," I mumble to myself, mentally willing Mars into a comeback. I know there's some kind of honourable gun-less battle taking place, but can I throw a rock? You can't beat a good rock. Mars' real name is David, Jacoby's a bit of a Goliath. It feels right.

The punches stagger him for just long enough that Jacoby can throw him along the ground. He rolls several times into a shaken stupor by the time he gets to his feet. Mars dodges two kicks from Jacoby and falls backwards, completely disappearing into the thick, scratchy bushes. For a moment, Jacoby and I are probably both wondering where he's gone and whether he's OK. Out of nowhere, an extended foot flies out of the green scrub at an unprepared Jacoby.

This is it – the badass action hero move to end it all. Or not.

As if he's in *The Matrix*'s slow motion, Jacoby sidesteps the flying kick and throws a perfect punch into Mars' rib cage, producing an audible crack. I watch him fall to the ground, landing awkwardly on his ankle. Not wasting any time, Jacoby sits on Mars legs, taking away possibly his greatest weapon. He throws punch after punch into my friend's midsection, as he protects his face with two raised arms, taking each blow to his cracked ribs as best he can. The punches slow down and I wonder if Jacoby is getting tired, but then as Mars' arms begin to droop it becomes clear he's the one losing energy. Jacoby's thrusts move from his abdomen and chest towards his face, with Mars' limp defence only slightly shielding the hard punches.

He told me this is his fight and I know he would want me to have already escaped in the chaos, but I can't just walk away. I've done that once already and I can't let another friend die as I pursue my own objectives. I can tell Mars wants to own this showdown, to defend his family honour and avenge his father's death. But I can't face Alison if I have to return with yet another of her loved ones fallen victim to the cause.

Growing tired of throwing punches, Jacoby rises to his feet and places Mars into a seated position. He reaches under Mars' battered arms from behind and grasps his own wrist, then stands and begins dragging him away.

He's a tough guy and I know the Spectral Suit can absorb a lot of damage with its high-tech weave, but there's no way to train a man to take repeated strikes to the face.

As the sounds of struggle fade, a bird's nearby squawk is the only sound accompanying the constant dragging of Mars' heels along the concrete. I realise Jacoby isn't just setting up his next move. He's taking Mars to the closest steep drop at the side of the clearance.

"Hey. Hey!"

Jacoby ignores me.

"Hey! Yo!"

"I'll deal with you in a minute," he says, continuing to move Mars' limp body. I run right up to him, intending to tug on his arm, but he hits me with a side kick as I approach, knocking the wind out of my guts. From the ground, I can only watch as he nears the edge of the SWAN roof. Mars finally puts up a fight, grabbing over his shoulder at Jacoby's head and neck, but it's no use. Jacoby is too smart and too strong. Mars' eyes connect with mine for a brief moment and the corner of his bleeding mouth curls into the slightest of smiles, as if he's trying to tell me everything will be OK. For a split second, it puts me at ease, as if he's got a way out of this, a plan to reverse the outlook.

But this brief moment ends when Jacoby throws him off the cliff edge, plummeting into the trees and rocks below.

Chapter 26

The Edge

"No!"

My shout falls on deaf ears and it's far too late to make a difference. Jacoby leans over the cliff face, making sure no superheroes swoop in to rescue Mars before he splatters into the turf. My instinct is to run towards Jacoby, to pummel him senseless and make him apologise for killing two of my friends.

Maybe it's Mars' words echoing in my ears, telling me to escape, or it's a subconscious desire to get back to Jin and make sure this isn't all for nothing. Whatever it is, my fight-or-flight response takes place and I start looking for ways to survive.

"Get back inside," Jacoby says, turning from the cliff to face me. He looks no more satisfied now that the fight is over. I ignore him, scanning the clearance for some way to escape. I shuffle away and scan the sky, wondering what's happened to Jin's flying gyrocopter. I realise I can hear it but can't see it, and I take off running through the trees to find a better view.

"Maven!" Jacoby calls out, taunting me like a horror movie villain. "I can't have you getting hurt now. You're my last bargaining chip."

I decide not to respond, even though I have a great quip, just in case it gives me a longer window to avoid him. I trip over and skin my knee on the concrete, only realising once I stumble to my feet and feel it throbbing with every stride. And now I don't know which way I came from. Darn it. I go with my gut and push through the scrub in the direction that feels right. After a few yards, I stop just short of a steep decline. I could slide down and make my way off the mountain, but it's too risky to make the leap without knowing the terrain below. I trace the cliff's edge, hoping to come across a staircase or perhaps a hang glider. That would work. I could try that.

I toe around a satellite dish, camouflaged like everything else, and a long cable stretching from a short stanchion down into the jungle. It stands out to me because there's been no attempt to hide it, although it is thin enough to pass for a vine if you weren't actively looking for a high-tech research facility in the middle of the Chiang Dao District.

"Maven!"

I don't answer. A rustling in the nearby bushes startles me enough that I consider jumping or at least sliding down the slope. The only thing stopping me is the bed of rocks below, looking about as friendly as my prom date's father when I turned up at her house in my cousin's Datsun.

"Maven."

I continue to ignore him, crouching down and hoping he'll pass me by.

"I'm right here. I'm standing... right next to you. Look at me."

I look up and see his brown eyes staring deep into my soul, telling me it's all over. If I can overpower him, I can make it somewhere that Jin can find me. But I just can't. All I have left is my voice.

"You did it," I say. "You beat Mars."

"What can I say? You bet on the wrong horse, man. You lose."

I stand up, looking into his eyes and pausing to consider my words.

"You killed him," is all I can come up with, but I'm still surprised to see Jacoby's remorse is non-existent.

"You heard him before. That was the deal. Him or me."

"Yeah."

"This ain't no game, man," he says, noting my defiance. "I told you I was serious about this. Now, get your other friend to hustle over here or–"

"I'm done with this. You know you can't kill me."

"You want to test me?" Jacoby draws his gun, stopping short of actually pointing it at me. "You think you're tough now, do you?"

"No. I'm just sick of thinking you're something you're not. You're meant to be one of the good guys."

"Listen, man," he snarls, casually pointing the gun at me as he talks. "You can put a top hat on a monkey, that don't make it a magician. I am who I am. Don't get sad just because you got it wrong."

"You know something, when I met you I thought you were Denzel in *The Equalizer*. But you're actually Denzel in *Training Day*."

Jacoby takes a second to think, staring up into the blue sky. If I had any hope of bringing him back to the side of good, that small chance has slipped away. I couldn't find the right words to say, or maybe he was just too far gone.

"That's your problem – you're trying to understand the world through the lens of your own experience. But I'm not Denzel. I'm not Rust or Mars. I'm Jacoby Hirano. I'm Agent X. And this is it. I win. It's over. You made this bed and now you've got nowhere to lay."

I reach into my pocket and feel my necktie, wrapping my fingers around one end. I try to do it subtly, but Jacoby's definitely noticed. He just doesn't care. He's not threatened by me or anything I can possibly do.

"Jacoby. I'm sorry about your people in Chicago. I think we could help them, you know? If things work out, we can make some real change with a big platform. People would listen to us. We could do something, instead of just taking the easy option – you know what I mean?"

He doesn't know what I mean, judging by the sideways look on his sweaty, smooth face.

"But there's no chance to do anything like that when you're doing all this crazy stuff."

"I mean... I'd like to believe you, Maven, but I can't see how your pals and I can work together anymore. Surely, you don't think that's possible by now. After all this."

"When I met you, you told me that you sometimes have to look a man in the eye and make a decision about him. You've had so many chances to trust me and work with me here."

"Yeah... but no. It's too late. This is the end, man."

"OK. I don't know what to tell you. Except, thanks for not killing me."

Jacoby's smirk morphs into a silent gasp as he realises I'm going, going, gone – all the way down to the jungle floor, riding the telephone wire as a zip line with my graphene microfibre tie.

The strongest material known to man.

I have to admit, it feels great flying through the air, even if everything else sucks. Rust is gone. Mars is gone. I have no idea where this wire leads and I'm zipping at breakneck speed to find out. With my luck, it'll be a pit of quicksand, which would be a fun way to discover they do actually exist in real life. Saturday morning cartoons really led me to believe the threat of quick sand would be far more predominant in the adult world.

The funny thing is I wouldn't have had the courage to try this if Jacoby didn't throw me down a zip line back in Panama. He prepared me for this moment. I wonder if he's impressed, although I suspect he wouldn't tell me either way. It's hard to be excited when I know that making it out of this would leave me to track down Jin and get back to Alison, then explain to her how I managed to get her husband and son killed within half a day. She's nice enough, but she does scare me a little. She's a Fox, after all.

I look up at the tie wrapped around my knuckles and wrists, making a mental note to thank Jin for this handy gizmo. Just when I think I'm safe, I feel a bullet tear through the meat of my thigh, setting my nervous system on fire. Yet still I hold on, gripping my tie hard as I pick up speed.

It's only one bullet. A warning sign. Jacoby isn't giving up.

I reach the end of the wire, slowing down as the incline steadies. I'm not great at estimating distance, but I must have slid five hundred yards through the treetops, taking the odd branch to the face, before I come to a stop at a roadside telephone pole. It looks like the same road we drove on yesterday, likely only a few miles apart. Now I just have to get down from here.

I look around for a safe landing until I realise the bullet in my leg is a growing problem and I need to act fast. Not only are the pain and bleeding making it even harder to hold on, the fall from this height would cause major issues to the wound.

But I don't really have a choice. I need to drop. Or maybe not. I swing my legs towards the pole until I can wrap my feet part way around it. If I can shimmy my hands closer, I can slide down the pole like a fireman, using my tie the way I've seen locals use rope to climb trees for palm sugar and coconuts. It works well. I get about halfway down until the pain in my thigh overcomes my grip and I fall into the bushes.

A branch scraping down the length of my back is my only extra injury, but it's still not enough to take the focus off my throbbing leg. I wrap my tie around my leg, trying to reduce the blood flow. I don't really know what I'm doing. I skipped first aid training when I worked at *The Post*, but I know this is meant to help. My tie is proving worth its weight.

I roll out of the bushes and crawl through a dewy patch of grass. It's hard to know whether I should stay here and let Jin find me or if I need to move to avoid becoming Jacoby's prey. Either way, my leg is bleeding and it hurts like hell. I squint into the sunlight, searching for a speck in the sky and listening out for the drone of the gyrocopter. I've got nothing – just bird sounds and blowing branches. Whether it's the pain or the complete lack of sleep, I feel like I could nod off right here with the sun burning down through the trees.

"Bro."

If I close my eyes, I can even hear Mars' voice in the distance, calling out to me. It feels like a week since I had a legitimate sleep. It's very possible I'm already asleep right now. I can't remember the last time I just lay in the grass. It's kinda... nice.

"Bro."

My body shakes with a startled jump as a hand grabs my shoulder. I look up and see Mars standing above me. Am I dreaming or delusional from the blood loss? Or is he seriously here right now?

"It's all right. I survived."

"You... look fine," I say with confusion, examining his body for injury from the multi-storey drop.

"I am fine. I mean, I had the wind knocked out of me for a while. But this suit took care of the rest."

I squint closely, examining his Spectral Suit with care.

"The neck. There's like a subtle V print."

"Yeah, it's a new suit. Prototype. Grabbed it at the SWAN with Mom."

"Why didn't you use it in the fight?"

"It's a prototype. They designed it to withstand extreme impacts, like explosions and falls. It detects your movement through the air, you know, velocity. And then *phhhwt* – exoskeleton activates."

"Exo, huh? That would've been useful when Jacoby was beating the crap out of you."

"Yeah, he rattled me real good," Mars says, gently touching the raw marks on his face. "But what about you? I saw you flying out of there. That was badass, my friend."

"He shot me."

Mars looks down at my leg and winces. "Ooh, yeah. Nasty. Let's get you out of here."

"Can you call in Jin? Where is she?"

"No idea," he says, peering through the trees above us. "That jammer is somehow still active. It's probably why your telephone wire zip line was hardwired into the SWAN."

"Yeah. Probably." I get to my feet and remember there's something we need to discuss. "Mars. About your dad, look..."

"Not now," he cuts me off, looking more than focused on anything and everything else right now. "We'll talk about it later."

"I'm sorry."

"It's OK. Let's just get out of here. You can walk, right?"

"But where? I like a challenge, but... I'm probably not in hike mode right now."

"I don't know, we just can't stay here. That's a bad dude back there."

"He ain't back there," a loud voice barks from behind us. "He's right here. And he's pissed."

"Oh, geez."

Mars whips out a gun and I trip myself up turning around to see Jacoby lauding over us with his pistol targeting my chest.

"I already popped one in you, but I'm willing to give you another," he says.

"Haven't we been through this already?" Mars asks, more or less nonplussed. "You're not gonna kill him, and you're not gonna get away with this."

"Listen, man. My worst-case scenario is you fools getting out of here and finishing the job. If I die taking you out, at least my name doesn't get dragged through the mud."

Mars raises his gun with even more aggression, thrusting it towards Jacoby for emphasis. "Not. Going. To happen."

"But that's still my last resort. I want the data. And I'm here to get it."

"Do you see any hard drives, baldy?"

"I can wait."

"We can't. You see my friend's leg here?"

With his gun still trained on my chest, Jacoby peers down to my bullet wound, inspecting his work up close.

"It's a clean shot," he says. "He'll be fine."

"In this heat, without food or water, you know he's gonna need medical attention soon."

"I'll take my chances. Will you?"

Such a lack of compassion. Who is this monster?

"Do you even like dogs, Jacoby?" I ask. "I just don't know you anymore."

"I like dogs."

"Do you?"

"Yeah."

"Here's an idea," Mars interjects. "We all put our guns away, we get out of the heat, and we talk until we find a solution that benefits everybody. Maybe we find some dogs."

Jacoby's knitted brow tells me this idea won't work, but I know it's the only way we all leave the country breathing.

"C'mon."

"I... don't think so. Decisions have been made. Some... I might regret..."

"That's OK. We can–"

"The kid even said it. I'm the reason his old man is gone. You think I'm gonna trust that he'll forgive that and let me walk?"

Mars bites his bottom lip, unwilling to speak for or against Jacoby's reasoning. As helpful as it would be to say all is forgiven, he's not willing to commit the energy required for this particular lie. I groan in frustration, struggling to think of a way out that doesn't involve bullets.

"Jacoby, I know you think there's no meaning in life, but you've got to see how we all fit together. I was in a Panamanian hotel room, Mars vanished, and right when all hope is lost, you're there to save me and whisk me across the world with a chance to right so many wrongs... together. The crimes of the past don't compare to whatever we can bring people by shining a light to the truth. We can break the chains of corruption the New World Order has imposed over the entire planet. I honestly believe that. I think your family would understand that too."

Jacoby drops his head, perhaps equally disgusted by my naivete and rueful towards his own lack of faith in humanity.

"You still haven't figured it out have you?"

"Ye... Yeah?"

I'm not sure what Jacoby means, but I imagine he's about to tell me. He shakes his head and releases a short breath, the type you'd expect from a bitter man about to break off an engagement.

"It was him," Mars chimes in. I shoot him a look and see his eyes widening as he finds his words. "He took me in, back in Panama. Jumped me from behind. That's how I got locked up. That's how he found you and got in touch with Jin."

This should shock me, but deep down I knew it. Jacoby had made a half admission back in the parking lot when Rust was accusing him of sinister intentions. I must have just pushed the idea out of my head in the hope it wasn't true.

"It's like I told you. I've made a lot of bad decisions to get here. Don't think I'm not ready to make some more."

"That's it!"

Sensing Mars has reached boiling point, Jacoby draws a second pistol, now aiming one at each of us.

"Cool it. I told you, I'm not leaving without what I came for. And Maven, I will put a round in your sunburnt ass, if that's what it takes."

Mars takes a large sidestep to block Jacoby's line of sight, protecting me from any immediate threat of gunfire, evening the odds back to a one-on-one battle.

"You'll have to go through me, bro."

"Believe me, this will hurt you more than me."

Snapping twigs and panting breath from the nearby bushes pull our attention, causing Jacoby to point one of his guns to the side. Jin stumbles out, her arms scratched and bleeding with a look of panic in her eyes. If she had hoped to find us before Jacoby, she's not only far too late, but she's lost all potential for a surprise attack. A pistol pointed directly at her face will make sure there's no more kickboxing. She mumbles in Thai as she comes to a standstill, raising her hands in the air.

"You can't shoot all three of us," Mars says.

"I can damn well try."

"What about four?"

Alison pokes her head out from behind Jin, with her own gun pointed at Jacoby.

"Oh, geez." I can't believe it. "One of us is definitely dying today."

He adjusts his aim from Jin to Alison, so now everyone holding a gun also has one pointed at them.

"I really hope one of you fools brought that hard drive."

No one answers and it slowly sinks in that every threat in the world won't get Jacoby any closer to completing his goal. I tried to tell him, but he's done too much already to not take this as far as he possibly can.

"Where is it? Tell me, right now, tell me or I'll–"

"It's already uploaded," Alison says, without batting an eyelid. "You're too late."

"It is?"

I can't believe it. It's over. No matter what happens, that's it. We've taken our shot and there's literally nothing more we can do to convince anyone. My body tingles with adrenaline and relief as the struggles of the past twelve months flash before my eyes. It's all over.

Jacoby looks furious and now there's no bait on the hook to keep him going. There's nothing he can accomplish, yet there's no reason for him to keep me alive. Logically, it's time for us to go our separate ways and deal with the consequences, but the rage in his eyes tells me the science of thought isn't informing his actions.

"How many people in your family want to die today?"

Nobody answers, nobody flinches.

"Step aside. I'm taking Maven with me."

"Not gonna be able to do it," is all Mars has to say in response.

"Then you'll be seeing your father real soon."

Before I can even question what he wants with me, it's Alison's turn to step in front of Jacoby's gun, taking the attention away from her son. If it weren't for my leg, this would give us a chance to escape, but I know there's no chance Mars would ditch his mother after already leaving Rust behind.

"Oh, it's like that?"

"It's like that," Alison bites back. "Now either end this now, or turn yourself around and start over."

"Don't test me, woman." I've seen Jacoby in a lot of tense situations in a short amount of time, but I've never seen the utter loss of hope I'm sensing in his eyes right now. "I'm neck deep here and I've got nothing to lose. Give me Maven."

My jaw drops as Jin steps in front of Alison, forming a conga line of brave people ready to face the barrel of a gun, each deterring harm towards someone they care for. Unlike Mars and Alison, Jin isn't armed and offers no threat to Jacoby in her defiance.

"It's not true," she says.

"Jin."

She waves off Alison's stuttering attempts to dissuade her, instead focusing her eyes on our opponent. I reach a hand to Mars' shoulder and ask him to trust her. Jin's one of the smartest people I've ever known and she wouldn't do something like this without thinking.

"What the hell are you doing, Jin? Stand down."

"It's not true. What you said."

She must sense the same fragility in Jacoby's eyes, because it's only heightening as she speaks.

"You've got plenty to lose. We all do. I don't know why you did these things. It doesn't matter."

"Move. Now." Jacoby trains the two of his guns on Jin, signalling a shift from confusion and pity to contempt over her insolence.

"All that matters is what you do next," she says, projecting calm as well as affirmation. "I know you've done bad things. But you didn't kill Rust. You could have. It would have been easier."

"I'm *not* going to tell you again!" Jacoby bellows, raising his voice to a sickening scream. My heart is pounding as I anticipate the sound of a gunshot and all the consequences that would follow, with visions of an all-out battle, flying bullets and bloody corpses. But Jin's calming voice brings me back down.

"I know you are afraid of something out there. That's OK too," she reassures Jacoby. "No one knows what will happen next. We will find out together. And we'll face it together."

By now, Jacoby's two pistols are shaking in his grip.

"You're not alone."

"I am."

Exhausted, his arms slowly drop to his side, as his neck falls into a depressed downward stare. She's done it. Even with everything I've learnt, I couldn't talk him down, but she's done it.

"Jacoby." I peer out from behind my three heroes. "I meant it before. We can go and figure this all out. It'll be OK."

My heart skips a beat as he raises one of the guns to his bald head. He pressed the barrel into his temple and rubs it up and down, scratching his skin, then holsters both weapons before turning away from us completely.

"Hey. Jacoby."

He doesn't respond. After a few seconds and one long breath, he begins walking away, looking slightly over his shoulder to say two words before he disappears into the trees.

"I'm sorry."

Chapter 27

____

Corporate Espionage

"That's it?"

It seems too simple to win this way. The cost has been high, but everything I've learnt has pointed towards a violent defeat for one of the two sides. The reality is a bittersweet compromise for Jacoby and a lingering sense of closure. This pleases the pacifist in me, even though I'm feeling a lack of karmic justice towards the man largely responsible for Rust's downfall.

"Should we, like... go after him?"

Jin and Alison embrace, finally overwhelmed by the situation as Mars shakes his head in response to me. He doesn't need to explain his reasoning because I saw the same thing in Jacoby's eyes. It was defeat, with a hint of acceptance. The demons he's facing and the consequences for his family will haunt him through the foreseeable future, even if he's not called to account for his crimes.

It's impossible to predict what will happen when the news gets out. Thinking about it gives me flashbacks to this time a year ago, back in Kansas when we uploaded the original whistle-blowing video. Our expectations fell completely flat. The difference this time is we have proof, or the closest thing in existence. I know it's possible former Metric agents will be fully exonerated for following government orders, but it doesn't seem like Jacoby will risk the drama. He won't show up to find out, and I don't blame him. As much as the truth will finally be undeniable, the New World Order is still out there pulling strings and running the country. It won't be easy to shake the target on our backs, and I wonder if any of us will ever feel truly safe in America. But we have to go back now. For the first time in a year, home can be home again.

I hug Jin and thank her for coming back to save me. She says something about how we've all saved each other. It's a nice moment with her head against my chest. I can't remember the last time I was in such a genuine physical embrace.

"Your heart is beating so fast," Jin says.

"Yeah."

"You OK?"

"Yeah. I'm good."

"Your face is red."

"That's probably sunburn."

"Oh, your leg!" She pulls away, remembering my injury.

"Yeah, it really hurts. I got shot."

As Jin inspects the wound, we briefly talk about how she found the words to calm Jacoby. She planned it, she says. She knew it would come to this. I don't know how, but that's her story. She asks about the shooting and is thrilled to hear about my necktie zip line.

"I told you it would be useful."

"You did. But you also told me Coppard was chasing us with water guns."

I turn my attention to Mars and Alison, realising this is my first chance to explain what happened to Rust.

"You're probably wondering..."

Alison stops me, saying Jin has already described the situation and passed on Rust's parting words.

"Yeah, but, you know... I'm sorry. I'm really..."

"It's OK," Mars says, with a hand on my shoulder. "I knew as soon as he walked out of that hospital room. He was all in. All or nothing. We could see it in his eyes. We could hear it in his voice. We've made our peace with it. That's exactly how he would've wanted to go."

"I just feel terrible. If we had time, we could've–"

"Andrew, please." Alison looks hurt but stoic, having accepted the reality long ago. "Everybody has an expiration date. I've been preparing for this day since I married Bryan. When they took me here, I wasn't sure I would ever see him again. I made peace with my life without him. I mourned for that loss already. But you brought him back to me and let me say goodbye. Thank you."

I nod, choking back platitudes and clichés that won't do any good right now. "I miss him," is all I can come up with.

Alison smiles. I don't know what she's thinking as she looks to the sky, but I think she's pleased that someone could spend enough time with her husband to see through his grizzled exterior to recognise his humanity.

"I told them he was a hero," Jin says, before drinking from a canteen previously attached to her waist. I can't help but chuckle at her choice of words, as she hands the drink to me.

"He always hated that label. *Hero.* When I met him... he was a true patriot. But in the end, he was so much more than that. You know, a patriot loves his country, and yeah, Rust was as devoted as they come. He fought for Metric. He went after his own flesh and blood." I point to Mars, remembering their battle in the rain. I can't bring myself to make eye contact with anyone. This might seem an odd place for a speech, but I feel compelled to say something worthy of the man who changed my life. "It seemed like there was nothing he wouldn't do for Metric and the allegiance he felt to America. But then he threw away his reputation to tell the truth, to expose the lies. The man who gave his life right over there, all he cared about was finding his wife and reuniting her with his son. And yeah, he wouldn't say it, but I know it took him his whole life to realise what mattered the most. But he figured it out. He knew it. And he sacrificed himself so we could have a chance for normal lives. All of us. He always fought for what he believed in. And thanks to him, we can stop fighting."

I pause to open the canteen and think carefully about my next words. I didn't realise how much I needed the water until I started drinking.

"If it's possible, if we even have a hope for normalcy, it's because of what he's done for us – not just today, but for the past year. And history might not ever show that. Ever. Even if it makes it onto paper, no one will ever know what that sacrifice meant. They just couldn't. But we know. He was a hero in a world where there are no heroes. That's what I'll always remember."

Mars nods solemnly, also avoiding eye contact as he reflects on his father's sacrifice.

"*Mighty Mouse.* That's what I'll remember," he says. "Rust... Dad wasn't there a lot. We didn't do much together. But I remember watching *Mighty Mouse* with him... in the back room with the old brown TV."

He looks to his mother and she cracks a smile, saying he couldn't have been more than five years old. I realise my understanding of Mars' relationship with Rust started when I met them both, but there's a whole history of good and bad memories before that. There's been a lot said about his absence, so it's touching to know Mars can reflect on good times as well.

After a few moments of silence, Alison thanks me for my kind words and we all agree to make our way to our getaway car nearby, where Alison parked before finding us in the shrub.

"How did you know where we were?" I ask her, toying with the redundant Nano GEAR deep in my pocket.

"I just called Jin's cell phone and she told me."

"Ohh, cell phones. Of course. I can't wait to use a phone again. I'm gonna have so many unread emails."

"You've got more than emails to catch up on, bro."

"What about you, what's next?" I ask Mars, hoping he'll return to America with us. As much as I miss my old life and my old friends, he's one of the only people who understands what I've been through and the thought of separating from him again leaves me a little unsettled. "You wanna open a bar together? Taco stand?"

"I guess it depends how the US government takes the news. I'd like to go back to the CIA. Those were good days. And I have a lot of new skills."

"Maybe corporate espionage then."

"Maybe."

"Painting," Alison says. "Gardening."

"That sounds nice," Jin says. I know her uncertainty for the future is dwarfed by her relief to be free from the shackles of Metric and Bhandit. Maybe I could persuade her on the pros of returning to American living.

I slide into the car and pick up my backpack. I know the data has been safely transferred, but I want to make sure everything else is still inside.

"Yes!"

Every face turns to understand my excitement.

"Sorry. I just remembered I've got a blue Gatorade here waiting for me."

"You said we could split that," Jin says.

"That doesn't sound like me."

"Never mind. It's so warm by now."

"I don't even care. I'm no scientist, but I believe warm electrolytes are still electrolytes."

Epilogue

———————————

"Is that Takashi Hirano?"

"Speaking."

"Mister Hirano. I'm sorry to call you at home, but I'm glad I found you."

"OK."

"My name's Andrew and I'm... a friend of your son."

"OK. Terry?"

"Jacoby."

"Oh. Ohh. Is he all right?" I can hear the realisation sink in. Just as I expected, Mr Hirano isn't accustomed to conversations about his estranged military son.

"To be honest, I'm not sure, sir. I haven't spoken to him for a while, but I did spend a lot of time with him recently. I just wanted to talk to you about him, if you've got time to listen."

"OK..."

"It's complicated, but there's a lot that you don't know. You might've heard or read a few things, and I really think you should hear the full story. He spoke about you a lot. Your family."

"Really? That... Yes, I would like to... Do you know where he is?"

"I'm sorry, it's been about six months since I saw him. But if you want to meet me, I can be in Chicago this weekend. How does that sound?"

"Oh. Well..."

"It's OK if you want to think it over," I say, understanding how strange my offer must sound. I have no idea how Jacoby's father could have reacted to the Metric information leak. "I'm a journalist. My name's Andrew Maven, if you'd like to look me up. This isn't for material. I'm not reporting on anything. I just think we would have a lot to talk about."

There's so much I can't explain about this situation. First of all, I still don't know exactly what I'm going to tell Jacoby's family, but they deserve to understand how much he cares for them and the extremes he took in his effort to help them. Secondly, I don't know how I'm going to justify it, but I'm adamant about helping them financially the way Jacoby wanted to. I'm getting them out of Englewood.

And to round out the trifecta of uncertainty, I really don't know what's motivating me to do any of this. It could be my gratitude towards Jacoby for letting me walk when he was so close to undoing everything I'd worked towards. But then again, he was the only threat and the reason we were in that situation to begin with. By the typical karmic standards, he doesn't deserve this help or any resolution. Lucky for him, I don't subscribe to karma. Maybe this is my way of proving to myself I've forgiven what he did to me, to Rust. Maybe it's my way of letting go and proving I would've worked with him to help his family, if only he gave me the chance. There's a decent chance he'll never find out about it, but it's possible that one day he'll see I helped him accomplish his goal. My motivation, as usual, is quite possibly mixed and tainted by my own ambition. So perhaps it's guilt, because I know his intentions came from a good place. Maybe deep down I recognise Jacoby was right, and there wasn't much difference between us. Who knows, maybe we were both doing what we needed to do to help ourselves and the people we care about. Maybe none of that matters.

I just know I need to do this.

Life has been strange since I came back in America. It was obviously strange before that, but it's a different kind of strange now. It's like everything in my old life was moved three feet to the left. It's all here, but there's something off. I expected my apartment to be gone, my friends and family to disown me, my bank account to be empty. Everything was basically as I left it. Even my cat is here, after spending a year with my landlord.

Indisputable evidence makes a heck of a difference. Now everybody wants to hear the stories. *An Evening with Andrew Maven* sells out every time I summon the energy to make a public appearance at a college campus. I'm also quite big in Europe, strangely enough, and almost prefer to do the Skype session gigs where I don't have to leave my apartment or wear deodorant. I've had dozens of book offers and this time next year I imagine I'll have written out as much of the story as people will ever believe. But there's no rush of excitement from the fame. It's shallow. These same people were ridiculing me a year ago. You won't believe how many contemporaries in the media world have told me they always believed in me.

"Hey Andrew, I vouched for you."

"Andrew, I knew you were right."

"I tried, Andrew, but my editor wouldn't listen."

It's all lip service. I nod and smile, make a joke of it, but I remember how few genuinely reached out to me in the days after Kansas. It's all turned around now and I'm happy that people want to know the truth. There's just an emptiness to sharing the world's dark reality over and over again, with little hope of seeing it change in my lifetime. The New World Order is like a shark in the ocean, hiding in the depths and picking its moments to strike from below the surface, taking out unsuspecting victims that go unnoticed. This is a better alternative than the previous regime that simply assumed direct control of everything that mattered, but it's far from the freedom, justice and American way that we were taught about as children. I know they're out there in the shadows. And now everyone knows it. My message has an audience. It's a loss of innocence, but it's also a new enlightenment. It reminds me of that shift in time from parents letting their children roam the streets to the modern era of helicopter parenting. I'm glad I've had an effect and can see people are finally listening to what I've been telling them for so long. I know there's a huge downside to this revelation and people will naturally pine for the ignorant days of the past, but the new attitude comes from a new understanding of what's taking place in the world out there.

I never had a finger on the pulse of the New World Order so I can't say I know if it has a discernible personality. Still, I imagine they would have to feel undercut and less powerful now that people are actively looking for their fingerprints and questioning the organisations they've controlled for so long. As far as I'm concerned, this is the best result we could've hoped for.

This is my message now, with my goal to motivate people to keep the NWO running, and there are certain phrases or points I make sure I proclaim every time I have a video camera or dictaphone held to my face. This is what I tell students and teachers, business leaders and politicians, anyone who will listen to me. I always echo Jin's wisdom: "If you shine a light on evil, it hides or it dies." It's true and it's what kept me going through every dark moment, knowing the light was always near, even when I couldn't sense it.

Secondly, I always bring my message back to a personal level – it's about family and community. Mars and Alison are now working together as special-division consultants. My parents have returned to America, leaving New Zealand and Middle-Earth behind. Jin returned to her family in southern Thailand, but I think she will be moving here soon – at least, I hope so. And we know how far Jacoby went to fight for his people too. Good folk just want to live a good life alongside those they love, earning what they deserve to have, and trusting there are no other powers at play to take that away, or make it harder than it needs to be. There's NWO conspiracy to discuss at every level, and layers upon layers of reasons why Metric's atrocities of the past have taken place in the name of American prosperity and private interests. But I don't think we could ever comprehend it and I certainly don't try to explain it to people who aren't ready to believe it. It's easy to boil it down to "how does this impact my life?". I just think a global community deserves better than the self-centred past we've justified for too long.

Lastly, I always mention Rust's name as much as I can. I want to make Bryan Fox famous, and since he's not here to complain about it or deal with the consequences of that fame, he's the perfect icon for this movement. Better even than me. As much as I'm appropriately considered a maven of the movement, it was the spy who made it happen. Rust died for this. He gave his life for his family, to give them a community they could feel safe in, and a future where they could build something meaningful. He threw away his lifetime of work, his honour and his reputation in Kansas as the first face in the revolution, to confess the sins of Metric and the NWO. He was a true patriot, but above that, a father and a husband who knew what mattered most.

I try not to think about my own legacy. My identity has been reinvented too many times over the past few years to assume it won't continue to evolve or be turned upside-down at some point. But I am proud of my role in all this. So much has changed that I can barely relate to the person I was two years ago. Sometimes I think back to that timid and naïve news reporter, searching for a scoop, and I yearn for such innocence. Life was simple. It was good. I really think that person was someone the world would like more than who I am now. But I'd rather know the truth and let it change my life than live the lie of ignorance.

It's been said that clichés are cliché for a reason and I gotta say, the truth really does set you free. It does more than that though. It shines down on you like the sun and warms your spirit. Knowing truth is so much more than holding facts. When you're sure of what's inside your heart, that's when you can bask in the truth and let it inspire the change you want to see. I'll never stop chasing that feeling. Never. It's the story of our time. When fake news abounds, and history is dictated by imperfect memories and skewed perspectives, objective truth is no longer accepted. You have to decide what this means to you and whether to share it with the world.

All you have is what you hold onto. Whatever you believe is all you'll ever have.

www.ingramcontent.com/pod-product-compliance
Lightning Source LLC
Chambersburg PA
CBHW020128120726
47903CB00007B/2155